SIONNA FOX
SHARI MIKELS

Mated

A PARANORMAL
ROMANCE SHIFTER ANTHOLOGY

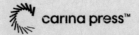

carina press™

CONTENTS

SAVING HIS WOLF   5
Kerry Adrienne

WOLF SUMMER   111
Sionna Fox

DRAWN TO THE WOLVES   219
Shari Mikels

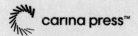

carina press™

ISBN-13: 978-1-335-89009-2

Mated: A Paranormal Romance Shifter Anthology

Recycling programs
for this product may
not exist in your area.

Copyright © 2017 by Harlequin Books S.A.

The publisher acknowledges the copyright holders of the
individual works as follows:

Saving His Wolf
Copyright © 2017 by Kerry Adrienne

Wolf Summer
Copyright © 2017 by Emily Kilduff

Drawn to the Wolves
Copyright © 2017 by Sharon Muha

www.CarinaPress.com

Printed in U.S.A.

SAVING HIS WOLF

Kerry Adrienne

**Also available from Kerry Adrienne
and Carina Press**

Waking the Bear
Pursuing the Bear
Taming the Lion
Claiming His Lioness

I'd like to dedicate this novella to my mom, Phyllis, who passed away October 2016.
Though we had a rocky relationship, she was still my mom and I miss her every day.

Dear Reader,

I hope you enjoy *Saving His Wolf*. Observing the world through the eyes of a heroine who is blind was a new challenge for me but I enjoyed it. I've gained new appreciation for the gift of sight and all the things I take for granted just being able to see.

For returning readers, thank you for joining me in the realm of the Deep Creek shifters again. You may recognize a few references to some of the characters from my Shifter Wars series, including Shoshannah, Griff and Amy, and the Green Glen wolves. This novella is completely stand-alone, however. If anyone wants to learn more about the world of alpha-bear park rangers, sneaky wolves and cocky lions, please check out Shifter Wars, which starts with *Waking the Bear*.

Love and light,

Kerry

Chapter One

Streaks of pain seared through Olivia's ankle as she slipped on the sharp rock. She bit her lip to stifle a yelp, but a weak moan managed to escape. If she didn't keep quiet, the rest of the wolves would find her. She was already at great risk in human form since she wasn't able to shift, but it couldn't be helped. Never had she wished for the ability more than as she trudged down the path tonight. She batted away the snowflakes freezing on her eyelids.

Being blind hadn't ever been more dangerous than it was now.

The icy snow gave way underfoot, and she began to slide down the embankment she'd fallen over when she stumbled off the path.

Despite the snow, she'd had to leave the pack.

She grasped for anything within reach that would break her descent, but the slush and ice covered everything in a glaze of slippery wetness she couldn't hold on to, and she continued to slip down the hill, her ankle twisting loose from the rough rock that had broken her initial fall.

From what she could tell, the rock was more of a boulder, perhaps one that had sheared off recently and left jagged edges more damaging than a serrated steel trap against her skin. Her ankle pulsed as her boot tightened around it, a sure sign of swelling. She'd be lucky if her ankle wasn't broken.

Arms spread-eagled, she tried to slow down. She whimpered, snow edging under the hem of her coat and damming against her abdomen.

She grabbed at the ground as she slid, her gloves snagging on something twisty and knotted. A root or branch of some sort stuck out from the ground, and she clutched it with both hands, her throbbing ankle now useless as an anchor. Tears burned her cheeks as she dug her other foot into the snow to hold herself steady.

"I had to leave," she whispered, laying her cheek on the cold snow for a moment of rest. *No choice.*

Staying with the Green Glen wolves wasn't an option since Alfred had decided to take her as one of his mates. He'd made the announcement, and no one had spoken up in protest, not even those she called friends. Everyone was afraid of him. He was the cruelest creature she'd ever known and she could never love him, even if he was the last wolf on Earth. He'd threatened to force her to mate, and he meant it. Everyone knew it.

She shuddered.

Blind and lost in a snowstorm with an injured leg was better than being with Alfred. Freezing to death, alone, was better.

A long, low howl sounded in the distance, and icy fear slid up Olivia's spine and gripped her in frozen panic. She clung to the root tighter, her knuckles aching at the tension.

Alfred.

No mistaking that howl. Part monster, and part...

something else, his howl strangled her soul, and made her wolf want to curl into a ball and hide forever. She pushed her hair from her face and listened. How close was he?

And more importantly, how long did she have before he found her? Maybe he would stay on the trails while he looked for her. He'd never believe a blind wolf would dare leave familiar ground. Not that she'd planned to, but the snowstorm had messed up her internal map, and she'd gotten off the path and gone right over an embankment. She adjusted her toehold in the snow. She was stable for the moment, but she needed to come up with a plan.

Alfred howled again, but sounded no closer.

Other howls answered. One, then another, and another. All different, all long and low and piercing. Deferring to him. They sounded out from different areas of the forest, yet converged as they overlapped and echoed through the snowy tree boughs.

They're searching for me.

And they'd find her on the embankment, as they triangulated her position methodically. Wolves hunted in packs and they always found their prey. They'd drag her back and she'd be Alfred's forever. Once back at the pack compound, he'd make damn sure she'd never have the chance to escape again—telling everyone it was for her own safety but, in reality, using her blindness to control her.

Alfred took advantage of weakness and used it to gain and maintain control. That went for anyone the wily wolf came in contact with, be it wolf or human or shifter. She'd scented his *modus operandi* the first time she met him, and it'd grown stronger as he'd matured.

His younger brother, Claude, might be the head of the pack in name, but it was Alfred who reigned.

She shivered, more from fear than cold, though the slow seeping chill of her damp clothing pressed against her skin and sent goose bumps racing over her stomach and chest.

She'd be hypothermic soon if she didn't find shelter and warm up. She almost laughed. She didn't know where she was or how far she was from Oakwood, so the chances she'd make it to town were slim.

The snowflakes stung as they hit her cheeks and forehead, and the wind tossed her hair across her face. The shivering had become almost rhythmic and her teeth chattered. Her leg ached from holding her body weight on the snowy hill, and her other ankle had gone completely numb.

If only she could shift. Then she could run, despite having one gimpy leg. But that wasn't meant to be. No, she was going to have to get out of this predicament like a human.

She tried to push herself up with her good leg but couldn't get traction, and she was growing more tired by the minute. Things could be worse. The wolves weren't howling, so they weren't close, and the snow would mask her scent a little.

At least for a while. Eventually, they'd find her. The question was, would she be alive or have frozen to death?

I want to live!

She yanked at the root to readjust her grip and punctuate her feelings. The wood gave way in her hand, pulling loose from the embankment.

With no time to scream, she covered her eyes and

let go, hoping she wasn't about to tumble off a cliff. Her ankle bumped and banged as she rolled, and snow flew in her mouth and nose as her braid slapped her in the face.

She hit the flat ground at the bottom of the hill with a thump, the fresh snow cushioning her fall enough to keep her from getting the breath knocked out of her. On her back, she lay still, listening, her heart slamming against her chest wall as adrenaline flooded her system like a warm cappuccino.

Alive!

She could've just as easily slid down a bank and dropped a couple hundred feet to her death. Her moment of gratitude was short-lived. The wolves howled again, the low voices almost lost on the wind or blocked by the cliffs.

Alfred wouldn't give up. Once he had his mind set on something, he kept at it till he had what he wanted. And he wanted her. She'd gone against his wishes and he'd make her pay.

The snow had picked up, and it bit into her face as it fell faster and the wind whipped it against her. She imagined the flakes as little spears swirling in puffs of air then attacking her bare skin. She had to move before she froze. Willing her legs to move, she lifted them one by one, her injured ankle sending aftershocks of pain up her leg to her thigh.

She sat up, feeling the ground around her body with her hands. Her wet gloves stuck to her palms, and she mashed her fingertips against the ground, trying to figure out where the ground ended and a cliff began.

One wrong move and she could fall to her death. She pulled her hood around her face, the faux fur trim tickling her cheek. The flush of adrenaline was wearing off and the shakes set in.

Do or die moment.

She slid to the right, dragging her bum ankle, which had numbed to a hard block of flesh. Feeling the solid ground again, she inched a bit more. A few more times, and sweat had formed on her back, though she still shook from the chill of wet clothes and falling snow. She tugged her scarf tighter, trying to keep her neck protected from the elements.

Hope I'm going in the right direction. If she could get to the embankment she had tumbled down, she could figure out how to climb it. Moving incrementally, she continued to slide toward what she hoped was the hill. The wind whistled as it swept around the cliffs and through the trees.

The wolves had gone silent.

Her wet pants, soaked through from sitting in the snow, began to stiffen. Warmth filled her legs and she closed her eyes.

The darkness was blacker than usual. She yawned.

She breathed deeply, scenting the pine amongst the snow. Always a peaceful scent, and one that reminded her of her mother. If she were alive, she'd never have allowed Alfred to lay claim on Olivia. She'd have fought him herself if she had to.

So tired.

The shivers and shakes were continuous but she ignored them. The embankment had to be close.

There!

She touched the incline. Steep at the bottom, it would take a lot of energy to haul herself up. And she was exhausted.

It's not so cold any more.

Was that a wolf howl? Or a bird call? She leaned against the bank and listened to the muted sounds in the snowy forest. The air had warmed. When had it gotten so warm? She could take a little nap before trying to climb the embankment.

Yes, a short nap. A few minutes.

The crunch of heavy footsteps sounded, and Olivia struggled to stay awake, her heart picking up speed at the thought of Alfred.

"You there. What are you doing out here in this blizzard? And all alone at that?"

The voice, a man's, was commanding and firm.

And not Alfred's.

"My ankle," she whispered.

"What?" More footsteps. "You're injured."

His voice melted over her like warm honey, and she waited to hear him speak again. She could listen to him forever…she took a long deep breath and the world silenced.

"Oh no you don't."

The voice jerked her back into wakefulness. No longer cold, she couldn't remember why she'd even worried.

"I need to rest for a few minutes." She curled on her side. "I'm so sleepy."

Chapter Two

What the ever-loving fuck was he going to do with an injured wolf? Powell dropped to his knees and pushed a long strand of the woman's blonde hair out of her face. He yawned and tugged his toboggan over his ears.

Yawns really are contagious.

He could use a good nap himself, but he was on patrol duty for most of the month while the other park rangers rested, and of course all the excitement happened on his shift. Finding an injured wolf wasn't on his agenda for the day. Yet, here she was, and her wolf was so close to the surface; the sensation was almost palpable.

The scent of her washed over him like a warm wave of summer air, and he breathed her in and savored the feeling for a moment.

But she was *wolf.* He scowled and peered closer. Not one of his normal rescues, that was for sure. Wolves were dangerous and conniving.

Her full lips mouthed something, then her head lolled to the side and she went limp. With skin almost as pale as the snow, save the bluish tint of cold around her pink lips, she might be in serious danger.

"Dammit." He scooted closer.

Was she still alive? He placed two fingers on her neck to check her pulse. Slow, but then again, she was a wolf, so that was somewhat normal. Hypothermic, he was pretty damn sure of that. He wiped the falling snowflakes from her face.

Why the hell was she out in the woods alone during a blizzard so bad he could barely see six feet ahead of him? And in human form too. The wolves weren't known as the brightest creatures, but this was a pretty dumb move. Shifters healed more quickly in their animal form, yet here she lay, all human, sprawled in the icy cold.

He shook her gently, but she didn't respond. He'd heard the wolves howling—maybe they were looking for her. They'd sounded agitated as their howls reverberated through the snow-laden forest, and that was never a good thing. If they found her with him, injured and passed out, they'd leap to conclusions that could be extremely dangerous for a lone bear. He couldn't take on numerous wolves at once.

He sniffed again, pushing through the honeyed warmth that wafted from her, to the deeper scents. *Blood.* Faint, but he smelled it. She said she'd injured her ankle. The snowstorm obscured most scents from his sensitive nose, but the metallic trace of blood pulsed in the crisp air.

Fresh.

If he didn't get her help soon, she'd die.

A long lone howl sounded in the distance. The sky was already darkening as dusk approached. It'd get dark more quickly in this snowstorm. He shook her, again, more forcefully. No movement. Her puffy coat was saturated from melting snow, and her body temperature would drop quickly if her skin got wet. He moved her wet scarf from her face.

Wolf, dammit!

He fisted his hands. Continuing his patrol and letting the wolves find her would be the right thing to do. If she died, well, that was on them for not keeping up with their own.

What did he care if there was one less wolf? He was always dealing with them stealing sheep and chickens from farms that neighbored Deep Creek, and they often sided with the lions and lied to the bears. They told people what they wanted to hear then did as they wished.

A wolf's word wasn't worth the breath that it was uttered on.

Not one good reason he should help her.

She moaned, almost too faint for him to hear.

Duty.

"Dammit." He'd never live with himself if he didn't try to help her. As a park ranger in Deep Creek, he couldn't leave her to die. Maybe he could move her to a more obvious place, like back on the trail she was following. Then, her pack could find her more quickly.

A compromise.

After unzipping his parka, he slid it off and over her, then scooped her into his arms, pulling the coat around her like he was wrapping a baby in a blanket. Limp in his arms, he held her close to his chest and headed back toward the path that led around the embankment.

Why she'd tried to climb the hill when she could've made her way out more easily along the lower path, he didn't understand. The snow must've been falling more heavily when she took the tumble down the small hill.

Maybe she'd hit her head.

Another howl sounded, this one closer, more plaintive and piercing. Then another. The wolves weren't happy.

His breath caught in his throat and he scanned the forest.

No wolves except the one in his arms.

His boots crunched with every step and he moved quickly through the forest. Snow muffled most sounds, and the world turned into a peaceful place when Deep Creek was alight with the glistening ice of winter.

Powell preferred patrolling in winter. He rarely saw another bear. Occasionally, a buck would gallop through the brush or a hare would thump the ground, but mostly he was alone.

And he loved it.

He paused on the path, the snow well over his ankles and still piling up. If he was going to leave her on the path, now was the time to do it. The snow had picked up, and a chill settled over him and was working its way into his core. He had to get to shelter soon or he'd also be hypothermic.

"Shit." No way he could leave her. If he could carry her as a bear, he would, but she wasn't able to hold on to him in her current state. She wasn't heavy, but if they ran into the other wolves they'd be in trouble.

A screech owl hooted and its echo multiplied through the trees. He crunched over a dead limb and trudged on. He'd take her to his cabin for now. Figure out what to do with her after he warmed up. With the forest on the verge of nightfall, he didn't have many choices.

He trudged on, sniffing the air for male-wolf scent and hoping he'd make it home before the forest was completely dark. The female wolf hadn't stirred. Her long hair, mostly in a braid, swung like a pendulum as he walked. He adjusted her in his arms.

Not much farther. His arms burned under the effort of carrying the wolf, and his face stung from the icy cold air and falling snow. Most of the bears would be napping now, content and warm under their blankets. Snoring.

He smiled at the thought. Glad that the Deep Creek bears didn't fully hibernate, yet happy that the long gray winter was a time of rest and rejuvenation. Much of the park was closed to tourists and only some roads were open. A glorious time to hike and run free.

A howl, much closer. Then another. Powell sniffed the air, his pulse racing and breath coming in cloudy bursts. Not much range for scenting with the snow heavier than before. Hopefully the wolves were having the same trouble. Sharp yips sounded. Then repeated.

Too close for comfort.

He pulled the injured wolf up over his shoulder in a fireman's carry so he could move faster. Sure the wolves were behind him, he took a big breath of cold air and ducked into the wind, the snow pecking at his face and eyes. His cabin porchlight shone in the distance, like a yellow firefly in a mason jar. Thighs and back burning, he jogged toward home, careful not to bump the wolf's injured leg.

Sweat dripped down his back as an icy gust pierced every pore of his exposed face.

He'd never been more glad that he'd taken the most remote ranger cabin when it became available. Tonight, that decision probably saved his life.

And hers.

The snow had accumulated several more inches since

he left, and his footprints from the cabin were mere hollows now. He tromped up the steps to the wooden porch, hand on the rail as he fought to maintain his balance on the slippery stairs.

A lone howl sounded from the forest, this one an octave higher than the last, and farther away.

Good. The wolves were not following them. He reached into his pocket, grabbed his key and pushed it into the lock.

Finally, home. The door swung open and a blast of warmth rushed over him. His cat, Narcissus, meowed in protest, fur askew in the chill.

"Not now, Nar."

The cat hopped onto the sofa back and padded his front feet. Powell pushed the door closed with his foot then carried the wolf to the couch and laid her on it. She was still out of it.

After removing his gloves and hat, he locked the door. They'd made it and the wolves hadn't caught up with them.

Thank the gods.

He moved the fire screen out of the way so he could get a fire going. He'd learned a couple of winters back to prep a fire in the fireplace before he went out on patrol. Coming home and lighting a match was a lot easier than building a fire from scratch. He lit the wadded paper under the kindling and stood back a moment, making sure the fire spread throughout.

Nar rubbed against his legs. "I'll feed you in a few minutes, buddy. We have a guest. I need to tend to her first."

The cat meowed and purred.

Powell gave him a quick pat on the head. The cat had

kept his loneliness mostly at bay. He'd found Nar as a kitten, flea-infested and scrawny, wandering around the Dumpsters in Oakwood. Taking the little thing home hadn't even been a choice.

He couldn't leave him to die.

Powell glanced at the couch. Seems like he was developing a habit of rescuing lost and wounded animals.

This one isn't staying.

Powell moved to unwrap the wolf from his parka. Despite having her coat on, he could feel that she was thin and lean, like a dancer. After unzipping and slipping off her coat, he set both coats near the fire to dry. He set her scarf beside it.

The wolf still hadn't woken, though she was breathing.

He headed for the bedroom. Maybe he should call someone, let them know about the injured wolf in case the other wolves made an issue out of it. Griff was likely awake, but Powell hated to take the chance and wake him and Amy both up.

Powell sighed and dragged some clothes out of the laundry basket of clean clothes he hadn't gotten around to folding. If she was still around in the morning, he'd let the bears know. No point in making a fuss tonight. Not like anyone would be getting out in a blizzard to come see her. And he could tend to her ankle.

He quickly pulled off his boots and changed into a T-shirt and flannel pants. After he slid his slippers on, he grabbed an extra pair of socks and padded back to the living room.

She hadn't moved.

She lay on her back, eyes closed, her arms draped over her chest. Powell set the socks on the couch beside her then added some larger branches to the fire. Nar had curled up near the hearth already—warmth replacing food as his comfort.

He went to take off her boots.

Which ankle was it she hurt? He sniffed. Though the wound wasn't bleeding any more, he scented the tang of blood. He unlaced the boot closest to him and pulled it off. Her sock was soaking wet and he peeled it free. He couldn't reach her other leg as easily, so he kneeled by the couch and reached carefully over her and slid her pant leg up, revealing a long scratch that disappeared into her boot top. The blood had dried but the cut needed attention. He untied the laces of her boot and loosened them.

He winced as he tugged at the boot. It had to hurt. Her foot had swollen and the boot didn't budge, so he unlaced it completely then wiggled it to and fro till it came off. She groaned as he pulled the sock down, but didn't stir. Better that she not be awake while he tended to her ankle and the long cut.

Examining her ankle, he found no evidence of an open fracture, but she had a lot of swelling and some purplish blue spots forming around the anklebone. The cut ran the length of her shin.

Powell washed her foot as gently as he could, then put antibiotic ointment and a bandage over the cut. She'd heal quickly as a shifter, but no need to risk infection.

Her ankle needed compression bandaging, and he wrapped a dressing around it to help support the swelling, careful not to wind the fabric too tightly. When he was done, he pulled her into his arms to adjust the pillow underneath her. Her body stiffened in his arms.

She awoke and attempted a scream and flail, but he

held on. Her voice cracked and she coughed, her body shaking.

What was he going to do now? His mouth went dry. "I'm trying to help you."

She looked up at him, long lashes surrounding pale blue eyes, wide and cloudy with a hazy fog covering her irises.

"Who are you? And where am I?" Her voice, weak and shaky, shot straight through him.

No! It can't be. A warm rush of adrenaline burst through his core.

Mate!

Chapter Three

Olivia struggled against strong arms that held her tight, but not painfully so.

"Take it easy. Everything's okay." His voice warmed her from the inside out, like a shot of fine, aged whiskey. Smooth with a slow burn.

Exhaustion gripped her and the day's tension had tightened every muscle in her upper back and neck. Something about the man comforted her, and slowly she relaxed in his arms until she went limp, unable to hold her own body up or fight against the unseen any longer. If he was the Big Bad Wolf, then she'd not be able to fight him today.

No, he wasn't Alfred. Her legs dangled off the edge of a soft chair or couch or something, and her ankle was numb. She'd never been so tired, and so confused. Surely they hadn't gone all the way to Oakwood. Her luck had never been that good, and there was no reason to think it was going to change today. Besides, even a shifter couldn't have made it so far in the bad weather.

The air warmed her, and there was no wind slapping her hair on to her face, no sound of twigs snapping under an icy load. The lack of noise was deafening. He must have brought her inside.

Somewhere.

"Who are you?" She sniffed, her breath catching in her throat. *No!* Sniffed again, scenting bear, not wolf. The chill returned to her gut and she shook. Bears and wolves had a tenuous peace, and she'd heard plenty of stories about what the bears did when they wanted something.

They took it.

Not sure whether to be afraid of the bear or happy he wasn't Alfred, she licked her lips and waited for his response. At his mercy to some degree, she listened for anything that might help her escape if she needed to. An opening door or a piece of furniture she could hit him with if he tried to hurt her. Blind, and with an injured ankle, she was at quite a disadvantage.

"I'm a park ranger here in Deep Creek." The man's voice, strong yet worried, resonated inside her. "You can trust me."

"Says who?" Her voice came out weak and uneven. Dammit, the day hadn't gone as planned.

"I didn't hurt you. I found you."

"I wasn't lost." She pulled from his grasp too hard and fell backward, then quickly sat up. The cushions were soft, like a couch. And there was a fire—she hadn't noticed it before but as the heated air brushed against her skin, ripples of sensation crawled up her arms. She turned her face to the heat, palms out, closing her eyes for a brief moment to savor the warmth. The room echoed with the crackling and popping of the fire.

Still so tired.

The bear harrumphed. "Well, excuse me. What were you doing, pretty much face down in the snow? Checking for buried acorns?"

She felt his weight lift off the couch then heard his footsteps cross what sounded like a wooden floor. Where was she? A house in Deep Creek, maybe. But where? Could she escape? The mocking tone in his voice set her nerves aflame and tears filled her eyes. She wouldn't cry in front of this bear. Typically, she held it together well, even with Alfred picking on her.

This bear was no match for what Alfred could inflict, but she was so exhausted, she didn't have the strength to continue the banter with him.

So what if he rescued her? She didn't owe him. The next thing he'd tell her would be that he'd called Alfred and the wolf was on his way to claim her. Her chin quivered and she couldn't stop it. Her whole body shook, and her muscles ached.

Had she planned and escaped only to be turned back to the pack? She'd spent too much time figuring out when to leave—when the wolves were busy and less likely to notice. The only miscalculation had been the weather.

It may have cost her everything, and she should've taken into account that the weatherman was often wrong about how much snowfall Deep Creek was going to get. She should've waited till later in the season to leave, but the fear that Alfred might set a wedding date sooner than later had been enough of a catalyst that she wanted out as soon as possible.

How long had she been lying in the snow before the bear found her? She'd heard footsteps as she closed her eyes. That must've been him approaching. She was lucky he'd seen her, or scented her.

"What were you doing face down in the snow?" he repeated.

"Obviously, I fell."

"So you needed me." The grin in his voice was as apparent as the scent of masculinity that flooded off him.

She sniffed again, and the smell of bear, and fire, and wood permeated her senses. No wolves had been in the room in a long time, if ever. Maybe Alfred didn't yet know where she was. The hope was almost painful in its intensity.

"I didn't say that." She fought against the urge to cross her arms and chew her bottom lip. The last thing she wanted to appear as was a petulant child.

The ranger poked at the fire—she recognized the sound of metal against wood and the scrape of coals on the hearth. A blast of heat washed over her as the fire was stoked higher. "Well? Why were you out in the snowstorm in the first place?"

She smirked and crossed her arms anyway. If he was going to prod her, she was going to push back. "None of your business." Her tears dried on her cheeks.

"Fine, I'm merely trying to help."

"You can help me by telling me where I am. I need to get to Oakwood."

"I brought you back to my ranger cabin. Wrapped up your ankle and treated a nasty cut on your shin." His back was still to her—she could tell by the muffled tone of his voice. His voice grew louder—he must've turned around. "I got some warm dry socks out for you, if you want them. I was about to put them on your feet when you woke up."

"Yes, thanks." She nodded, teeth clattering. Once she got warm, she could go back to being perturbed at him for taking her to his cabin without her consent. "I'd like some warm dry socks."

"Don't think you'll be heading to Oakwood tonight. Not on that ankle and not in this heavy snow. I wouldn't go out on ranger duty unless it was an emergency."

Who did he think he was? The Deep Creek park rangers were always messing in the wolves' business. She felt beside her for the socks.

"They're right there..." His voice held a question.

Cold dread settled in her stomach. He didn't know, but he was figuring it out. Quickly. And he was probably pointing to where the socks had landed. Could she fool him? She felt for the socks on the cushion she sat on, acting like she was merely pulling at the hem of her shirt.

Her hand warmed when he covered it with his own, and tingles shot up her arm at his soft touch. She jerked her hand away like she'd been burned by fire. She could sense his presence, close. He didn't move away and she breathed in a deep breath, unable to stop herself from scenting his intoxicating manliness. The dread in her gut spread and bile burned the back of her throat.

She was the enemy.

Injured or not, he probably didn't like that she was wandering through the forest on the bears' turf. The wolves were as territorial. It was as if Deep Creek were divided by magical lines delineating territory. Bears, wolves, lions.

He towered over her—she felt it. Yet, he didn't say a word, which made things worse. How could she respond to something when he stared at her without questions?

She swallowed hard. "What is it?" she whispered.

The socks were shoved into her hand and she clutched the thick ball of fabric.

"You can't see, can you?" His voice was warmer

than the fire and low, full of empathy. Compared to Alfred's shrill whine, the bear was downright soothing. She wasn't used to anyone feeling sorry for her. Most thought she was a drain on pack resources and were glad she was going to be wed to Alfred, put to use providing heirs. In their eyes, she was finally giving back.

She was the disabled wolf among a pack of warriors and thieves.

He cupped her cheek, his rough thumb tracing the line of her jaw, then he pulled away.

She shook her head. Now what? Would he take advantage of the poor blind wolf? Her heart fluttered in fear, and she tugged the sock on to her good foot in silence, the popping and crackling of the fire the only sound in the room. Maybe she should've expected as much. The wolves always did say the bears were barbaric.

"I'm sorry." His words no more than a whisper, his fingertips trailing up her arm.

"Not your fault." She turned away from his touch, unsure of what to think. He'd felt comforting, not frightening. But that went against everything she'd learned. She eased the other sock over her tender ankle, wincing as it passed over the bandaged area. Surely, her shifter ability was already helping it heal faster.

Not quickly enough.

Maybe by morning she could escape.

"Meow?" Then a bump against her leg.

A cat? Olivia froze, then sniffed the air. Yes, she should've scented it immediately. Sure enough, the bear had a cat.

How unusual.

"That's Nar. As in Narcissus. And I'm Powell."

Powell moved away, and she cooled from the loss of his presence. The shivering returned, and she ran her hands along her pant legs—her clothes damp from the wet snow.

Despite her discomfort, she smiled, though she hid it as much as she could. The idea of a huge bear taking care of a little cat amused her. She didn't know why. Who was the alpha? Wasn't the cat usually the one in charge? She ducked her head to suppress a giggle and smoothed the oversize socks. Her feet already thanked her for the fuzzy warmth, though her injured ankle began to throb as feeling returned in the thaw.

After straightening the other sock over the bandage on her ankle, she tugged her shirt straight. How much should she tell the bear? Sure, he'd rescued her, but that didn't buy him her trust. For all she knew, he'd take Alfred's side. "Olivia. I guess I owe you my life. You're right, I wouldn't have survived long out there, so thank you."

"I thought you wanted to be out in the snow." His words carried a smile. "I can dump you back out there if you want, but I don't think you'd make it through the night."

"You wouldn't dare."

"Try me. Is that what you want? I can arrange it." His levity spread.

"I don't want to leave right now, but soon. I have to."

"You aren't going to be able to walk for a while. Even with super shifter healing power, it's going to take some time."

"It won't take that long." She'd show him. Maybe she couldn't see or shift, but she'd always healed quickly.

"We'll see." His voice held plenty of skepticism.

"I heal fast."

"So do I, but there's a massive snowstorm outside to complicate things."

"I won't be here long." She tugged the elastic hair band from her hair and finger-combed the braided tangles. Yeah, the snow would be a problem, but she'd worry about that when it was time.

"You can stay here at my cabin while you heal. I'll sleep on the couch."

"I guess I don't have much of a choice, do I?" She shifted on the couch, rubbing her hands together. Her skin was so dry. "I appreciate you bandaging my ankle." He must've removed her gloves while she was passed out. And her coat and scarf.

"I could still toss your backside out in the snow." The humor returned to his voice. "If you don't want to be here."

"I'll stay inside." She wouldn't give him the benefit of a smile. "Where it's warm."

"Let me get you a blanket and some coffee or something to eat."

"A blanket would be great. But I'm not hungry."

"Maybe later, then." He walked away and she heard a sound from the other side of the room. The cat jumped up onto something, small thuds followed by claws on wood.

"Maybe." If she had her way, right now she'd be sleeping not eating. She yawned.

"Get down, Nar." Powell came close, and then she was surrounded by a heavy blanket on her shoulders.

"Thank you." She tugged the blanket tight. Whatever had happened—whether she'd hit herself on the head and knocked herself out or what, her current situ-

ation could be a lot worse. Would Alfred find her at the
ranger cabin? She turned in the direction she assumed
Powell was standing. "Where is your cabin located?"

"In Deep Creek. On the fringe of the southwestern
edge of the forest. We're pretty far from what you'd call
civilization now that there's so much snow, and until it
lets up, we aren't likely to be going anywhere."

"We aren't near Oakwood?"

"No, not at all. Why? I have plenty of rations. We
won't starve."

If she waited for Alfred to show up, he'd kill Powell.
Alfred didn't want anyone to be near her. With Powell
alone, he was vulnerable. "I have to go." She stood then
immediately fell back onto the couch, streaks of white
pain shooting up her leg.

She cried out.

"Silly wolf. Why'd you do that?" His hand was under
her elbow, guiding her into position on the couch.

"I need to get to Oakwood."

"Not tonight."

"But—"

"Sit still. You can't walk yet, much less to Oakwood.
Let me get you some coffee and pain medicine. Then
you need to rest."

She set her mouth in a line and sighed. Staying and
waiting for Alfred to come pick her up was not accept-
able. She had to be proactive and get away from the
cabin, and into Oakwood. The prospect of hiking in
the snow wasn't pleasant, given what had happened
already. Still. She needed a plan.

"Where are my boots?" She asked.

She heard the tinkling of silverware and glass. He'd
walked away.

"On the floor, but you can't put them on till that swelling goes down in your ankle." He bumped around in what she assumed was the kitchen area. "Relax and get some rest. Tomorrow we can call your den. Find someone to come get you if the snow isn't too deep. If that's what you want."

"You haven't called anyone?" She tucked strands of hair behind her ears, sure his gaze was piercing through her.

"No, I'm sorry. I've been busy tending to you."

The aroma of brewing coffee wafted through the cabin. The cat hopped up beside her and curled against her leg. She stroked his head and scratched under his chin, and he purred. A crack sounded outside, and she whipped her head toward the noise, though she couldn't see it.

Was it Alfred? Another burst of adrenaline shot through her. She'd run from Alfred until she dropped dead if she had to.

"I need to go." She gripped the edge of the couch.

Powell was right. She wouldn't get far in the dark and in a snowstorm. And with a bum foot, it wasn't likely she'd make it to Oakwood in three days much less one. Staying in the bear's cabin meant they were all sitting ducks in a game where she was both the target and the prize.

"Not tonight, you don't. We can talk tomorrow. Tonight, you rest." He approached her, his footsteps soft on the creaking floorboards. "Here, take these."

He took her hand, opened her palm, and dropped tablets into it.

"What are they?"

"Ibuprofen. And I've got a glass of water. Let me

know when you need it." His voice soothed her, though she didn't want to be soothed. She wanted to be away. Out. In Oakwood where she could figure out how to get to Florida where her aunt lived or anywhere but Deep Creek. Anywhere away from Alfred.

"How do I know you aren't lying?" She turned her face toward his voice. He could poison her, and that would be it. Or sedate her to turn her over to the pack.

"I guess you don't. But I've done nothing but help you. Take the medicine and let me get some more wood on this fire. And stop this nonsense about going out in the snow tonight."

She held her hand out and the cool glass was shoved into it. She popped the pills then chased them with a gulp of water. Then another. Thirsty, she drank the rest then held the glass out. She felt Powell take it from her hand.

She listened to him return to the kitchen area and set the glass down then come back and heft a larger piece of wood onto the fire. Lots of sputtering and popping as the wood hit the flames, and a blaze of heat seared her.

"That ought to last a while." He sat beside her, but at the other end of the couch. "Coffee will be ready soon. Then we can go to bed."

Her blindness couldn't hide her embarrassment. Powell snickered.

"Don't worry," he said. "I'll sleep on the couch."

"Fine."

"I can tell you're anxious. I'll protect you while you're in my care. I promise."

She didn't respond. What would the bear expect in return for all his *kindness*?

"You haven't told me what's up with the wolves but the howls didn't sound happy."

"Is it that obvious?"

"Yes."

"Don't call them, okay?" She hated the pleading tone to her own voice. Nothing worse than sounding weaker than she already felt.

"If you don't want me to, I won't."

"I don't."

Nar meowed from somewhere across the room.

"What does he want?" She turned her head in the direction of the sound.

"He thinks I'm going to let him out in the snow but I'm not."

"It's too cold outside for a cat." She fought to stay awake. Her clothes, now dry and warm, plus the heated air, combined to make the day's exhaustion set in hard. So much more comfortable than being outside in the cold. She yawned.

"Yes." He stood. "He can go out when it's daylight. Are you ready for coffee?"

"No." She shook her head. "My ankle aches, and every muscle I have and some I didn't know I had hurt like crazy. A good night's sleep will help."

"You didn't hit your head when you fell?" His voice held the serious question. "No chance of concussion?"

"No, just my ankle. I'm so tired, I want to sleep."

She heard Powell yawn. "I am too. I agree. Rest tonight, fresh start tomorrow. Hold on."

Arms slipped under her and before she could protest, he'd swept her up and was carrying her…somewhere. Part of her wanted to lean against him and let him take care of things and part of her wanted to punch him in the nose for being so presumptuous.

Before she could decide, he dropped her on a soft bed.

"The cabin is small, but adequate. This is my bed. There's a bathroom right here to the immediate left."

She wasn't sure what to say. The bear was being super nice to her. All the stories she'd ever heard were about how bad the bears were, with few exceptions. "Thank you," she managed.

"Lie down."

She obeyed and the covers settled over her. He tucked her in all the way around, then laid a heavier blanket or a quilt over her. The bed seemed to sink in and the warmth from the blankets soothed her aching muscles. *So comfortable.*

"I'll be in the next room if you need anything." His footsteps retreated. "We'll deal with everything else in the morning."

"Okay."

He paused at the bedroom door and it squeaked as he started to pull it shut. "You realize how lucky you are?"

She nodded. She needed sleep, so much sleep.

"Not much longer out in that weather and you'd not be alive."

She yawned. "Thank you, again." She tugged the covers higher around her chin, and the scent of him washed over her, setting her insides jumbling. Of course a bear would give her a stomachache.

"I'm going to feed Nar and turn off the coffeepot." The door squeaked closed after his whispered words. "Stay put till morning. We'll get you home."

She didn't answer, though. The wind rattled the windowpanes nearby, and she listened as ice crystals pelted the glass.

Thank the gods, she was inside, safe and warm. Even if it was in a cabin somewhere unknown in the forests of Deep Creek. A good night's sleep would help a lot before she continued her journey.

A howl began, far away then seemingly nearer, its purpose and intent clear. Olivia belonged with the Green Glen wolves. She belonged to Alfred. Unless she found a way to get into town with an injured ankle, she'd need to hide out. Shifter healing had already begun, but she'd messed her ankle up and it would take some time for it to heal enough for her to be on the move again.

She wouldn't be running the next day unless she had to.

Alfred bayed again, insistent. Persistent. The sound trilled on the wind and through the bare tree branches, which clicked together like secret code in the icy wind.

Olivia...where are you?

My Olivia...

Chapter Four

How long had he lain awake, thinking about the beautiful wolf in his bed? How many times had he fed the fire in the night? He wasn't sure when he'd finally fallen asleep, though the pinks and oranges of dawn had lit the room in a pale glow. Now past midday, he needed to get moving. Powell sat up and pushed the blanket away. She was exactly what he liked in a woman. A little sassy, with a sense of humor to match his own.

And she was his mate.

Dammit.

He didn't want a mate. He'd never wanted a mate. Mates were for other bears like Griff and Derek: bears that wanted to settle down and have cubs and a house in the woods with a split-rail fence and flowers growing along the walkway; bears that were much more emotionally equipped to take care of a female and not screw things up—not forget how to love or what to do.

He rubbed his eyes and studied the remains of the fire, the embers glowing like crusted lava with feathers of blue and yellow flame flaring up occasionally. He could whip the fire back into a blaze if he wanted—there were enough coals—but it was still plenty warm in the cabin already. Besides, poking around in the coals would mean breaking his reverie, and he was enjoying the quiet reflection.

Delicate as the fine branches that sprouted from the trees in spring, Olivia had charmed him immediately. Her lips, so pink and wet, begged to be kissed, and he wanted to wrap her hair around his hands and clasp on to her as he moved inside.

I've got to stop thinking about her as a lover. She's a wolf.

As long as his mate remained a daydream, he could handle her. Reality was another thing entirely. The risk was getting daydreams and reality mixed up. If he was honest with himself, he'd admit he needed to feel her in his arms. His very essence ached to protect her, hold her, comfort her. And yes, make love to her.

Muted sunlight reflected off the bright white snow banks into the living room. The sun had definitely climbed to midday, and he needed to get up. He moved to the window and pulled the curtain back to look out. Birds pattered everywhere, enjoying the peanut butter and birdseed logs he'd made for them and set up along the narrow fence that lined the walkway to his porch. Cardinals and a couple of blue jays and tons of little nuthatches and sparrows pecked and bartered over the feast.

Patchy clouds blotched the sky, and snowflakes swirled and danced on a much lighter breeze than the night before. His snow gauge measured twenty inches, but the snow drifted much higher in places and another round of snowfall was expected in the late afternoon, though the gravid clouds of precipitation hadn't rolled in yet. He dropped the curtain into place.

He loved the way winter hugged the forests and

mountains of Deep Creek and brought a peace over the valleys. Most of the bears stayed inside even when awake in the cold weather, but he took long hikes in the fresh air to enjoy the blanket of solitude the cold brought to the park.

Time to wake Olivia. He'd been waiting, hoping the extra rest would help. Her ankle needed to be re-bandaged. The cut was probably already healed, but in case, he'd check it and dress it again if necessary. Maybe the swelling had gone down some too. He walked carefully to his bedroom and rapped on the door.

No answer.

After calling her and knocking louder with no response, he turned the doorknob and pushed the door open.

An icy blast burst forth, punching him in the face. The room was still dark, as all the shades were drawn closed. Why the hell was it so cold?

"Olivia." He used his loudest whisper. He didn't want to startle her, but something wasn't right.

He moved closer to the antique bed and reached to tap Oliva on the shoulder. When his hand hit the lump of blankets, the fabric collapsed onto the mattress.

Olivia was gone.

"Dammit!" His yelp was loud enough to be heard in the kitchen. He closed his eyes to breathe through the rage that filled him. Gods, the woman was stubborn as hell.

Worse than he was.

What made her think she could travel in the snow that had washed over the forest overnight? Not only was she blind, her ankle was injured. She'd barely be able to move, much less trek through deep snow on one leg.

Stubborn.

He checked the window. She'd mostly closed it, but that had been her escape route. The window was close to the ground and it would be easy to slip out. Had she gone out in the snow without shoes?

Dammit. He'd slept through her escape.

His bear paced, huffing in frustration. *Mate in danger.* The urge to shift almost drowned him in nausea. The pull, so strong, to find her and bring her back. Now he understood how Griff had done what he'd done to Evers. Having a mate was nothing to joke about, and a bear would do anything to protect her. Anything.

Mate is life.

After slamming the window shut and locking it, he went into the living room and stripped and dropped his clothes on the floor then headed out the front door, sliding into his bear as he pulled the door closed behind him. He paused on the porch, where the icy chill blasted him as his body shifted.

Breathe.

His bear fought to surface, pushing aside man with a growl that reverberated through his body. Never had his bear been so eager to take charge.

Mate.

Blues and hues of purple swirled in front of his vision as he relaxed and let his body take on its natural bear form. Fur warmed him and long strong legs formed like columns. His head ached with the stretch, and he gnashed his teeth, nipping at the spiraling snowflakes that filled the air. Curved claws raked through frosty air.

A growl sounded from deep in his gut as his eyesight cleared to a precision unmatched by human vision, and his hearing sharpened. A thousand twitters of birdsong rang in his ears, and close by, the pattering of a rabbit heart sped by.

He swung his head left then right, scanning his fence where yard met forest. In some places, snow drifted almost as high as the four-foot posts. He growled and loped off the porch in search of Olivia. She couldn't have gone far in the deep snow.

He rounded the cabin to the side where his bedroom window perched a few feet off the ground. She'd put on his boots, apparently, and dragged a quilt with her, by the look of the tracks in the snow—though the tracks had filled in a bit, which proved she'd left in the morning. He glanced up at the sky. Gray storm clouds swirled and now covered the sun.

It'd start snowing again soon.

Footprints led to the west, and he hurried to follow them out of his yard and into the deeper part of the forest. He paused to sniff a tatter of his quilt that had caught on a branch and torn off.

Smells of mate.

His bear heart thumped with the sudden rush of blood. He never felt as alive as he did when he was all bear. Snarling, he moved on. He'd find her and bring her home.

The wind whistled as it bore down on the forest, tipping ice-laden branches into graceful curves and crystallized evergreen boughs arced almost to the ground like tunnels of magic. In the dim light, the snow sparkled. As soon as the forest thawed, the trees would spring back upright, tall and majestic.

Resilient.

Mouth open, he panted then paused to sniff the air. No scent of Olivia or any other wolf. Where could she have gone? The footprints into the forest were less defined, and Powell moved more slowly as he tried to track her.

The steel-gray sky began to spit snow, and chunks of ice wedged between the pads of his toes and clumped to his claws. Bears knew better than to be out in this weather for long. Though he had a warm coat, eventually the cold would penetrate to his skin. He shook, sending a shower of loose snow flying in all directions. Everywhere he looked it was white, with interruptions of brown and an occasional green.

No Olivia.

He reared onto his hind legs and scented, again.

Pine. Birds. Some small mammals. And a faint hint of frigid water crashing over smooth boulders in one of Deep Creek's many streams.

No Olivia. Following the fading tracks was his only option.

He continued onward, unable to get a fix on how long it had been since she passed through the area. The snow came down hard now, no longer light flurrying action. He picked up his pace.

Rage fueled his movements and he growled as he ran. What a dumb thing for her to do. She could easily die of exposure. Hadn't she learned her lesson when she fell down the embankment? Hell, he would've helped her get to town if that's what she wanted. She didn't need to feel like she had to do it all herself. She didn't need to run from him.

Women!

This type of behavior was the exact reason he had never wanted a woman of his own. Or, if he listened to how Griff or Derek described it, a woman would own him, regardless of what he thought. Sure, he'd still protect her and take care of her, but her wish was always the man's command. His bear snorted. Either way, it was too much trouble.

He didn't need the stress.

The fur down his back bristled. No, he was a single bear and intended to stay that way. Just because he had met his mate didn't mean he had to marry her. Besides, she was a wolf and didn't seem to have any clue that he was her mate.

Maybe it didn't work that way.

Maybe he was wrong.

Maybe wolves didn't know who their mate was at all. Olivia had shown no sign that he was anything more to her than a man who'd rescued her.

And would rescue her again.

He padded on.

He shook his head, his ears flapping as the snow went everywhere. *Mate.* Whoever came up with the idea of a fated mate needed a head check. Commitment was for the birds. Too much trouble, too much work. He slowed his run, tired and achy, and ready to leave Olivia in the woods and hope someone else came across her.

Serve her right.

A pang of guilt stabbed him the moment the thought crossed his mind.

Of course he wouldn't dare leave her alone in the snow. He wouldn't leave anyone to die, much less Olivia. He'd only known her a day, and mate or not, she'd consumed about every waking thought and had walked in his dreams.

His ears pricked.

Hey, what was that?

A red round object peeped from beside a large elm tree ahead, and Powell slowed to check. Maybe a woodpecker. Whatever it was, it stuck out like a stop sign in the white snow. No, it was something that he'd seen Olivia wearing—her scarf! She must've limped into the living room to get it before she left. Her coat must not have been dry since she had left it behind.

Or she didn't want him to notice it was gone.

Sure enough, it was her. She leaned against the tree, the quilt wrapped around her and a pair of his boots bulky and loose on her feet. He picked up his pace and rushed to her. Why the hell was she in human form? She hadn't shifted into wolf—and she could've frozen to death because of it.

He nosed her in the side.

She screamed.

Dammit! He'd startled her.

He'd forgotten she couldn't see. He nudged her again. How scary to be in the woods alone, cold, and lost—and not be able to see. He couldn't imagine. An all-encompassing urge to protect her washed over him.

"Powell?" Her voice weak, shaky. She reached for him, taking his head in her hands. "I'm so glad it's you."

He leaned against her, hoping she felt some security in his touch. She trembled with cold. Good thing he'd found her. The quilt was covered in a layer of snow, and the precipitation continued to fall at a steady rate. They needed to get to the cabin.

She climbed on his back, groaning as she moved her leg, and laid her head on him, her arms around his neck, still clutching the quilt. He waited on her to stabilize herself and turned toward home. Shocked that she trusted him to carry her, he headed back to the cabin, careful to balance her and not let her slip and fall. The warmth of her on his back and the slight weight of her body felt right. His bear hummed in approval.

Mate.

The sky had almost completely darkened with clouds, though it was only late afternoon by the time they got back to the cabin, and he eased her onto the porch. She slipped off him and entered the cabin without a word. As he morphed back into his human body, he wondered if she was sneaking out the back door while he shifted. Surely not. She'd seemed genuinely glad to see him. The cold air hit his exposed skin like frozen needles, and he rushed inside to get warm, shutting the door behind him. She wasn't in the living room. He grabbed his pajama pants off the floor and pulled them on.

Olivia limped out of the bedroom with Nar in her arms.

"I don't know what to say." She stroked the cat. Her hair lay around her shoulders and down her back in a mess of wet tangles, and her cloudy eyes stared into oblivion.

He pulled his T-shirt over his head and down over his abdomen. Anger bubbled in his gut, but it was mixed with relief. She could've died.

"Sit."

She felt around and hobbled over to the couch then sat. Nar lay beside her, and she pulled the blanket over her legs. "I thought I was healed enough. I could walk, somewhat."

"Did you think so?" He poked at the embers and added some small wood and sticks. "Because I thought it was pretty obvious that you weren't ready. It's a long walk to Oakwood, and correct me if I'm wrong, you don't know how to get there from here."

She didn't respond.

He jabbed the tool at the embers, sending sparks up the chimney. For someone who seemed so damn smart, she had done something pretty stupid. Twice in two days.

Nar hopped up onto the hearth and swished his tail, eyes questioning the anger in Powell's voice.

"Meow?"

"Yes, I'm working on it." He petted the cat on the head then scratched him behind the ears. "It'll be hot in here soon."

"Working on what?" Olivia asked.

He looked back to her. She'd pulled the blanket up to her chin, shivering. It was a wonder she hadn't caught a cold by now. Or gotten frostbite. If she'd been human, she would've, for sure.

Being a shifter had saved her life.

"Building a warmer fire." He grabbed the last log off the hearth, a small piece of wood only about two inches in diameter. "I need to get more wood off the porch. We're out in here. It's starting to get dark, so I want to have enough for the night in case the snow piles up more."

"I'm sorry for dragging you out in the cold. I didn't expect you to come after me."

He sighed and put his hands on his hips.

Seriously?

"Of course I'm going to come after you. I'm not going to let you freeze to death." He set the log on the fire with the tongs, then moved to sit beside Olivia on the couch. "But I don't understand why you felt like you had to sneak out."

She shrugged but said nothing.

"Why can't you wait a couple days? I'll take you to Oakwood. And why didn't you shift into a wolf to stay warm? Why stay in human form when you could fight the elements so much better as wolf?"

She turned her face away. "It's a long story."

She'd tensed up and locked down, her knuckles white from tightly grasping her shirt hem.

"I've got time. Tell me. It makes no sense why you wouldn't shift. Unless you thought the wolves could track you more easily? I've kind of guessed that you're running from them."

She shook her head.

Nar jumped up between them, and Powell petted him till he purred and flopped onto his back. "I think I deserve to know why you left a perfectly warm house and went out into the freezing cold with an injured ankle. Are you psycho? If you are, I'd like to know it."

She smacked him on the arm and smirked. "No, I'm not crazy."

"Then why not shift? What reason could you possibly have to go out in the cold by yourself? In a blizzard—blind and injured?"

She pushed her hair behind her ears. "I'll give you the short version, but you have to promise not to pity me."

"I promise." He scooted closer, her scent filling his nostrils and wending through his brain. Pity was the last thing on his mind.

"I'm engaged to Alfred."

It was as if she'd given him a lobotomy with an ice pick.

"What?" Had he heard her correctly? She was engaged to that scrawny asshole? That red wolf without a conscience? What the hell?

"It's not by choice," she added. "The pack thinks it's what's best. No one would want me. I'm damaged goods. And Alfred, well, he can have more than one wife since he can take care of more than one and well, they decided I wouldn't be a burden to him—" Her voice hitched in her throat.

"That is the most ridiculous thing I've ever heard of! Isn't polygamy illegal? Especially forced polygamy?" Anger surged through him, and the desire to rip Alfred's head off consumed him like a flash flood. He fisted his hands and tamped down the feeling, gritting his teeth so he wouldn't scare Olivia. "What the hell is damaged about you? You mean because you are blind?"

She nodded. "That's part of it. There's another reason."

"What?"

She squirmed, her chin quivering. What had Alfred done to her? Powell would kill him.

"I can't shift." She turned her face to him, her milky gaze full of tears.

"Oh." He wiped the tears from her cheeks and pulled her to him, her head on his chest. "Why can't you shift? Did something happen?"

"I've never been able to. It's probably because I'm blind." She sniffled. "At first, I agreed with the pack about marrying Alfred. I figured I'd be taken care of. But then I heard about his sexual sadism, and I can't..."

He gripped her arm and took a deep breath. "And you won't have to. I'll see to it."

Not sure whether her inability to shift or her betrothal to Alfred upset him more, he gritted his teeth. No wonder she was scared. Alfred was an asshole.

"But the pack is strong. They'll find me and drag me back. I won't have a choice."

A long, low howl sounded outside and Olivia tensed in his arms.

"Shh. They aren't close. It'll be evening soon and they are out hunting, that's all. They don't know you're here, and there's no reason to think they will find you, especially with the snow piling up and covering scents. I'll protect you, but you've got to trust me and give me the chance to figure out what to do. We'll handle this together. I need your promise to stay put and let me work up a plan."

"Okay." She relaxed into him.

He stroked her hair. "Everything will be okay. We'll get some dinner and rest."

A loud buzz sounded followed by a snap—then everything went dark in the cabin except for the orange glow of the fire and the faint light coming in the windows from the setting sun.

Chapter Five

"What was that sound?" Her heart thudded and she gripped him. Was Alfred on the porch? *Oh my goddess, no.* He'd kill Powell without hesitation, and she'd be back with the Green Glen wolves before she had a chance to do anything.

"The power went out." Powell's voice held a hint of wariness. "That's all. No need to worry."

"I'm scared," she whispered. And she was. Her palms dampened. Was it possible that Alfred had cut power to the cabin? Would he and the others attack while the power was out and they had the advantage of darkness, killing Powell and taking her back to the pack?

"It often happens when there's a storm. It's gone out quite a few times." He patted her knee. "The power lines get heavy with snow and ice and snap, or the transformer blows. The cabin is so remote, it doesn't take much to cause a problem. And we've gotten a lot of snow. We have a fire to keep us warm, though. We'll be fine."

"Are you sure that's all it is?" Her voice caught. She chewed her bottom lip. Nothing worse than feeling helpless. She was so tired of having to rely on others to take care of her. If only she could shift, she could fight.

"Yes, of course. What else could it be?"

"Alfred." Maybe she should return to the pack and stop all the stress. Be Alfred's wife. Maybe she didn't deserve more. Who would want to be with a blind wolf who couldn't shift, anyway? She'd always be a burden.

"No offense, but he's not that clever." Powell rubbed her arm.

"I wouldn't put it past him. When he wants something, he's pretty insistent."

"He's not going to get his paws on you unless it's what you want."

She shook her head. As much as she didn't know what she'd do, she didn't want to be under Alfred's control. "No. Definitely not."

"Good. I don't want you with him, either." He squeezed her hand and stood. "I need to get more wood from the porch so we can keep the fire going all night. We'll need it to stay warm since the heat is out."

"Okay." If he could tell how frightened she was, he didn't show it. "Do you have enough wood set aside?"

"Yes." He laughed. "There's enough wood for a semi-hibernating bear to sleep away the winter by the fire. Not a little fire, either. A roaring bonfire. Plenty of wood."

She let out a breath. Maybe things would be fine. "If you say so."

"I do. Once the fire's going, we'll find some food. I'm sure you're as hungry as I am. I'll be back."

She pulled the blanket higher, rubbing the softness against her chin. "Please hurry. I don't want to be alone."

"I'll be right here in the living room stacking the wood as I bring it in. You aren't alone. Nar is here too."

"Meow."

The cat rubbed against her, purring. Olivia smiled. She'd never have guessed that she would befriend a cat, ever. Wolves and cats usually didn't get along. But Nar was different. He wasn't all scratchy and bitey like the few other cats she'd met scavenging around the pack fringes. Nar liked her.

She patted him, running her hand down his back. Being a wolf, she'd not had much close-up experience with cats at all, though she'd heard that black cats were even more unlucky than other kinds. A wolf had once told her that the color black was what she saw all the time—the darkness she lived in. It was the absence of color. Surely Nar was different. He was too nice not to have color. One thing was certain, petting him calmed her in a way not much else did.

Powell made several trips in and out, dropping armloads of wood on the hearth and floor, and she listened to the wood hit the ground and roll or crack as it landed. He brought in a lot, surely enough to last the whole night. She'd not realized it took so much to keep a fire going. With the door opening and closing, the warm air had escaped, and now the living room was freezing.

Powell hadn't pushed her about shifting.

What had he thought about her inability to transition to a wolf? Did he feel sorry for her? More than he must already because of her blindness?

The blanket wasn't enough to keep the chill away, and she shivered as she tried to cover herself. As she bent her leg, her ankle ached. So frustrating. She never should've tried to go out in the snow. Healing was likely slowed down, and she'd have to wait longer before she could hike to Oakwood, not counting the stupid snow.

If she could shift to wolf form, the ankle would heal much more rapidly. She sighed.

The late day was full of reasons to feel sorry for herself. Powell must take his ranger duties seriously for him to take her in and tend to her injuries.

She was lucky he had been the one to find her.

He tugged the door shut with a thump and clasped the lock.

"That should do it." He coughed. "I think the snow is letting up. But it's pretty deep. Good thing we don't have to get out."

Icy air hung in the cabin. Nar walked across her lap, pausing a moment before jumping down.

"I want to go to Oakwood as soon as possible." She leaned forward. "You shouldn't have to take care of me. I know I'm a burden."

"You aren't a burden, and it's not a problem. It's my job to take care of people lost in the forest, remember?"

She heard him toss another log onto the fire and poke at the flames. A burst of heat raced across the room. So that was it. She was a duty. An obligation to Powell. Nothing more than another lost soul in the forest who needed tending.

The realization made her heart ache, but she didn't know why.

"I'm sorry. You shouldn't have brought me here." She held her head in her hands. The sooner she could leave the better.

He sat beside her and pulled the blanket over them both, his thigh warm against hers. "Olivia, what's wrong?"

She turned away. How to explain to someone what it

felt like to never feel wanted? To never be good enough? To always be the one holding everyone else back?

It sucked.

Hot tears filled her eyes, and she set her chin, trying to keep from breaking down. That would be the topper to a great day—crying in front of her twice-rescuer. He surely couldn't pity her any more than he already did.

"Olivia?" Powell's voice, calm and warm, seemed to come from inside her.

She wiped her eyes. "What?"

"I don't know why you're so upset, but I hope you aren't mad at me."

"No." She paused. "Why would I be upset with you?"

The fire popped and crackled, and the scent of pine filled the cabin. He must've put a fresh pine bough on the fire.

"I don't know. But you are on edge, and I don't know why. I wondered if I'd done something to upset you."

She smoothed the blanket over her legs. "No. I'm sorry. I must seem ungrateful. Thank you for rescuing me. Twice."

"You're welcome. Happy to do it. But please don't leave, again. The snow has reached dangerous levels out there."

"I'm concerned about Alfred. He won't be happy if he finds me here. And he's mad that I left. I'm sure it made him look bad that one of his promised wives ran away."

Powell took her hand, and she savored the warmth of his palm seeping into her skin. So strong. So firm.

A man who knew what he wanted. Yet…one that didn't force his will on others.

"I don't understand why Alfred is being assigned

wives and in the plural. Since when are wolves polyga-mous?" He rubbed her hand with the pad of his thumb.

"They aren't. He's taking all the unwanted girls in marriage. It's supposed to be a mutual thing. He takes care of them and they…take care of him."

For once, she was glad she was blind and couldn't see his reaction. She was ashamed she'd considered the proposal. From the outside, it was absurd. At the time, most pack members made her feel like she was lucky to have Alfred. Now, if she went back, she'd be shunned. If Alfred still wanted her, she'd be punished.

"How many wives does he have?" Powell's voice re-mained low and unaffected.

"Oh, only two right now. I would've been number three." The fire's heat warmed her cheeks. "He's the only wolf that has more than one partner, though. Be-cause his family is in charge, though I think most of us know that Alfred runs the pack. Claude is weak."

"That's ridiculous, you know that?" He squeezed her hand. "Having more than one wife—and not being in love, that's my assumption?"

"Oh, he doesn't love anyone but himself." She tried to pull her hand free, but Powell held on, gently squeezing.

"What about true mates? Love? Hasn't he heard of that?"

She shook her head and relaxed in his grip. "He doesn't believe in fated mates." Her heart pattered at Powell's proximity. Why did he have such an effect on her? He was a bear, for goodness' sake. But every time he was close, she broke into a light sweat and her heart did mini flips. And she craved his closeness.

He cleared his throat. "Unacceptable. True love and fated mates are…essential beliefs."

"That's why I left. I want more. Well, and I don't want to be a burden."

"You deserve more. Much more. You won't have to go back, I'll make sure of it." His voice picked up an urgency she hadn't heard before. "You aren't a burden to me, Olivia."

Every bit of her essence wanted to believe him. But how could he help her? He was a bear. She was wolf.

A damaged wolf.

They didn't share the same urges. On the cold nights of winter, she ran with the moon and he napped by the fire. She wiggled away, pulling her hand free. Napping by the fire was something she could get used to.

If only...

She sensed him before she felt him. Warmth then soft lips touching hers, his hand sliding behind her head and pulling her toward him. Off balance, she inhaled deeply, filling her lungs with his scent and tumbling head over heels in her mind as she reached for something to grab on to. Her wolf howled inside like it had been set free from a trap.

He tugged her close, planting kiss after kiss on her lips and cheeks till she responded, sliding her tongue along the seam of his lips. He welcomed her tongue and met it with his own, thrusting with a strength and passion she'd not imagined was possible.

After a moment, she pulled back. He didn't speak. What was he thinking? What cues would his facial expression provide, if she could see?

"I'm sorry." He offered no other words but pushed the blanket away, then stood and walked away.

Chapter Six

Powell shoved the iron poker at the fire, lining up the burning logs with precision. The flames surged and sputtered. What the fuck had he done? He couldn't bear to look at Olivia. She'd trusted him.

He'd betrayed her trust. He was no better than Alfred, forcing himself on her.

Blind and injured, she was his responsibility. Not because he was a park ranger, but because he was her mate. Even though she didn't seem to sense they were mates, he was sure they were. Hell, maybe wolves didn't know when they met their mates. Maybe it took longer than a first touch for them to know.

It didn't matter. He'd taken advantage of someone in a weaker position and that wasn't his style. Kissing her when she was in such a vulnerable position had been out of line.

Dammit.

Sorry wasn't enough, but what else could he say? She was stuck in his cabin for the foreseeable future unless they got out the snowmobile and tried to get to town. With her injury, the last thing they needed was to have to deal with an accident. They needed to wait until the snow stopped before snowmobiling, that would be safer.

He'd gone out on rescues when the snow was pouring down, of course, but he didn't want to risk his mate.

He peeked at her.

Blond hair splayed across her shoulders, blanket pulled up under her nose—she looked like a child hiding from a scary movie. Yet he knew how strong she was. The fact that she'd set out, blind, not once but twice, into the forest to get away from an unimaginable fate with her pack proved that.

She'd had a rough couple of days.

The flickering fire their only light, she was bathed in oranges and yellows, more beautiful than any girl he'd ever seen. Knowing she was his mate cast her in a different light, for sure, but he'd dare say she was gorgeous inside and out.

He'd kissed her because he couldn't resist. He'd never been in that position before.

Way to go.

Now he felt like a first-class asshole. Never mind that she'd kissed him back. That might have been habit from dealing with Alfred, responding out of fear of repercussion if she didn't. Anger rose in his gut.

If that damn wolf had harmed her, he *would* kill him. It wasn't an idle threat. The bears had dealt with the wolves before, and Powell already knew what a scheming jerk the red wolf was. He'd used his own injured brother to gain the bears' sympathy and scope out intel to take to the lions. Probably had been paid well too.

He breathed out slowly. Getting ahead of himself and letting his imagination run wild wasn't going to solve anything. He didn't know the truth about Olivia's relationship with Alfred, other than she didn't want to marry him.

She hadn't said the wolf had done anything to her or

physically harmed her, though clearly he'd been emotionally abusive. Powell shouldn't leap to conclusions until he knew the whole story. Still, he couldn't help but want to rip Alfred's throat out for thinking about touching Olivia.

His bear reared up inside, pawing and begging to be released to go after Alfred.

Having a mate was complicated. Being a bear and having a mate that was a wolf?

Impossible.

For now, he'd have to make the best of things with Olivia. She'd be staying with him for a little while, until she was healed enough to get around on her own. No more trudging through the snow with a bum ankle though—he'd see to that.

"How about a sandwich for dinner?" Lame, yes, but practical. Plus, fixing dinner gave him a chance to think and maybe figure out a way to redeem himself. A way to apologize. He had to start talking to her again, somehow.

"Sure, that sounds good." She pulled her legs up onto the couch, gently easing her injured ankle onto the pillow. "Thank you."

No mention of the kiss. And she was talking. Good signs.

"Give me a minute to set the table." He placed the fire poker back into its holder. "Peanut butter and honey sandwiches okay? I know I have both."

"Yes, I love peanut butter." She kicked her legs forward and started to rise then winced and fell back into the couch. "I'm sorry I'm not much help."

"You relax and let me fix dinner. You're injured. I can make sandwiches." Relieved she didn't seem mad, he headed toward the kitchen.

The open-floor plan of the cabin allowed him to keep his eye on her, and he grabbed a candelabra off the bookcase and set it on the table then lit the candles. She leaned back on the couch and closed her eyes, folding her hands under her cheek. She rested a few minutes, and he retrieved the honey from the pantry. When he returned, she was sitting up.

"Powell?" Her voice rang out, clear and firm.

"Yeah? What is it?" He grabbed the loaf of bread and pulled the peanut butter from the cabinet.

"When we're eating, I want to talk." She twisted the edge of the blanket with her fingertips, worrying the edges.

He swallowed and pulled out two plates from the cabinets beside the sink. "Of course. Why wouldn't we talk?"

"About the kiss."

He paused. "Okay." He opened the silverware drawer and took out a knife, swallowing down the fear rising in his throat. "Whatever you want to talk about."

A woman who'd turned down Alfred wasn't going to let Powell get away with an unexplained kiss. He couldn't blame her. If only he knew more about the mating of bears and wolves, he might understand what was going on, because he definitely felt a strong sense of protectiveness when he was around her. He couldn't fully explain it, but it was something he'd never felt before.

A need to be near her. An urge to shelter her from anything that might hurt her.

A desire so white hot and pure, it could consume him if he let it.

* * *

Powell watched Olivia take a bite of the sandwich and set it back on the plate in front of her. He'd helped her to the table, letting her lean on him as she limped across the wooden floor. It'd taken every bit of willpower he had not to pick her up and carry her, though she was getting around better than a human would be so soon after an ankle injury. The last thing he needed to do was force her or overpower her. Make her feel weak around him.

He needed her to trust him. No, more than that, he *wanted* her to trust him.

The fire had heated the cabin, but a chill still filled the corners and dark areas, so he had retrieved one of his sweatshirts for Olivia. The gray shirt dwarfed her but provided some warmth, he hoped. She pushed her hair behind her shoulders.

"It's good," she said, mouth full. "I didn't realize how hungry I was."

He pulled the strips of crust off his sandwich. "Me either, though I'd rather be having a juicy steak than a peanut butter and honey sandwich." He laughed.

She sipped her water then set the glass down, smiling. "Me too."

He ate in silence, waiting on her to start the conversation he dreaded. The fire popped across the room, and occasionally, the wind whistled through small cracks around the windowpanes. Olivia was quiet, eating and seemingly lost in thought. Though blind, it didn't take her any time to figure out and remember where her food and drink were on the table.

He wiped his mouth and set his napkin down, his sandwich gone. After a long yawn, he drank another gulp of water. Things had been too exciting for winter.

His body was tired, and he was used to napping much of the winter away. Lying awake the night before hadn't helped. Exhaustion crept through his muscles and he stifled a yawn.

If he had to stay awake, he would. For Olivia, anything.

"You kissed me." She pushed her empty plate away. "Why?"

He opened his mouth then closed it. Her straightforwardness both shocked and pleased him. Never a fan of games or passive aggressiveness, he was still a bit taken aback. He cleared his throat. "I wanted to."

"I see." She seemed to think about his answer for a minute.

He stood. "I'm going to put our dishes in the kitchen."

"Okay. But we aren't done talking." She drank the last of her water. "Aren't you afraid of Alfred? I mean, that you kissed me. He'd kill you for kissing me."

"No, I'm not afraid of Alfred. Are you?" He gathered their plates and set them on the kitchen counter. "Besides, I thought you didn't want to be with him."

"I don't, and I won't. But I'm still afraid of him. He's…mean."

"I can handle him. You don't need to worry. We're safe here."

"I wouldn't want something to happen to you." She shivered and rubbed her arms.

"I can take care of Alfred if I need to. You don't need to worry. Let's go back in the living room by the fire where it's warm."

"Yes. Please."

He took her by the arm, and she leaned on him as she limped. He breathed her in, trying not to be too obvious. If she'd allow, he'd take her in his arms and kiss her again. But he didn't get a read on whether she'd liked the kiss or was upset by it. He couldn't risk another one.

Not yet.

She sat on the couch.

"I'll be right back. I need to grab something from the bedroom." He glanced at the fire to make sure the wood situation was okay. The fire blazed, the wood filling the fireplace.

"I'll be here." She yawned. "Not like I can go anywhere. But you know that."

"Yeah, we're stuck. Give me a minute."

He headed to his room and grabbed his hairbrush off the dresser then returned to the living room. She had her head leaned back on the edge of the couch, her eyes closed, her neck bare. His pulse quickened at the sight of her exposed neckline, pale and long. He reached out to run his fingertips along the skin, but pulled away.

Did this mate thing always make bears crazy? It seemed like he was barely in control of his actions. Olivia was like a strong magnet—stronger than any he'd ever been around. And he was pure metal.

He moved to sit beside her and she turned to face him. "You're back."

"Yes. I'd like to brush your hair." He used his low and calm voice. "If you'll let me."

She raised her head. "Is it that bad?"

He smiled. "It's a bit of a tangle. I thought we could talk while I do it."

"Okay. That'd be nice. Thank you. What do you want to talk about?"

"Turn to the side." He helped her move. "I don't know. What do you want to talk about?"

"Not snow or winter or injured ankles or Alfred."

He brushed her hair in long strokes from scalp to end. The pale strands glistened in the firelight as they fell from his fingertips. Maybe she'd relax. His father used to brush his mother's hair, and Powell saw how much she'd loved it. He never thought that one day he'd use the same technique to try to relax his mate. He took a deep breath and steeled himself against a possible pushback.

"Let's talk about your shifting ability. I'm curious to learn more about it." He stopped to pick at a tangle.

"You mean my inability to shift." She winced. "Ouch."

"Sorry. That was a pretty tight tangle." He continued. "So you've *never* been able to shift? Not once? Not even when you were a child?" Shifting had come so easily for him, he couldn't imagine not being able to change into his bear. In fact, he couldn't remember a time when he had to think about the process. It was always accessible. A part of who he was. His bear was right there, waiting to come to the surface and take charge. He'd assumed that was true for all shifters.

"Never. And I've tried. Really hard. I simply don't have the ability." Her shoulders slumped. "I'm simply not meant to shift."

How to respond to her? He brushed another section, detangling the knots and straightening the length. Never shifting? He couldn't deal with that. Being a bear was such an integral part of who he was—not to be able to shift? He'd want to die.

"Are there other wolves that can't shift?" He tried to keep his tone light, but she was bound to feel lonely. Being among shifters and not sharing the ability was a fate he wouldn't want to suffer. Maybe he shouldn't push it, but he wanted to know what was going on.

"Not that I've ever known or heard of. I'm the only lucky one." She turned her face toward him, smirking. "And bonus! I'm blind too. Don't you think I'm incredibly lucky?"

A burst of wind rattled the windowpanes, and she turned her head toward the sound. He sensed her fear rising.

"It's the wind. Nothing more." He paused his brushing.

"I guess I'm a bit jumpy."

"Understandable." He ran his fingers through her hair. "You've had a lot of things going on. And Alfred isn't someone to mess with. You're right, he's dangerous."

"If I could shift, I would be able to fight him on my own. Or escape without falling down an embankment."

"To be honest, I think you can shift. I think you have the ability inside you, somewhere. You're a wolf, and wolves are strong creatures. Majestic. Maybe you haven't found your magic yet. But I'll bet it's there."

"I don't think so. Otherwise, I would've found it by now. It's not like I haven't tried."

"Maybe you haven't been looking in the right place."

"Maybe. But maybe my being blind keeps me from seeing what I need to see to be able to shift."

He placed his hand over her heart. "I think you can see everything you need to see right here."

She touched his hand for a moment, her hand trembling. "I don't know, Powell. I've tried everything. Maybe it's time to accept that I'm damaged and I'm simply not like the other wolves. It happens, right?"

"You're definitely not like any wolf I know. You're better." He took a deep breath. "If only you could see what I see in you."

She moved her hand and ducked her head. "You're as blind as I am. Maybe more so."

He started brushing again, and she closed her eyes as he twisted the silken strands gently. Anguish nearly consumed him. He hurt for her. Yet she was kind and empathetic. She hadn't turned out bitter and hardened as some people would. She accepted things and made the best of them, and when things happened to her that she didn't like, she made an effort to change them. Running from Alfred had taken more courage than most people could imagine, much less muster.

He ran the brush through her hair, teasing out each tangle. Every brush stroke sent an electric impulse skittering up his arm. It was as if her wolf called to him. Her heart beat a rhythm composed especially for him. His bear paced, growling for release.

And Powell wanted to answer that call.

He did think she knew how to shift, somewhere deep inside. She needed help. A clue where to begin. How could he help her? There had to be a way.

The sudden realization made his mouth go dry, and he set the brush in his lap.

"What about Shoshannah? Maybe she could help you." Excitement coursed through him. The ancestral spirit might actually be able to help Olivia shift. Healing her would be exactly the type of thing Shoshannah would do. She might cure her blindness, though that was less likely.

Olivia's shoulders drooped. "The cave spirit? I thought she was merely a legend until Alfred said she helped Claude when he was shot. But I didn't realize she helped anyone. Especially someone like me."

"She helps shifters. Not everyone, but some. She also offers advice, kind of like an oracle of sorts. You should talk to her. She might help."

Olivia tensed. "And she truly heals people? Alfred wasn't lying about Claude?"

"She does. She takes care of all the shifters of Deep Creek. Sure, she mainly helps the shifters who guard the cave, but yes, she did help Claude. No one knows how she picks and chooses."

"It's hard to believe."

"Yes, I know. But it's true. I've seen her."

"What does she look like?" Olivia cocked her head. "I've heard she's very beautiful and pure. Of course, I'll never see her."

He paused. "When I've seen her, mostly she's been a large white bear, sometimes made of smoke or light or rain. White, like the brightest light. She often speaks aloud and occasionally in a person's head. Sometimes, a shifter might go and meditate all day and she won't appear. She's not a simple creature, but she knows when and who she wants to help."

"Hmm. Definitely sounds magical. I wonder if she would speak to me."

"I don't know. If she could help you, that would be great. We should go to her and find out." He moved the brush onto the pillow beside him. "It wouldn't hurt to ask her, anyway. If you want to, that is."

He waited for her response, hoping she would agree though he could tell she wasn't fully buying the idea of a cave spirit. He couldn't blame her.

Nar leapt onto the couch. "Meow."

He reached for Nar, but the cat hopped down.

"When can we go?" Olivia's voice betrayed her excitement. "If she can help me see, or shift, I don't want to waste any more time. I want to talk to her. As soon as possible."

"Maybe tomorrow if it stops snowing. We can take the snowmobile and be at the cave in no time. If Shoshannah can help, it could be the miracle you need to free you from Alfred's grip."

"Do you think she can? I'm afraid to get my hopes up."

"It's worth a shot. What have you got to lose?"

Olivia nodded. "Yes, I want to go. I hope the snow stops soon."

"Me too."

Chapter Seven

Olivia turned over in the bed and pulled the ancient quilt up to her chin. The fabric, softened by years of use, had thinned, but the batting was compressed and warm and the flannel back smooth against her cheek. Powell had to retrieve another one from his cedar chest since she'd dragged the one he'd had on his bed through the snow.

The air in the room stilled with the chill, the heat from the fire barely radiating to the far corners of the cabin. Still, she'd insisted on sleeping in the bedroom, and they'd propped the door so the warmth could trickle into the room. The couch wasn't comfortable or large enough for the two of them to rest comfortably, and she didn't want to be alone.

Powell snored beside her, his breath rattling in his chest. She'd asked him to lie down with her, both to share warmth and because she was frightened. Though used to the dark, something about having no electricity made the world seem darker and scarier. She worried that Alfred was waiting outside to pounce on them at any moment, though that made no logical sense.

They hadn't heard any howls at all, only the gusty wind as it beat against the little cabin and the distant crackling of the fire that warmed the space enough to keep them from freezing to death. Nar lay between her and Powell, curled up in a perfect circle of fuzzy warmth. Olivia stroked him and he purred louder.

She wiggled her toes and moved her ankle. It felt so much better than when she'd taken off hiking. Such a stupid idea. She'd known she wouldn't make it to Oakwood, but she'd thought she was protecting Powell from Alfred and the other wolves.

The bear changed things when he was around. Her dark world seemed to light with color.

Since he'd first wrapped her ankle she'd known he was different. Initially, she thought it was because he was a bear. Slowly, she'd realized it was more than that. With each gesture to make her comfortable, to help her, or simply listen to what she had to say, she became more aware that the growing spark in her gut was something special.

And now she was more certain of it. She'd wondered what it was about Powell that made her stomach turn flips when he was around. The feelings were so trite to describe and yet so wonderful to experience. She'd never thought she would have them, being an outcast in her pack. But obviously she'd been wrong because it had happened. Faster than she'd thought possible too.

Mate.

It had become very clear when he kissed her but she didn't say anything or admit the realization to herself, it'd been so unexpected. She'd barely had time to let the possibility form in her mind before he'd pulled away and acted like he'd kissed a frog.

Why did bears act like wolves had leprosy?

Had he felt anything when he kissed her? He hadn't acted like it. Nothing beyond lust, anyway—certainly not that she was his fated mate. Her questioning him hadn't revealed anything, either.

Surely he'd have said something if he felt they were mates, wouldn't he? Men were so confusing.

Not lust, though.

Lust was a feeling she understood a lot more since Alfred was always sniffing around her. Thank goodness he'd been holding off till marriage to claim her. She shuddered.

She could never go back to Alfred, that was for sure. Especially since men like Powell existed. Even if he didn't realize they were mates, the gentleness with which he treated her was enough for her to realize she did deserve more than Alfred.

She tugged the quilt higher.

Odd that her mate would show up when she needed a rescuer, but she'd heard the knight-in-shining-armor story a million times.

He'd agreed to take her out in the deep snow, through Deep Creek, to the ancestral spirit's cave. She could ask for healing. Olivia tucked her hands under her cheek on the pillow.

What would she say to Shoshannah? She didn't feel worthy to speak to something so special. What if the spirit took one look at her and offered her a place in hell, instead? A shifter who couldn't shift?

Defective.

Why would anyone offer to help when there were many who were more worthy?

That wasn't supposed to be Shoshannah's style, but she also wasn't known as a spirit to simply hand out healing. She might pity Olivia or she might tell her to live with the blindness because wolves were considered evil. No way to know how she would respond or if she'd appear to them at all.

Anxiety gripped her and burned in her gut. The sooner the sun came up, the better. She'd barely dozed all night, and it was bound to be morning soon.

Olivia reached for Powell, putting her hand on his side and feeling the rise and fall of his breathing. He seemed to have not a care in the world, and she had the weight of everything on her shoulders. She took a deep breath and began to count backward from one hundred.

"Liv?" Powell's sleepy voice broke the silence. "You awake?"

"Meow." Nar rubbed against Olivia's knees.

"Yeah, I'm awake." She pulled her hand away.

He coughed and the bed shook as he moved to turn. Nar meowed then hopped down. "Looks like we made it through the night, but the power isn't back on yet." He got out of bed and she heard the curtains rustling. "The snow's stopped."

"Is there a lot?"

"Oh yeah. It's beautiful. The woods are white and pristine and pure."

"And cold." She giggled and burrowed into the quilt.

"Yes, very cold. Glad you're inside." He yawned. "I'm going to go toss more wood on the fire. Be right back."

"Okay." She listened to his footsteps. Bare feet on the wooden floor. He had to be chilly.

She lay still, waiting on Powell to return, hoping they'd be able to go see Shoshannah after breakfast. Hoping she'd be able to heal her. Olivia held more hope than she'd had in a long time.

And it was all because of Powell.

"That should heat us right up." Powell walked into the room and sat on the bed. "How's your ankle feeling?"

"Much better today." She lifted her foot under the cover. "I think I might be able to walk."

"That's great news. You are a shifter, after all."

She felt the tone of happiness. Yes, things were looking up. "Are we going to go see Shoshannah today?"

"I think we can make it to the cave, yes. The snow has stopped, and it won't take long to get there on the snowmobile. If you're up to it."

She sat up. "Oh, yes. I can't wait to hear what she has to say. I hope she can help me."

His voice lowered. "I hope so too."

Olivia licked her lips. Though the power was off in the cabin, there was electricity in the air. Charged with emotion, she wanted to act on her desire. Touch Powell. Have him touch her back. But what if he refused her?

Nothing would be more humiliating.

She sighed.

"What is it?" He scooted closer on the bed. "Are you nervous about meeting Shoshannah?"

"Sure I am. But that's not what I'm thinking about." She rubbed her face.

"Well, spill it. What are you thinking about?"

"The kiss—"

"Not that again." His voice held a level of exasperation she'd not heard from him. "I'm sorry I kissed you, Olivia. Can you drop it? I didn't mean to upset you."

"It's not that. I—I *wanted* you to kiss me." Her heart nearly pounded loose from her chest.

For a moment, he didn't speak. "You did? I couldn't tell."

He didn't believe her. Did that mean...he had wanted her? For real? "Lean this way." Surprised at the strength in her voice she reached her hands toward him. "I want to touch you."

The bed rocked as he moved close, his knees touching her thigh. She put her hands in the air and felt for his face, and he guided her hands to his cheeks. "Right here," he said.

She cupped his cheeks, warm with exertion or embarrassment or merely life, the scruff of a day or two's beard. Mouth parted, she ran her index finger around the curve of his jawline. Strong and angular, he must be very attractive. His lips were smooth and soft, but she knew that from the kiss. When she ran her finger down the bridge of his nose, he shivered, and she lightened her touch, feeling one eyebrow, the other, then feathering each row of lashes.

"Mmmm." He let out a groan. "That feels good. Like your touch is healing or stress-relieving."

She didn't answer but continued to trace his features in the darkness of her mind. She splayed her fingers in his hair, then moved on to his neck and his broad shoulders, massaging and feeling the strong muscles. No wonder he'd been able to carry her so easily. Her breath quickened.

"Powell?"

"Hmmm?"

"Kiss me?"

He leaned in, his lips meeting hers, and she arched against him, opening her mouth to let him explore and to revisit the magical sensations his kiss had brought to life the day before. She wouldn't stop and she hoped he felt the same. He growled and pushed her back onto the bed, lying alongside her, his hand in the small of her back and keeping her pressed against him.

She kissed him back and tugged at his shirt, trying to pull it off and feel him at the same time. He pulled away, and for a brief moment she worried he didn't want her—then he came back, his mouth crushing hers. She wrapped her arms around him, and her hands found bare skin, hot to the touch. Muscles flexing and moving as he kissed her jawline and down her neck.

He pulled back again, his breathing ragged. "Are you sure you want this, Olivia? I don't want to take advantage of you. I couldn't bear to hurt you."

"Yes!" She tried to tug him toward her. "Please. I need you."

"Shit."

"What is it?" A lump lodged in her throat. Did he not want her?

"I don't have any condoms."

She smiled. "Wolves know when their fertile times are, and this is not my time. And you know shifters don't carry human disease. We don't need a condom." She tugged at her shirt hem. "I want the warmth of your skin on mine. I want to see you with our touch."

"I've no argument with that." He slipped off her shirt and bra, giving a quick kiss to each nipple before pushing her back on the bed and sliding her pants and underwear off. She'd have had to be deaf not to hear his intake of breath. Was he pleased?

What she wouldn't give to see him.

He stood and she heard clothing hit the floor, one piece after another. A louder thump.

His pants.

Her legs quivered from excitement, a little fear, and

the chill in the room. She held her arms out to him. "Hurry. I need to feel you."

"Honey, you're going to feel me, all right. And you're going to love it." He clambered back onto the bed, and it shook under him.

She giggled. "Is that so?"

"Have I ever lied to you?" He placed his hands on either side of her hips and slid her toward him.

"Well, not that I know of."

He pinched her thigh gently. "I don't lie. If I promise you something, I mean it."

"Then make me love it." She let her legs fall open.

"Not so fast. I need you to be ready."

"I am ready." She tried to sit up but he pushed her down.

No sooner than her head hit the quilt, his fingers traced her inner thighs and streaks of pleasure raced up to her core. Feather-light touches followed, growing ever closer to her sex, and she panted in anticipation.

"I want you to enjoy this." He stroked the fine hair on her mound, dipping inside little by little.

"I am." She breathed, her hips automatically responding to his touch and pushing forward, seeking more.

"That's it. Relax."

Eyes closed, she watched the colors of pleasure swirl in her darkness. When he slid one finger inside her, she cried out and bucked her hips forward. This was what being with one's mate felt like? Nothing else would ever come close.

She was sure he was smiling, so she lay still except for her body's growing need to push against him. He had two fingers inside now, or maybe three, and his thumb pressed rhythmically on her clitoris. She strained to capture the pleasure, pushing against him. Slowly, the snow disappeared then the cabin, the room, the bed… and all that was left was Powell and his fingers.

The orgasm hit her hard and fast, and she cried out without shame as waves of sensation pulsed through her. Powell wasted no time. As soon as she relaxed he moved between her legs and positioned his cock against her then pushed.

She breathed in as he entered her. She'd not ever seen stars except in her dreams, but she saw them behind the window shades of her eyes now as he thrust into her again and again. His weight on top of her didn't give her much room to move, but she tried to meet every thrust with a counter of her own, taking him as deeply as she could, savoring the long strokes as he made love to her.

How long had they been together? She couldn't tell. Maybe it was nightfall or a week later. Powell's love-making had made her lose all sense of time.

He sped, the thrusts shorter and faster. Warmth spread through her, like a puddle of sunshine, and she tipped her head back to savor the sensation. He kissed her throat and nipped at her collarbone and she giggled. With another push, long and strong, he paused and laid his head on her shoulder as he came undone with a long, low groan. She wrapped her arms around him and held him close.

Was it possible for a bear and a wolf to mate forever?

If anyone could, it had to be them. Powell felt so perfect. So right.

She'd ask Shoshannah.

But not yet. Now, she would enjoy Powell some more.

Chapter Eight

Powell zoomed through the woods, the snowmobile gliding easily over the fresh-fallen snow and Olivia clinging to his back. He smiled and took a deep breath of crisp air, scented with pine and ice. The rush of speed, coupled with the natural beauty of the forest, and the knowledge his mate was holding on tight all came together into a happiness he'd not felt before.

Making love to Olivia had been better than he'd ever imagined it could be, with anyone. He was sure the stupid grin on his face was now a permanent fixture. He squeezed the gas and the snowmobile raced ahead over the path.

Fortunately, he had two helmets in the basement from riding around with Derek to check out the far reaches of the park when the snow was deep. And thank goodness she had healed enough to be able to walk again and wear her boots. He'd had the snowmobile out recently when he'd scoped out Deep Creek during ranger duties, so it was ready to go.

"Shit," he mumbled, his voice lost under the grumble of the engine. He'd not sent in his log or updates on his last check of the park. He'd meant to email before the power went out. Not a big deal, because the other rangers would understand and not worry. Still, Powell would've liked to report the brewing issues with the wolves.

He was sure the bears had heard the wild howls the last few nights and wondered what was up. The howls were definitely echoing each other and not the normal "howl at the moon" crazy shit the wolves usually did when they were bored.

Most of the bears were likely napping or gorging themselves while bingeing on TV cop shows anyway. With the gates now closed to the public and the one open road impassable because of the blizzard, Deep Creek would be quiet.

A wonderland.

He slowed the snowmobile to go over a mini hill between two large oaks that bowed over the path like a tunnel.

"Hold on tight," he hollered.

Olivia clutched him as they sailed over the hill, the snowmobile plunking into the snow on the other side of the hill with a spray of fine particles fanning into the air like sparkling rain. He felt Olivia laugh and he leaned back into her. She squeezed him tighter.

He held the moment in his mind, savoring it. True bliss—the purity of the snow settled over Deep Creek, the echo of Olivia's laugh, and the warmth of her body pressed against his.

He turned the curve on the path that led toward the cave. The woods grew denser and blocked more of the sunlight, but the sun that did get through laid down notched shadows across the crystalline ground—rows of shadow branches like a fractured landscape.

If he hadn't been out patrolling, he'd not have found

Olivia down the embankment. With her injury and the amount of snow that had fallen, she'd have surely died of exposure. Not much chance the wolves would've found her.

Even if they had, it would've been bad for her. Amazing how things seemed to work out the way they were supposed to. Meant to.

Alfred wanted her as a toy, nothing more.

Anger pounded in Powell's temples and he throttled the snowmobile, edging the speed up. If he ever ran into that smarmy red wolf, he'd kill him. The thought that a wolf, anyone, believed he could prey on the disadvantaged for his own pleasure? It enraged him.

Olivia scooted closer, holding tightly, and he slowed down, willing himself to calm, and edged the snowmobile to turn eastward. They'd be at the cave in no time. He couldn't meet up with Shoshannah while angry with Alfred. He needed to focus on Olivia. He took a breath of cold air and let it out slowly. Then, he could focus on the mating bond.

He hoped Shoshannah would help her. If not, Olivia was perfect to him.

Slowing to cross the earthen bridge over a small stream, he gazed at clear water rushing through an ice dam of snow and leaves and sticks and slippery rocks, creating a cascade of cold beauty. If only Olivia could see it too. A pang of guilt pierced his heart and he hit the gas. He'd figure out how to share the beauty of Deep Creek with Olivia, one way or another.

She could hear the birdsong and the splash of water. She could touch velvety moss and rough bark and smell the natural composting of leaves. He'd help her feel the beauty in every way he could.

Maneuvering the snowmobile was more difficult as he eased through the dense copse of trees as he neared the cave entrance. Where were the Sentinels? Even in winter, bears guarded the cave entrance. Powell knew where they stood guard, but he didn't see them.

They'd be there somewhere, though, hidden from plain sight. With the lions pawing around, the security threat was high.

He slowed more as they approached the cave, looking for a place to stop. He'd have to leave the snowmobile close but not by the entrance. Ah, there was a Sentinel in a tree stand. He nodded his head, hoping he'd be recognized under the helmet then realized they'd know his snowmobile.

He drove as near to the cave entrance as he could then killed the engine and unbuckled his helmet. They'd have to traipse through the drifting snow to get into the cave, but it wasn't far.

No one shoveled the path. In fact, the bears had covered part of the entrance during winter to keep snow from blowing into the cave, and the snow had piled several feet up the barrier.

Olivia struggled with her helmet, so he helped her pull it off. He set it on the seat of the snowmobile.

"We're here?" She took in a deep breath. "That wasn't a long ride."

"Not too far, but a long way to walk." He set his helmet beside hers. The freezing air bit at his throat. "It's always warmer in the cave, so let's go inside."

The cave, like most, stayed at a constant ambient temperature—not warm but not freezing, either. There were some areas deep in the tunnels where warm spring water increased the humidity and warmed the air more, but the main part of the cave where the lake was stayed at around fifty-five degrees Fahrenheit. Winter or summer, it was a tad cool but not cold.

His teeth chattered as he scanned the woods for signs of anyone besides the Sentinels. Always on the lookout for infringing lions or wolves, he relaxed at the virgin landscape. Apparently no one had ventured out in the snow—even the small animals that usually filled the trees and underbrush with scurrying and scampering seemed to be hunkered down in their dens. The woods lay pristine in their covering except for the snowmobile tracks that led to the cave area.

"I'm all for warmer. Lead the way."

A bright pink flush settled over her pale cheeks from the snowmobile ride, and her hair, in a loose braid when they left, was now in a tangle from the helmet and the wind.

Goddess, she was beautiful.

She held out her arm, and he took it in his own and guided her through the deep snow. Knee-deep near the cave, the snowfall had varied from a foot to several feet throughout the park. As much as he loved the snow, his bear loved it more, and he wanted to shift and play. But now wasn't the time. He didn't want to make Olivia feel bad that she couldn't join him, either.

"I hope she'll appear." He guided Olivia into the cave's entrance, helping her duck under the narrow part that wasn't blocked for winter. "We may have to wait a while."

"Me too. I'd heard talk of Shoshannah before, of course. The wolves never mentioned that she might help me." She'd lowered her voice to a whisper.

Powell grabbed a flashlight from the bears' stock in

the anteroom to the lake and then lit a lantern as well, setting it on one of the tables. Though he'd been visiting the cave since he was a cub, he still didn't feel comfortable being inside in total darkness.

He'd never be able to handle the world Oliva lived in. She was stronger than he'd suspected.

"I don't know what she can or can't do, but we're going to find out. Sometimes it takes a bit for her to show up. I'm going to grab a couple of blankets."

"You bears are prepared."

He chuckled. Yes, that was one word for the bears. Prepared. Well, they tried to be. Speaking for himself, he surely hadn't been prepared to stumble on his mate in a snowbank on a cold day when he felt like napping.

He grabbed two dark wool blankets from the chest then closed it, setting the blankets on top.

"I'm going to need a little help carrying this." He pushed the flashlight into Olivia's hand. "Hold this for me and hang on to me. My arms are going to be full."

"Okay." She took him by the waist and turned her face up to him, eyes closed.

He kissed her on the forehead then hugged her. "Whatever happens in here, don't forget that you'll always have me. No matter what. It doesn't matter to me if Shoshannah helps you. I mean, I hope she will, but if she doesn't, it does not change the way I feel."

"Always?" She laid her head on his chest. "Do you mean that?"

"Always. That's what mate means, isn't it?" He stroked her hair. He'd said it aloud. *Mate*. A thrilling sensation raced through him and he wanted to shout. *Mate!*

"You feel it too?" Her voice cracked. "Really?"

He brushed her hair back and planted kisses on her forehead, cheeks, chin, and finally her mouth. "I felt it the first time I held you in my arms."

"I wasn't sure bears—"

"Oh, yes. I knew you were my fated mate, even though you're a wolf. I wasn't sure wolves knew if their mates were bears."

She laughed. "Yeah, but I was afraid to believe it. I mean, of course we know when our fated mates are wolves. But there aren't many instances of fated mates being other shifter species. We're in new territory."

Her voice echoed in the chamber like a thousand tiny bells, sending shivers up his spine. He'd seen Griff completely smitten by Amy and thought it was all hogwash. Now, he was starting to understand. He was sure Griff and Derek would rag him about it. But he didn't care as long as he had Olivia in his life.

The other rangers could tease him all they wanted. He'd still be the winner.

With a single finger, he traced the sides of her face. "Believe it, Olivia. Since meeting you, I can't imagine life without you. I can't explain why things have changed, only that they have. And I don't know all the details about how we'll deal with our den and pack, but we will. Whatever it takes to be together."

Her smile was so big, he thought he might burst open with happiness. He traced her eyebrows. "I know you can shift. I feel your wolf so close to the surface. She wants to be set free."

"I hope you're right."

"Let's go talk to Shoshannah."

"I'm ready."

* * *

Powell stretched, his back aching from sitting on the ground for so long, his muscles stiff from the penetrating cold. Why hadn't Shoshannah appeared? He looked to Olivia. Her shoulders slumped and her head down, she looked like someone who'd lost a loved one.

Defeated.

He'd made a mistake bringing her to the cave. Getting her hopes up. For some reason he'd thought Shoshannah would help. Now what?

"How much longer should we wait?" Olivia's voice turned down in despair. "I don't think she's coming."

He sighed. "I don't know. I had hoped she'd show up."

"I told you I wasn't worth it."

"You are worth it! We never know why Shoshannah chooses to do what she does or show up when she does. I'm sure it isn't you. I know plenty of bears who've sat here for days at a time with no response."

"I wish I could believe that." She propped her arms on her knees and laid her head down. "Tell me what the cave looks like, Powell. Every detail. I want to know."

He scooted close to her and put his arm around her back, tugging her close in an embrace. "Okay. Let's see, where to start. The area we're in is the largest, I guess you'd call it a room. The cave is open here and in front of us is the lake I told you about. It spans most of this area, though we're on an elevated part that is somewhat like an entryway."

"Okay. Are the walls all stone?"

"Yes." He glanced up. "I can't see very far with only the light of one lantern, but the ceiling and walls were hollowed out a long time ago by the river that ran under the mountain. Water still drips through from above sometimes, especially after a heavy rain and when the snows melts in spring. The rocks are slick with moisture, almost always, and we keep a few boats by the lake in case we want to cross the water or go out to one of the small rocky outcroppings in the center." He paused. What point of reference did she have for all the information he gave her?

"Go on. Please. Tell me more." She turned her face upward, as if she was gazing at the stone ceiling.

He kissed her on the forehead. "Okay, well... There are a few tunnels in the cave that spoke out from this main room. A few of them are waterlogged and some are on higher ground and dry. We store things deep in select caverns and crannies, and we bury our dead in an area that we use for catacombs. There are many shifters buried there. Bears, wolves, lions, and more."

She nodded and laid her head on his shoulder. "When's the last time you saw Shoshannah?"

He started to speak but, just as he did, a white light filled the cavern, rippling off the surface of the water and casting bright wavy reflections on the walls.

"What's that?" Olivia clasped his arm. "I feel something. Is it Alfred? Did he find us?"

"No, it's Shoshannah," he whispered. "She's here." He squeezed her tightly.

"Oh goddess, I don't know what to say. Is she wolf or bear?" She sat up, her voice quivering and her eyes wide.

"I don't see her yet, only her light." He stood. "But she's coming." His heart raced. Thank the gods, Shoshannah was coming. If only she would help Olivia. Dare he hope? He couldn't stand the thought of Olivia being let down again. If he could offer his own ability to shift to her, he would.

A voice called out through the light. "Powell, go."

"Don't leave me." Olivia scrambled to her feet. "I'm scared."

"I need to speak to Olivia alone." Shoshannah's voice came from everywhere and nowhere at once.

He took a deep breath. Shoshannah would not harm Olivia. She would help her or give her guidance. He needed to convince Olivia that everything would be okay.

"We need to do as she asks." Powell took Olivia in his arms. "She won't hurt you. But she won't help you if I stay. I'll wait right outside with the snowmobile."

"But—"

"I won't leave you, I promise. This is a chance that might not ever repeat itself so we need to do as she says."

"Go." Shoshannah's voice grew louder.

"I need to go. Will you be okay?" He leaned close. "I will be right outside."

"Okay. I can do this." Olivia trembled.

"Yes, you can. You are the bravest person I know."

"Thank you. I don't feel very brave."

He kissed her quickly on the lips and when he opened his eyes, a twinkling of white lights had locked together to form the shape of a wolf. Larger than life, the creature stared at him, teeth bared. Shoshannah meant business.

"She's a wolf, sweetheart." He kissed Olivia on the head again. "Call to me when you are done, and I'll come back for you. Don't try to leave on your own or you may end up in the lake."

She smirked. "I won't fall in the lake. I'm not so blind I can't sense things other ways."

He smiled. She'd be okay. One more quick kiss, and he headed toward the cave exit and the snowmobile.

As he made his way outside, he prayed to the gods and goddesses that Shoshannah would help Olivia.

Chapter Nine

Olivia couldn't stop the tremor in her body. She shouldn't be scared. Powell said Shoshannah was a good creature, and that there was no reason to be afraid. Still, the unknown of the situation made her doubt her reasons for being there. What if the ancestral spirit was mad?

"Shoshannah, are you there?" Olivia called. Powell had said she was in wolf form. That had to be a good thing. Right?

"I'm here, child."

A cool breeze washed over Olivia's face, scented with lavender and roses. She breathed it in and felt her body relaxing.

"Why have you summoned me?"

Shoshannah's voice seemed to come from inside Olivia's head and from loudspeakers in the cave too. Olivia crossed her arms and took a deep breath. Where to begin?

"I hoped you would help me," she began.

"If your need is true, I might." The spirit wolf's voice was hypnotic, low and soft. Loving yet authoritative. Familiar.

"I'm blind." Anxiety almost caused her not to try,

but the thought of Powell waiting outside in the cold pushed her onward. "I hoped that you could make me see. I also cannot shift, but I don't know why. I know it is a great thing to ask, but I feel like my life would be so much more fulfilling if I could be more independent."

"These problems are connected." The voice floated on the scented air.

"Yes. I'm supposed to be able to shift, but I can't. I think it's because I'm blind." Olivia took a deep breath and waited. "Will you help?"

Shoshannah paused before replying. "You are partially correct, my child. You cannot shift because your heart is blind, not because of your eyes. Once you remove the blindness you have placed there, you will be able to shift."

"What does that mean?"

"It means I cannot help you. You must help yourself."

"What about my eyesight? I can't fix blindness. It would take a miracle." Hot tears formed and dripped down her cheeks. Shoshannah wasn't going to help. The whole day had been a waste and Powell would be so disappointed.

"I cannot help with that, either. Your problem is not so simple, but it can be solved. You must find a way to remove the blindness from your heart, and then you will run as wolf. That's all I can tell you. I give you the guidance of the gods, and they are never wrong. Trust yourself. You will find your answers."

"I don't know what to do!"

"Peace be with you, child. If your obstacles cleared easily, you wouldn't appreciate the gifts you have. Trust yourself." Shoshannah's voice trailed off and the scent of lavender and roses dissipated.

Olivia strained to hear an answer, but the only sound in the cave was the dripping of a fountain or something nearby.

"Please, won't you help me?"

No reply came. Shoshannah was gone.

Tears streamed down her face unabated. Shoshannah had not helped her. If anything, she'd confused things with her riddles. If the spirit knew her, she'd know how hard Olivia had tried to shift. So many nights, as a cub, she'd stayed up and tried, hiding so that no one would make fun of her. What would she do now?

Well, time to call Powell. Tell him the bad news. Would he stand by her, knowing she couldn't shift and would never see? She wiped her tears away. In all the sadness and disappointment, he was the one thing that had been solid, unwavering.

She had to trust her mate.

"Powell?" Her voice rang through the cave, echoing off the walls. She waited but he didn't come. Could he not hear her from outside? They'd come through a couple of rooms on the way in. She called to him again but no response.

Despite what he'd said, she'd have to go outside herself. She could find her way. He misjudged her ability to navigate. Well, barring snowstorms.

She felt along the cold stone wall of the anteroom and made her way toward the cave opening, following the rush of frigid air to its source. Had Powell left the lantern and taken the flashlight? It didn't matter. Tears continued to flow, and she laid her head against the damp cave wall and sobbed.

She didn't want Powell to see her crying.

Broken.

Unfixable.

Blind and unable to shift, why would Powell want her as his mate? He'd said those things when he thought Shoshannah was going to fix her. He wouldn't have been so emphatic if he knew she'd never be able to shift.

Trust your mate. Shoshannah's voice sounded in her head.

What if their pups were also blind and unable to shift? How tragic a life to lead. Shifter babies almost always took on the species of the mother. What would Powell and the bears do with a bunch of blind babies who couldn't shift and learn all the things that shifters did?

Would she want to condemn offspring to her fate? Would Powell?

Trust him!

She wiped her eyes. She'd surely been a disappointment to her own parents. No one wanted a child as damaged as she was. She should go back to Alfred while he would still take her.

Her brief moment of happiness with Powell would have to sustain her for her whole lifetime. A time spent in ignorance of the burden she'd become once they found out she wasn't ever going to be able to shift.

Somehow, the little bit of hope she'd felt at the possibility of Shoshannah helping her had made her situation stand out in stark contrast to normality. Being with a bear wasn't possible. She'd been kidding herself. The other bears would never accept a blind wolf into their den. They'd see her as baggage.

And she was.

She pushed aside Shoshannah's voice. This was reality, not some magical spirit wolf's life.

No, she was going right outside and telling Powell that she needed to go back to Alfred. He could take her on the snowmobile. They didn't have to tell Alfred anything about what had happened.

And she didn't have to tell Powell anything more than Shoshannah couldn't help her.

If she'd known the oracle was as crazy as the lady reading tarot cards at the street fair in Oakwood in the summer, she'd have not bothered. That lady spoke in riddles too. Alfred had stopped by with a group of wolves, and Olivia had listened to the reading. She couldn't make heads or tails out of it, and the wolves had laughed it all off as nonsense.

She knew how they felt. Laughing would be as effective as crying, and neither was going to change the circumstance.

"Hey, you! I saw you come in with Powell." A voice sounded to her right. A voice she didn't recognize. "You need to go! Quickly, before they come back."

She turned toward the voice. "What's wrong? Who's there?" She felt her way closer to the cave entrance.

"The wolves. They took him. Attacked me too. I've radioed for help but I need to get to the lake."

"Where's Powell?" Was that her voice screaming? She didn't recognize herself. Oh gods, what had happened? Alfred had taken Powell?

"I told you, the wolves attacked. A tall red one and some smaller greys. I know you're a wolf, but you're in danger. I assume they're after you—they kept asking for a she-wolf."

"Yes, they're after me. Is Powell okay?"

"I tried to help him, but they injured me badly. I'm losing blood." The voice headed away from her. "They hurt him too. He didn't have time to shift, either. They attacked him beside the snowmobile. There's blood everywhere. You've got to escape now before they come back."

"Where are you going?" Her heart thumped in her throat, and her tears dried on her cheeks. She had to get to her mate! Alfred had attacked and taken Powell. Back to the Green Glen den, no doubt. They'd torture and kill him if he didn't tell them where she was.

"I've got to get these injuries into the lake to heal." The man paused. "I've radioed that we have a man down and that I'm injured. With the snow, it'll take a while for anyone to get here. I doubt he has a chance unless those wolves need him for something. The big red one was asking for Olivia, but he wouldn't tell them anything. I assume you're her. If you can help save him, you'd better do it. Otherwise, he's a goner."

"But, I can't help him!" She pleaded, "You have to get the bears to come. They can rescue him from the den."

"Listen, lady, I don't know what your issue is that you can't tell I'm barely standing myself. I'd help him if I could. You'll have to excuse me, though. I need to get to the lake."

"I'm sorry I'm not more help. I'm blind." She chewed her bottom lip. "I'll be okay till reinforcements get here. You go take care of your injuries."

She paced a moment, her heart in her throat. If anything happened to Powell, it was her fault. He'd brought her to the cave. He'd waited outside while she made her plea to Shoshannah. Now, her mate was in peril. And it was entirely her doing.

My mate.

Though she was prepared to let him go, and defer to Alfred's wishes, she couldn't let Powell suffer because of her. She had to save him.

But how?

Energy flowed through her, like a shot of stamina, and she stood a little taller. What was it Shoshannah said?

Remove the blindness from your heart, and then you will run as wolf...

What did she mean? And she'd said *trust yourself.* What did she have to lose? With Powell's life in the balance, there was no time like the present to give it all or nothing. Failure wasn't an option, nor was not trying.

She began stripping. Could it be as easy and clear as it seemed? One way to find out. Push all her energy into the manifestation. This wasn't for her. It was for her mate.

She focused inward, reaching back to the warm feeling she had when Powell carried her out of the woods with an injured ankle, the comfort when he dragged her back to the cabin after she crept out his window. Then, she savored the taste of the peanut butter and honey sandwich he'd made her, and Nar's soft fur and the scent of burning pine logs, ripe with sap and spitting and popping in the fire.

Socks and pants came off, then shirt. She dropped them where they fell, trusting that she was doing what Shoshannah guided her to do. What she had to do.

She could almost sense the touch of Powell's fingertips along her spine, across her cheek, along the side of her breast...and feel the wetness of his mouth, his tongue hot against hers, their climax as they moved together. Chills raced through her, but not from the cold.

The mating bond was strong. Unlike anything she'd ever felt.

Her body hummed and she fell into the sensation, lost on the ride of emotion she could only term as love. Love for her mate who needed her now. Love for the man who'd saved her not once but multiple times, with very little complaint—and all of it in the best interest of her well-being.

It was happening! Her body moved under the thoughts of love and self-sacrifice for her mate.

Her legs and arms stretched and changed, and her face changed like warm clay sliding down a window-pane, realigning into something new. Olivia fell inside her psyche, over and over, her body struggling not to panic as it moved in ways it was meant to but never had. Shifting didn't hurt, but the buzz and burn was something new. Strength filled her bones as they lengthened and hardened into wolf bones.

She sensed paws at the end of strong legs and a long bushy tail.

She opened her eyes.

Her vision was so radiant and bright she had to squint. This was the white of snow that Powell had mentioned. She'd never imagined that a color could be so pure and bright. She placed a paw over her nose and eyes then peeked again.

By the gods, she'd not only shifted, but she could see!

The world, bright and new, held so much color, she could barely take it in all at once, though she didn't know all the color names. Pine trees were green, she knew that. But so many shades. Were they all green?

She shook her head. No time for enjoyment. Her heart thumped wildly, and she breathed faster as her blood pumped through wolf veins. She had to get to her mate. Save him. She sniffed the air, his blood rode the currents like a beacon.

Injured.

Alive.

Running would be the fastest way to reach him. She couldn't wait around for more bears to show up to help. Her clothes lay in a pile at the cave entrance, and deep snow greeted her feet as she dashed out into the light. Leaping into the air, she stared at the blue sky. All her life wolves had mentioned the blues of the sky. Such a color! With what must be clouds floating across the sun-lit sky, the sight was more beautiful than she could've dreamed.

She never would've imagined such glorious beauty in Deep Creek. Thank the goddesses that she was gifted the power to save her mate. And thanks to Shoshannah. The sun shining through the trees like bright strips of warmth would lead her west to where the wolves lived. She knew exactly where to go.

Where she would find her injured mate and save him from the wolves that would surely kill him once they were done questioning him.

She turned her nose to the air and howled, the sound echoing through her chest and throughout her spirit.

She was wolf.

Chapter Ten

Powell winced. The salty, metallic taste of blood filled his mouth. Ties bound his wrists, and he sat in a chair in the center of a room in the Green Glen wolves' pack compound. If only he'd had time to shift when they'd attacked, he might not be in this predicament. Shifting now would be difficult, if not impossible. If he could get the bindings off, he'd have a better chance. But as soon as they saw him shift, they'd likely kill him rather than face an angry bear. If only shifting were instantaneous.

Several pack members stood around, half-interested, half-afraid of Alfred. None spoke up against him. A scraggily bunch, they looked like the scavengers they were. Powell scanned them, looking for weaknesses. He'd figure out how to escape. Thank the gods, they hadn't captured Olivia. The Sentinels would've called for the bears to come, and if he held out long enough, they might make it in time to save him.

A slap brought him out of his reverie. Alfred stared at him, hand back, ready to strike again.

"There's more of that, if you need it. Or if I decide you need it." Alfred snarled.

Powell didn't answer, realizing that the wolf was posturing in front of his pack and nothing he said would help his predicament. He hoped Olivia understood that he hadn't left her.

"I'm going to ask you one more time." Alfred circled the chair. "Where is she? I know she was with you, I scented her."

"I don't know who you're talking about." Powell stared Alfred eye-to-eye.

If Alfred killed him, he hoped that Olivia had learned enough to fend for herself and not come back to the lunatic. And perhaps Shoshannah had helped her. He could only hope at this point that she was safe.

The punch came swiftly, and his cheek numbed under the blow as his head snapped back.

"I know you had her at your cabin. I scented her there too." Alfred bent and inched closer to Powell's face. "She's mine. And I want her back."

No way was he giving Olivia back to this monster. Hell, Alfred's own pack was afraid of him. What kind of leader ruled by fear?

A bad one.

He spat in Alfred's face. The wolf staggered backward, and a collective gasp rose in the room. The pheromones of anger wafted through the air. Tension grew, and Powell knew the wolves wouldn't bother keeping him around much longer.

Alfred wiped his face and howled a ragged, enraged human howl. Powell laughed.

"You'll pay for that!" the wolf screamed, crouching and prepared to lunge. "You bastard! No one gets away with disrespecting me."

Powell closed his eyes and waited for the blow to come. He'd gotten in a jab of sorts. And Olivia was safe.

The door burst open and a blast of icy air rushed in,

sending chills over him. He looked, and silhouetted in the doorway was the most beautiful she-wolf he'd ever seen in his life. His heart swelled and his mouth fell open.

White, with guard hairs tipped in silver sparkles, the wolf practically shimmered like a frozen mirage in front of him. She bared her teeth, fangs long and sharp, her guttural growl setting everyone in the room back a step. She walked into the room, and Alfred remained crouched, ready for combat, though his human form wouldn't have much of a chance against the she-wolf. She'd tear him to shreds.

He wouldn't have time to shift before she attacked.

Talk about karma.

She leapt. Powell watched her powerful legs propel her through the air and into Alfred, knocking him onto his back, his head hitting the floor with a pleasing thump and groan. Alfred pushed back against her with his hands, but her bites came fast and strong, and spatters of red dotted her white coat.

"You bitch!" Alfred screeched.

Powell couldn't take his eyes off the gorgeous white wolf and the way she took charge and dominated Alfred. Her strength seemed magical, super powered.

She tore into his throat, blood gushing from the wound, and a frothy blood-tinged spittle poured from his mouth. She shook him until the life had left his body and he lay limp on the floor. The other wolves stood back, and she panned her head from one to the next, daring any to move.

None did.

"Untie me," Powell called to the wolves, and one young man rushed over and worked at releasing his bindings. Powell pulled free, rubbing his wrists. "Anyone else want to fight? Or are we going to call this a day?"

Another man lunged toward Powell, and the white wolf snarled, standing between Powell and the others, crouched and ready to leap. After taking a look at Alfred, the man stepped back.

"Anyone?" Powell repeated.

The wolves looked down, none making eye contact. Clearly they were a bunch of scaredy-cats who followed whatever leader they had, without thought or regard to what was going on. Disgust filled Powell and he shook his head.

No matter, this fight was over.

Powell knelt. "Olivia? Is that you?"

The white wolf turned to him, her bright and clear blue eyes like lakes or patches of summer sky. His heart warmed and he hugged her neck.

Epilogue

Olivia panted, her paws still tender from being somewhat new to shifting. She dashed around a thick, heavily scented flower bush and stopped to wait on Powell. He was so slow. Moonlight lit the path almost as well as midday sun, and she glanced up to look at the pocked orb that shone, bright and ever-changing.

She never tired of seeing the stars and moon sitting in the sky like bright pinpoints of hope on a background of darkness. Ever since her victory over Alfred, she'd felt more alive and more independent. It wasn't her shifting powers or her newfound love for her fated mate that had opened her eyes to life, though those things helped. No, the catalyst for her metamorphosis was overcoming her fear and finding that she was stronger than she could've ever imagined.

Nothing could stop her now.

Powell loped up behind her, his bear large and not as graceful as her wolf. She smiled a wolf smile, her tongue lolling.

A nightly run had become part of her and Powell's bedtime ritual. The snowfall had melted and the forest had greened under spring's warmer temperatures and sunshine, and every night, her wolf and his bear ran through the forest together, scenting new things and exploring Deep Creek's grandeur. She imagined that any park visitor would think the sight of a bear and a wolf running together odd, but she didn't care.

He was her bear.

Her mate, forever.

She raced ahead, stopping on a large boulder and turning to wait. The scent of night jasmine filled the air, and a lone call of a hoot owl sounded from somewhere deep in the glen. The forest, alive with spring's rush, sang to her in new ways. Though she was only able to see when in wolf form, it was the most wonderful blessing and she was grateful for every moment of vision in the miraculous world of Deep Creek.

Powell caught up to her and leaned against her, panting.

I'm tired. His thoughts were clear to her, though he swore he didn't hear any of hers. He nuzzled her ear.

She licked his cheek and nodded her head in the direction of the cabin. Tonight, they'd cut the run short. Soon, she'd need to scale back on the running anyway, and she needed to tell him why.

Two new little heartbeats thumped their own cadences inside her. Baby girl cubs due by the second full moon. She lifted her snout and howled with gratitude. A long bay of respect for nature, Deep Creek, and the shifter bond.

Shoshannah had been right.

Love had broken the barrier that had kept her heart blind to her own power, and now that it was unleashed, nothing could stop her and her mate.

* * * * *

Acknowledgments

Many thanks to my editor, Anne Scott. She's exactly the right amount of patient for neurotic authors and her red pen is on point. I appreciate her professionalism and command of language and her author-whispering skills. I've been so fortunate at Carina Press. I'd also like to thank my agent, Marisa Corvisiero of Corvisiero Literary Agency. She's always working hard to keep me working. Aside from that, I'm thrilled to call her a friend. Also, many thanks to all my Facebook author friends who kick me off Facebook when I have a deadline, sprint with me when I need it, give me pep talks when I'm sure that my story is the worst and listen to me complain about whatever is bothering me. I only hope that I provide half the support they give to me. Last, thanks to my husband, who has been to every takeout place in Raleigh to pick up dinner and who hasn't complained (much) about picking up Japanese food at least once a week.

About the Author

USA TODAY bestselling author Kerry Adrienne loves history, science, music and art. She's a mom to three daughters, many cats and various other small animals, and spends a lot of time feeding everyone. She loves live music and traveling almost anywhere. Music and travel feed her muse like nothing else. She loves driving her Mini Cooper convertible on long, winding roads with loud music playing and no one else around.

In addition to being an author, she's a college instructor, artist, costumer, bad guitar player and editor.

You can connect with Kerry on her website (kerryadrienne.com), Facebook (Facebook.com/authorkerryadrienne) and Twitter (Twitter.com/kerryadrienne).

For information on upcoming releases, great contests, free books, cat pics and no spam, please sign up for her monthly newsletter here: eepurl.com/1T6PX.

WOLF SUMMER

Sionna Fox

For Bear.

Chapter One

It was a damn near perfect day. Work was slow, but it always was in the dead of summer. Callie spent a quiet hour doodling a cupcake asking for birthday cake money and taped it to the tip jar. It kind of worked. The regulars who filtered in and out were people she'd known her entire life. They were not fooled that she was spending her tips on cake, but left her cash and happy birthdays anyway. Add the handful of mid-week hikers who stopped in and were charmed, and she closed out with enough cash to buy her first legal drink, maybe two.

She had claimed birthday girl privileges to get control of the radio all day, and she was closing by herself, the music up loud, singing along, and doing a shuffling dance while she wiped down the steam wands on the espresso machine. She'd flipped the sign but hadn't locked the door, and a quiet laugh almost made her jump out of her skin.

"*Jesus. Fuck.* Goddammit, Sam!" She threw her wet, coffee-ground-flecked rag at her best friend.

He caught it neatly and grinned at her, the jerk, all white teeth behind his full beard and dust-streaked face. He must have been out doing trail maintenance all day.

He was covered in dirt from the top of his forestry services hat, down his shirt, to the hem of his standard-issue olive-khaki shorts, and over his muscled calves to his thick wool socks peeking out from his heavy work boots. He was her best friend, but she was still allowed to appreciate that he managed to make that uniform look hot. It was impossible not to notice.

"Stay off my floor with those boots, dude, or I'll make you mop it." She straightened to her full height, still several inches shorter than Sam's six feet, and put her hands on her hips, trying to look fierce.

He raised his hands in surrender and didn't move from the welcome mat. "Yes, ma'am." He leaned his butt against the door. She'd have to wipe down the glass again.

"Can you toss me my rag?"

He dangled it from between the tips of his thumb and forefinger. "This one? The one you threw at a potential paying customer? What would Melissa say if she knew you were yelling obscenities while the door was unlocked?"

He tossed it back to her and it landed with a wet plop on the counter after she completely missed catching it. "She's your aunt, why don't you ask her?" Callie turned around and dunked the cloth back into the bucket of warm water. The faster she finished the closing chores, the sooner she could get out of there and start celebrating.

"What's the plan, birthday girl?"

"Finish up here, go home, shower and head out. And you're going to the store, of course."

"Of course."

Even though, according to her birth certificate, Callie had officially been twenty-one for going on eight hours, everyone knew the clerk at the liquor store held a peculiar interpretation of the law that wouldn't let anyone buy alcohol until the day after their twenty-first birthday. Wayne did not believe in "on or before this date," only "before."

"Where do you want to start? Nachos? World Café? Jay's? The Tavern? We could go to the Public Room." For a small town, they had an awful lot of bars. Blame it on the après ski crowd.

"Let's go to Nachos. Five-dollar margaritas are about my speed right now."

"Like you're paying for drinks tonight."

"I'm not letting anyone buy me ten-dollar drinks. Unless they're huge. Like scorpion bowl huge."

"And since you can't get one of those in Pullman, I'll meet you at Nachos in an hour?"

She flicked her eyes to the clock. She could make it work. She wouldn't have time to do anything with her hair or makeup, but it wasn't like it mattered. She'd known Sam and everyone else in town since kindergarten. Not a one of them would notice or care if she showed up in her underwear. Or they would, but only to make fun of her. Such was life tagging along with Sam and his cousins. She was used to it.

"Sounds like a plan. Now get out so I can finish up."

Sam left with a clatter of the bells on the door and Callie locked up behind him. No more distractions. She turned up the stereo and finished her chores. When everything in the place had been emptied, wiped down and otherwise cleaned, she counted out the drawer and tucked the money in the safe, left a note for her boss to call the ice guy because they were running low, turned out the lights and left for the next two days. She'd traded working on her birthday proper for two days off in a row, planning ahead for the sure-to-be-epic hangover.

At her apartment, she dropped her shorts and black T-shirt and rushed through a shower, scrubbing the smell of stale coffee off her skin and out of her hair. She wound her wet hair into a bun at the crown of her head, threw on a pair of denim cutoffs and a loose white tank, slipped into her flip-flops, stuffed her wallet and the day's tips in her pocket, and was out the door to meet Sam exactly an hour after she left the shop.

Sam was tired when he came off the mountain. Beating back the encroaching forest from the trail network had a way of doing that. Tired was good. Tired meant the restlessness, the need to run, was calmed for another day. They were taught that early. Get tired, get physically exhausted, and the changes would be easier to manage, predict, control. There was no need to be a slave to the magic in their blood, but fuck, if it didn't feel good to run sometimes.

He dragged himself up the stairs to his room and sat down to unlace his boots. Every time he blinked, he saw Callie wiping down the steam wand, stroking it up and down, with a slight twist at the tip, while she swayed her hips in time with the radio. He scrubbed his hands over his face. Callie Anders wasn't for him. His father had a way of reminding him of that what felt like once a day. Best friend or no, some secrets he would always have to keep from her, for the good and the safety of them both. Sam would be paired off eventually with someone from their world in the name of alliance or power, and the best he could hope for was that he didn't actively loathe whoever she was when the day came.

Loathing was a strong possibility when every one of his senses pointed at Callie and whispered *mine* whenever they were in the same room. Even in his aunt's shop, with the smell of stale coffee and muffins thick in the air, he could pick out Callie's distinctive scent. The minty eucalyptus shampoo she used, the slightly salty smell of the sweat that made the red-blond hair at the nape of her neck curl into wispy spirals, and under everything else, the indefinable, warm, animal smell of her. He'd never been more simultaneously relieved and pained than the day in high school when she had gotten over the trend of covering herself with country apple-scented body spray and he got his first real whiff of her without the synthetic fruit.

She's not for you, MacTire. Never was, never will be. She thought of him like a brother. She always had. That wasn't changing. Couldn't change. Not unless she could. And even then, he still had obligations to his family. It was never going to happen.

He'd stripped out of his filthy uniform and tossed it into a corner of his room when his cousin Bren barged in. It was hardly the first time Bren had seen him naked, and it wouldn't be the last. A love of privacy and personal boundaries didn't fly in a pack. Still, he wasn't a fan of the way Bren's eyes trailed to his half-hard dick. He covered himself with a hand, but not quickly enough. He hadn't been able to shake the mental image of Callie stroking the steam wand while she waved her ass back and forth like a fucking red flag.

Bren snorted. "You going to take care of that before you meet Callie? I think she might figure out that you've had a crush on her since you were seven if you show up for her birthday dinner with a stiffie."

He shot Bren a filthy look. "Fuck off, Kealy." His cousin's intrusion had already done the work of deflating his cock like a pin in a balloon.

"Doing my job." Bren sprawled across Sam's bed. He was never sure if Bren was joking or if his father had honestly tasked him to run interference between Sam and Callie. "What time are we meeting her?"

"We?" Sam wasn't planning on letting the whole pack tag along for this. They'd come back to the house later and hang out by the fire pit, sure, but he wanted to celebrate with her first, be the one to buy her first legal drink.

"Dude, look at yourself, you can't be alone with her. Besides, she's my friend, too."

"I'm taking a shower." Sam turned at the door to his room. Bren was right, he shouldn't be alone with her. Not when he was feeling restless all over again, despite the day's physical labor. "Get everyone ready to go in a half hour. And send Colin to the liquor store."

Callie walked into the tiny restaurant that passed for Mexican food in their neck of the woods to find Sam, his brother and their cousins holding down a table with a pitcher of margaritas and a glass waiting for her. They immediately erupted into a spectacularly off-key version of the birthday song, like they were putting effort into being awful. She clapped her hands over her ears and cringed while yelling at them to spare her and everyone else their pathetic attempts to sing, but on the inside warm fuzzies washed through her. So she was a convenient excuse for them to come out and get drunk

on a Sunday night; they still came out. And Sam made
it happen.

Sam had showered and traded his baseball hat, uniform and boots for a black V-neck T-shirt and faded blue
shorts, both looser-fitting than his government-issued
olive drab. He still looked every inch the former var-
sity athlete who hiked and cut trails for a living. The
tattoo on his biceps peeked out from under his sleeve
when he stood up to wrap her in a hug at the end of the
song. He'd never explained the meaning of the vaguely
Celtic design, only said it was a family thing with an
air that never invited more questions.

Tucked against his broad chest, Callie took a deep
breath. They'd been friends since she was in kindergarten. He thought of her like the little sister he'd never had.
She'd spent her entire childhood rampaging through
the woods with Sam, Ryan, and their pack of cousins,
always tagging along. But she couldn't deny that he
smelled good. Not thoughts she needed to be having
about someone who thought of her like a sister.

Sam released her and sat her at the head of their
table. As he filled her glass from the pitcher, the waitress made a fuss of checking her ID and wishing her
a happy birthday. She clinked glasses with everyone
and drank down the margarita in a handful of swal-
lows and slapped the table for a refill. The night was
just getting started.

After a couple of rounds, they shambled up the road
to the guys' house. There was little about the place
to recommend it aside from the fire pit out back. The
house itself had been a bachelor pad for generations of
seasonal work crews and twentysomething guys and
had the mystery stains on the carpeting and the scuffed

and peeling linoleum to show for it. Most of the time, Callie avoided going inside at all. They had gotten their acts together at least about not leaving food sitting on the counter after Bren came face-to-snout one night with a fat rat that had been making itself at home in their kitchen.

Colin had filled the fridge and Bren got the fire going while the rest of the gang settled into the mishmash of weather-beaten Adirondacks and rusty lawn chairs, the kind that burned your skin on sunny days and might take a chunk of your finger anytime you tried to fold them. Callie helped set up a makeshift bar on the picnic table off to one side of the fire before she plopped into a chair with a plastic cup of cheap handle vodka and discount cranberry juice.

She was tipsy, on her way to drunk, in spite of the burrito Sam had insisted she eat. On any other night, she would have cut herself off, but she'd only have one twenty-first birthday and she didn't have to work for the next two days and she'd known these people her entire life. She had nothing to worry about with them. And Sam would throw around his big-brotherly weight if anyone gave her a hard time.

People drifted in and out of the yard and she lost track of how many happy birthday toasts she'd drunk. Things started to get hazy when Ryan started passing around a bottle of spiced rum and they were all taking swigs straight from the bottle. She stumbled up the steps to go to the bathroom and felt Sam's gaze follow her. He hadn't had much to drink at Nachos and had switched to nursing a beer when they got back to the house. It made her insides feel warm. He wasn't hovering, wasn't trying to tell her what to do, but he was watching out for her. Like her best friend. Like a big brother.

She looked up as she washed her hands and her face was doing that thing where it looked like a funhouse mirror and she didn't recognize herself. She poked her nose. Totally numb. *I should probably stop.* But when she sat back down, the bottle had come around to her chair and she took another swig. Ryan high-fived her and she stood up to take a sloppy bow, almost tipping the bottle and herself straight into the fire.

Large hands pried the bottle out of her fingers and leaned her against him. Sam's hands. Leaning on Sam. "Ooookay, Callie. I think maybe you're done." He put his hands on her shoulders and shuffled her over to the picnic table. "Sit. I'm going to get you some water."

She grinned up at him and nodded; her head felt like a bowling ball on the end of a pipe cleaner. She put her elbows on her knees and tried to prop her chin in her hands, but she slipped forward until she was bent in half with her hands brushing through the grass at her feet. It felt nice. It was the last thing she remembered.

Sam found Callie slumped over and nearly passed out when he returned with water, and forced her to sit up. She didn't want to. She tried to wrench her arms out of his grip but he was stronger and far more sober than she was. He hoped some part of her recognized that she was very, very drunk and he had done the right thing to pull her away from the fire and try to get some water in her. If she did, it didn't keep her from struggling to fold forward again.

"No. Was comfy," she whined.

"Cal, you need to drink some water."

"*Pfft*. I'm fine."

"Uh-huh. Says the girl who almost tipped a bottle of rum into the fire."

Her eyes went round. "Whoops." Apparently even this drunk she could understand why that was a bad thing.

"Come on, drink some water, then I think it might be time to go home."

"What? No." She screwed her face into a glare and if he wasn't worried about her, it would have been cute. "Don't tell me what to do, Sam. You're not actually my brother."

He winced at her slurred words. It was good to hear her say it, even if it took tequila and rum and God only knew what else she'd been drinking for the words to come out loud. "No, I'm not. But you're my best friend and you're wasted. I'm cutting you off and taking you home."

She wobbled to her feet. "Fine. I'm going home. You don't want me here anymore."

She'd gone from whiny and almost passed out to angry in the blink of an eye. Callie wasn't usually mean or dramatic when she drank, but maybe that last swig of rum got to her. He'd also never seen her this drunk. She was usually the responsible one, not edging too far past tipsy before she cut herself off and sent herself home for water and bed. She tried to make a grand exit, but tripped over her flip-flops and almost toppled over.

Sam rushed to her side and tried to help her but she kicked off her sandals and trundled barefoot toward the porch. He picked up her shoes and watched her shamble down the driveway. He wasn't even sure he should let her go home at all. He wanted to pick her up and take her inside where he would be able to keep a watch on her all night. What would he do if she went back to her place only to choke on her own vomit when she passed out? No. He couldn't let her be alone.

"Callie, wait up."

She was moving faster than he would have thought possible. She had made it to the end of their driveway and was in the middle of the crosswalk on Main Street when she turned around and stumbled. Sam would never be sure if he started running because she was about to fall in the middle of the street, or if he ran because he heard the rumble of a truck's engine moving way too fast through town.

It happened in slow motion. A black pickup, no headlights on, barreling down the street. He must have yelled, he heard his voice in his head. Heard tires squeal, the sickening crunch of impact, and the sound of a truck peeling out, fleeing the accident. Then flickering scenes. Callie's body on the ground. The feel of his knees hitting pavement. Her broken, bleeding body in his lap, the sound of her heart frantically struggling to beat, the gurgle of her lung, filling with blood where her rib had punctured the fragile flesh. She was dying in his arms.

Feet running up behind him. Bren's hand on his shoulder.

Sam pushed him away, the need to shift rising in him, driven by fear and desperation. He couldn't lose her.

"Sam, no. I'm calling an ambulance."

"She won't last that long." Her pulse was getting weaker, her breaths more ragged and shallow.

"Think about what you're doing. She wouldn't want this."

"She wouldn't want to die."

"She wouldn't want you to give up your life for her either."

Sam made a keening sound in the back of his throat. Her blood pressure was dropping as her body started to shut down. He could make them understand. Make her understand. But she had to be alive for him to have the chance. He'd accept the consequences—censure, exile, containment. Whatever they would do to punish him would be nothing compared to the pain of losing her.

"I can't let her go, Bren." He clutched her limp body and listened to the blood and fluid pooling in her lung and her belly while her heart raced against her tumbling blood pressure.

"I know." Bren put a hand on Sam's shoulder. "We need to get her out of the road."

Gingerly, they scooped her up and brought her into the shadow of the maple trees that surrounded the school fields where they'd spent their childhoods playing tag and throwing snowballs at recess. Sam let go, gave rein to his fear and let the wolf rise.

Chapter Two

The smell of blood and fear assaulted his nostrils. Callie's fading, frantic heartbeat filled his ears. Sam hesitated, hating that he would have to hurt her more to save her, before instinct took over.

He nosed at her thigh, raw and bleeding from where she'd skidded across the pavement. With a desperate prayer to save her, he tore into her leg with his own teeth, leaving punctures deep in the muscle. Dark blood welled from her flesh and he recoiled, watching the stain spread over her skin and soak into her torn shorts. But he'd had no choice. It was the only way. He licked her wounds, and curled at her side to wait.

"We have to get her out of here."

Bren's voice called him back to himself. He fought to shift back, the wolf determined to stay by her side and watch over her. Dazed, he pulled his clothes on. The coppery tang of her blood was thick on his tongue and he felt bile rise in his throat when he looked at the damage he'd done to her with his own teeth. But Bren was right, they couldn't stay out here.

"I'll take her in through the front door. Go ahead of me and keep everyone out of my way."

Bren nodded and loped across the street without a

word. Sam took a deep breath and scooped up Callie's limp body as gently as he could, keeping her injured leg to his chest, and hurried back to the house.

Upstairs, he laid her on his bed and settled in, leaning against the wall with her feet in his lap to wait and watch and pray that he'd done the right thing.

For hours, Sam watched over her while her body struggled on. He couldn't leave her side even to brush the taste of her blood from his mouth. Through the deepest hours of the night he waited, his senses on high alert to every infinitesimal change in her body.

Alone in the dark, he remembered the first time he saw her, arguing with a much larger, much meaner kid on the playground about cutting in line at the slide. She'd been fearless, a scrappy little freckled thing standing up to Kevin Lahout. Sam had picked her first for their recess kickball team after that. She'd been one of them ever since.

He was still there at dawn when Bren nudged his arm with a hot cup of coffee. Sam took it without a word.

"She's hanging on. That's got to be a good sign."

Sam grunted and put his ear gently to her chest for the thousandth time that night. Her breath was still shallow, but the gurgle and wheeze was slowly fading.

He'd made the mistake of looking up complications from fractured ribs. He could still lose her to pneumonia or infection. Or to the bleeding from whatever else her ribs had nicked as they splintered on the hood of the truck. Or to the surely severe concussion she'd gotten from hitting the windshield and then the pavement. For the rest of his life, he would never forget the sick crack of her skull as it hit the ground. He didn't know if the magic in his veins was strong enough to stand up to a traumatic brain injury. He'd looked that up, too.

"Do you want me to stay with her while you get some sleep?"

Sam tensed and growled from deep in his chest. He couldn't leave her side even if he wanted to.

"Didn't think so." Bren sighed and left the room.

Sam stared into his coffee mug and listened, as if, in the stillness of dawn, he would be able to hear Callie's flesh and bones knitting back together, healing, making her whole again. He thought of her face when she'd walked into Nachos and seen them all waiting for her. The way she'd looked in the loose white tank top and cutoff shorts that were now torn and stained with dirt and blood. He wondered if she would ever look at him with that simple joy on her face again. Would she still laugh at their off-key serenades? Or if she survived, would she hate him for what he had done? For the secrets he had kept from her? Or would she understand?

Somehow, he slept. He dreamed of her, of running through the woods with flashlights in the snow as kids, playing hide-and-seek. She'd always lost but never knew why. He remembered the night she finally bested him, the look of triumph on her ten-year-old face after she'd tackled him to the ground from behind. He dreamed of running through the woods with her on all fours, nudging shoulders and muzzles as they careened through the underbrush. He woke to fading sunlight and his cousin's hand on his shoulder.

"Wake up."

"Fuck. How long have I been out?" His neck and shoulders were stiff and sore from sleeping awkwardly slumped over Callie's feet.

"All day."

"Shit."

Sam held his breath and made a quick inventory of Callie's sleeping body. Her pulse was slow and steady, her breath shallow but clear. Her skin was warm to the touch and suffused with pink, no longer clammy and gray with shock as her body tried to conserve blood. She was healing. He inhaled deeply and almost sobbed with relief. Under the smell of adrenaline-laced sweat and blood, he picked up the faintest trace of the damp forest and musk scent they all shared. It had worked.

"Bren?"

"I smell it, too." His smile was tinged with relief and exhaustion.

"I should check on her leg."

Sam peeled back the covers and gently pushed aside what was left of Callie's shorts. Her skin still looked raw and scabbed-over in some places from road rash, and the dark purple bruise would take a few more days to fade, but even his bites were healing well. He'd tried to be gentle, to tear at her flesh only enough to make the change, to force the magic from his body into hers. His hands shook as he traced the outline of his teeth on her leg. She would heal.

Bren cleared his throat behind Sam. "We should get her out of her bloody clothes. She's going to be freaked out enough when she wakes up, seeing that won't help."

"Right. Get a T-shirt." Waking up in his bed would be enough of an additional shock. Her waking up naked would only make matters worse.

They carefully undressed her and wrangled her limp body into one of Sam's shirts. She made pained noises as they lifted her arms into the sleeves, but didn't wake.

They settled her against the pillows and she let out a tiny sigh before she slipped back into deep sleep. Sam stayed with her, not quite believing that he had done it and that she would be okay.

At around midnight, when her pulse was strong and steady, and her breathing subtly deepened as her lung and ribs continued to heal, Sam gave into exhaustion and curled up beside her.

Callie woke slowly from a dream of running through the woods, running for the sheer joy of it, feeling low branches whip by her face as she left the trail behind. She hated every second of awareness as she came back into her body. Everything hurt. She'd been hungover before but this was…something else. And that was before she realized she wasn't alone. There was an arm draped over her waist.

She scrambled to sit up and get out of the bed but every move sent waves of pain through her whole body and she tumbled over the edge and onto the floor. She landed hard on her ass and smacked her hand against the trash can next to the bed. Her sharp inhale of pain made her ribs ache like they would crack with one deep breath. She opened her eyes and wished she hadn't. Squinting through her splitting headache, she figured out where she was. Sam's room. She'd slept in Sam's bed.

"Oh, fuck," she whispered as she patted herself down. She had a T-shirt on. Not hers. Underwear was there. Shorts weren't. "Oh, fuck, fuck, fuck."

Sam stirred and sat up, looking slightly alarmed at finding her on the floor. How drunk were they last night? "Callie?"

He ruffled his hair and she would have sworn she smelled his shampoo with every shake of his fingers through the short brown strands. Shampoo and sweat, the kind that came with fear. She thought she heard his heartbeat pick up, but that was impossible, that was the racing of her own heart. Wasn't it? "I fell." She grimaced. "Why am I— We didn't, did we?"

He looked at her grimly. Oh, Jesus, fuck, they did. He sat up and moved to the foot of the bed. He pointed to the pillows and said, "You should sit."

Gingerly, she crawled back onto his bed and tucked herself up against the pillows with her knees under her chin. Feet pounded up the stairs and the door slammed open. It sounded like a gunshot to her hungover ears. Bren burst in and didn't look at all surprised to see her there. Perfect, they'd all been witnesses.

"I heard something hit the floor. Cal, are you okay?"

"I'm fine. I feel like I got hit by a truck, but I'm fine. No more rum for me. Ever."

Instead of leaving, Bren came farther into the room and pulled Sam's desk chair over to the bed. He looked at Sam, who looked back at him, both of them with an air of resigned determination.

Sam cleared his throat. "The thing is, you kinda did."

"I kinda did what?"

"There was an accident. You *were* hit by a truck."

"Oh, ha-ha." She cast her eyes between the two of them but the punch line didn't come. They both looked like they were about to tell her she had some sort of terminal illness. "Very funny, guys, fuck with the hungover girl."

"Callie, you were in a hit-and-run on your birthday. I saw it happen."

"This isn't funny, Sam. If I got hit by a truck, why am I here and not in the hospital?"

They did that thing again, looking back and forth like how would they break the bad news to her. She was fine. She was hungover and they were messing with her. This was some elaborate and poorly thought-out prank to convince her never to drink so much again.

"What's the last thing you remember?" Bren asked.

"The fire pit, passing a bottle around. Did I end up at the picnic table? I think I remember that."

Sam sighed. "I pulled you away from the fire after you almost upended the bottle and yourself into it." He scrubbed his hands over his face. "Fuck. I should have realized you were blacked out. I should never have let you walk off."

"What the fuck is going on, you guys? This isn't funny." A restless wave rolled through her and she wanted to run, in spite of how much it hurt to move. It did feel like most of the bones in her body were bruised, if not broken. Her legs twitched as the muscles in her stomach and back went rigid. "What. The. Hell. Is. Going. On?"

"It's probably the adrenaline leaving your system."

"For fuck's sake, Sam. You have to tell her."

"Tell me what?" she asked through a clenched jaw. She felt like she was going to explode if she couldn't run like in the dream. She needed to sprint through the woods and feel the wind on her skin and smell the trees and the earth.

Sam pried her hands away from her knees, where she'd left behind crescent moons, digging her nails into her skin. "Callie, look at me." She met his eyes, blue-green and deadly serious. It calmed her slightly. "You were in an accident. A pickup truck came speeding down Main Street, with no headlights on, when you were in the crosswalk, and it hit you. The driver must have been drunk. They didn't stop. You almost died." His voice broke like he believed what he was saying. Had someone slipped mushrooms into their beers and Sam hallucinated that she was dying? "I— You—" Sam's voice cracked again.

Bren made a frustrated growl. "He bit you, Cal. You were dying, your lung was punctured and you would have drowned in your own blood before we could get you to the hospital. He bit you, and now you're a wolf."

That was the punch line? She almost died so Sam turned her into a werewolf? If it hadn't hurt so much, she would have cracked up, but she managed a few snorts out of her aching chest. Both Bren and Sam were still watching her like they'd told her she had cancer. "Come on, guys. I promise I won't drink like that again. You will never have to share a mattress with me while making sure I don't choke on my puke, okay?" She nudged Sam with her foot. "What happened to my shorts, by the way?"

Bren held up a piece of ragged cloth. "You mean these?" He tossed them in her lap. Her shorts, shredded and bloody. From hitting the pavement? She automatically pulled the covers back and looked at her hip and thigh, dark purple and sore, covered with flecks of dried blood and healing scabs like she'd taken a good tumble. But still nothing like what would have had to happen to destroy her shorts like that.

"No." Her head bobbed back and forth and she felt the urge to *run* again.

Sam scooted closer and wrapped his arms around

her, stilling her twitching muscles. "I'm sorry. There was no other way. I couldn't lose you."

She planted her palms on his chest and shoved. He let go. "No. You're fucking with me. It can't— It's not real. You're not— You can't be. That's not possible."

"It's real, Cal." Bren stood up and pulled off his T-shirt and dropped his shorts.

"What the fuck, Bren?"

With a stretch of his back and shoulders and an uncanny twist of the light coming through the windows, a large gray wolf wearing Bren's boxer shorts sat on the floor in front of her. Its tail stuck awkwardly out of the leg hole. The pale fur under its chin mimicked the way Bren's scruffy beard grew in. It glared at her with Bren's eyes, as if to say, *See? I told you so.*

"What the actual fuck? This is a dream. I'm dreaming. This isn't real. Holy hell, I will never drink again." Callie ducked her eyes behind her knees, like she could possibly block out the image of wolf-Bren sitting in front of her.

In another instant, Bren was there, whole and human and in his boxers, sitting on Sam's floor. "You're not dreaming. You might want to keep the promise about not drinking, but it's real, Cal."

She shook her head and looked dumbly at Bren. "No. I've known you since I was five. I know your whole family. Your mom is my boss." She turned to Sam. "This can't— It's not real. It's not."

"It's real, Callie. I'm sorry but it is. That feeling like you want to run, like you want to sprint through the woods for miles because it feels good? That's the wolf. The adrenaline leaching out of your system doesn't help, but it's her and she wants out. It was the only way. We heal faster than humans do. I couldn't let you die, run over in the middle of the road by some drunk asshole. I couldn't let you die that way." She'd never seen Sam cry before but there were tears welling in his eyes. Somehow, his tears made it real—not Bren's magic trick, Sam's tears.

"I've known you my whole life. How could I not know this?"

The door crashed open for a second time that morning. Sam's father loomed on the threshold of his room. "Someone want to tell me what the hell is going on?"

Shit. Angus MacTire was intimidating on a good day and this was not going to be a good day. He was clearly furious, vibrating with it through every line of his body. Sam knew he had fucked up, had crashed through several of the laws they held most sacred by saving Callie. How was he supposed to explain that he just couldn't lose her?

"Dad—"

"Outside, Sam. Now." He turned on his boot heel and stalked out of the room. Callie looked like she was going to curl up in a ball and cry, Bren looked guilty.

"You called him."

"It's been two days. Shit, she was supposed to be at work this morning. I had to."

"You could have given me a few more hours."

"You think it would have made a difference?"

Sam sighed and got to his feet. He went downstairs and found his father surveying the backyard with an air of disgust and disappointment. Sam stood beside him and waited for the ax to fall.

"You want to tell me what the hell you were thinking?"

"Did Bren tell you what happened?"

"I want to hear it from you."

Sam stared at the ashes in the fire pit and searched for the right words. "She was drunk. I didn't realize how drunk or I would never have let her leave. I'd been keeping an eye on her all night."

He raised an eyebrow. "Why? Why do you feel the need to watch her so closely?"

Because she belongs to me. "Because she's my best friend."

His father snorted and Sam continued. "She was in the middle of the street and this black truck with no lights on came out of nowhere, over the speed limit, and slammed right into her, didn't even try to swerve, like they didn't see her at all." Maybe in time it would get easier to recount the moments when he thought he would lose her forever, but it was too fresh, the scene too vivid in his memory. "She would have died. Her lung was punctured, she was going into shock. I could hear her drowning in her own blood. She would have died waiting for an ambulance or an airlift."

"Maybe it was her time to die, son." He said it gently, but the words still cut, made Sam ball his fists and want to punch something.

"No. She's not supposed to die like a stray cat in the street."

"So you changed her."

"I saved her life."

"And disobeyed one of the fundamental tenets of our culture. You didn't give her a choice. You changed her when she had no idea we existed, should never have known we existed. She has to live with that now, because of you and your actions."

He'd fix it. Callie would be fine. She'd learn, he would teach her. "But she's alive. That's got to be better than ignorant and dead."

His father shook his head and strode back to the porch. "Come on."

Upstairs, Bren had put on some clothes and Callie was still curled around his pillow with a thousand-yard stare. His dad sat in the chair by the bed and spoke to her like he would a frightened animal, which he supposed Callie was.

"Callie."

"Mr. MacTire."

"Do you understand what happened Sunday night?"

Her eyebrows wrinkled together. Sam wanted nothing more than to soothe her, but he wouldn't be allowed to go to her until his father made his point. "Not really? I mean, I saw it. Bren showed me, I guess. But I can't— Wait, Sunday? What day is it? How long have I been out?"

"You idiots shifted in front of her? In front of a frightened, wounded girl? What the hell is wrong with you?"

Bren cringed along with Sam. "She thought we were messing with her, sir. I didn't know what else to do."

"Go downstairs, Brennan. We'll discuss appropriate behavior with the recently traumatized and changed later." Bren slunk out of the room and his father turned back to Callie. "I apologize, Callie. They should have brought you straight to me instead of waiting. It's Wednesday." He gave a quick, hard glance at Sam. He had broken that rule, too. But he knew she would have been more hysterical if she woke up in his parents' house with his father looming over her waiting to explain that she wasn't entirely human anymore.

"It's not Bren's fault. I didn't believe them. It was, um, pretty convincing to actually see it."

"That may be so. However, it remains that it was inappropriate and potentially dangerous." His father stood up. "You have a lot to learn." He turned to Sam. "She's your responsibility. You did this, you will own all of the consequences. Get her settled, then I want to know more about the truck."

"Yes, sir."

Sam slumped back onto the mattress as soon as the door closed behind his father but Callie perked up, her relief at being out from under his scrutiny palpable. "What was he talking about? Consequences? And what did he mean he wanted to know about the truck, you said it was a drunk driver."

"Oh, good. You're awake," he said sarcastically, and rolled onto his back. "I—I fucked up. We're not supposed to change people like that, unplanned, when they don't know what they're getting into. It was an emergency and you were unconscious, it's not like I had a choice." He scrubbed his hands over his eyes. "But it's not an easy thing to go through. I assume it was a drunk driver, but my father will investigate anyway, to be sure."

"You want to know what's messed up?"

"What?"

"I think I'm more mad that I never knew than I am that you—" she paused, struggling for the words "—changed me. You lied to me. Our whole lives."

"I had to. It's the first thing we're taught as kids, we keep our secrets."

"From your best friend?"

"From everyone who's not one of us, yes. There aren't many of us left; it's safer when people don't know we're their friends and neighbors."

"And I have to keep those secrets now?"

"Yes."

"From everyone."

"Yes."

"Fuck."

"I'm sorry. If I thought there had been any other way—"

"I know. I heard you outside with your dad. So, do I have superpowers, now? Will I howl at the moon uncontrollably? Live forever?"

Sam chuckled. That sounded more like Callie. "Superpowers, kind of. You'll be able to hear and smell more."

"Check and check. I thought it was the hangover making everything extremely loud and smelly."

"No, that's you." He elbowed her ribs gently.

"Ha-ha. Jerk."

"You'll only howl at the full moon because it's fun, not because you have to. You'll basically live a normal human life, with extras."

"That doesn't sound so bad."

"It's not. And there are a bunch of us around to help you. Come on. Let's get you back to your place and get you showered and fed." He wanted to clean away the scent of fear and blood from her skin and his, didn't want to ever smell it on her again. "You'll feel better, I swear."

"I'm already feeling way better than I did when I woke up."

"Highly accelerated healing. Comes in handy. Your ribs probably still feel pretty tender, and your head's going to hurt for a while. You hit the pavement pretty hard." He wasn't ready to detail her injuries and relive the nightmare again.

"Right."

He helped her into a pair of his shorts, since hers had been shredded to almost nothing, and walked her home. He'd lost her flip-flops, but she didn't seem to mind being barefoot. The wolf was already settling in. Callie would be fine.

The chorus in his heart, howling that she truly belonged to him, now more than ever, that was not fine.

Chapter Three

Taking a shower had never felt so good. Callie scrubbed away the smells of stale alcohol, terror and blood as her body knit itself back together under the stream of warm water. She still had the urge to run, but putting a name on it, even a name as incomprehensible and impossible as *wolf*, calmed her. Sam would take care of her. He would show her how to survive this.

His father had made it abundantly clear that she was Sam's responsibility and she felt a twinge of guilt. Sure, he cared enough not to let her die in the street, but it wasn't like he wanted to be stuck babysitting her for—well, she didn't have any idea how long he would be stuck with her.

The hot water started to run out, forcing her out of the shower. She slipped into the clean shorts and tank top she'd left on the sink and wrapped her hair in a towel. Sam was waiting for her when she emerged from the bathroom.

"I was beginning to think maybe you'd drowned in there." His smile was tentative, still worried, and he inhaled deeply through his nose.

"Are you—are you sniffing me?"

He blushed. Two new things today: Sam crying and

Sam blushing. "Sorry. It's—it's a habit. But if I never smell stale blood and terror sweat on you ever again, I'll be happy."

"A habit?"

His face was red from his hairline down to his beard. "You're—you're my best friend. You've always been practically part of the pack, even if you didn't know it. The sniffing each other out thing, it's part of it. So, um, yeah, I know what you're supposed to smell like."

This was a normal pack thing? She tested it out. That morning, she'd been convinced she was hallucinating when she'd smelled him running his hands through his hair but when she focused on filtering out everything else in the room, she found that she could pick him up. And she realized his warm, human male smell was familiar and soothing, and heat bloomed in her cheeks because his scent also kind of turned her on.

Sam cleared his throat. "You, uh, might find that you have some, um, strong feelings for a while as you adjust."

"Strong feelings?"

"If you're born to it, starting to shift usually coincides with puberty." His face was almost purple. Sam had never been a prude exactly, but they'd never had the kind of friendship where they talked openly about sex.

"Oh." *Shit*. He could smell that she was aroused.

"You don't— It's nothing to be ashamed of. It's best to, um, deal with it, though."

Oh God, her best friend was telling her to go masturbate. She didn't know what was worse, that or the fact that she wanted Sam to be the one to help her "deal with it." The voice that wanted to run through the woods told her to run and jump on him. *Down, girl.*

"Callie? You okay? I know this is awkward."

She could hear his heart. Racing, and not from fear. Anticipation? Something snapped. She was only half-aware of launching herself across the room and into his lap. She ran her nose up and down his neck, under his chin, through his beard, and that thing inside her curled up in contentment. *This is where you belong.*

Sam didn't touch her. He spread his arms and gripped the back of the couch, but she could hear his heart, feel his cock rising under her. A rational voice in her head told her that in spite of that, she should stop humping the poor guy who was saying and doing nothing to indicate that he wanted her in his lap.

She launched herself backward and landed smack on her ass again. She hissed as the impact jolted her ribs and her head. "Shit. Fuck. I'm sorry."

He let out a stuttering sigh and scrubbed his large hands over his face. "It's okay."

"It's not okay. I jumped you!" Her face was on fire and she wanted to crawl into a hole and stay there awhile.

"You're not in control. That wasn't you, that was the wolf. I know what it feels like, remember?"

"But—"

He cut her off. "You're not yourself. I won't take advantage of that. You're vulnerable and confused."

"And you're my best friend," she said woodenly. Her friend, only her friend. She had made a fool of herself and now he had to let her down easy. And he was stuck with her until whatever time his father deemed his responsibility fulfilled.

"I don't want you to hate me when this is over." He

got up and went to the door. "Meet me at the Pancake House in an hour, okay?"

"Okay." She lay back on the carpet and hid her face in her hands. The fact that he'd been kind and blamed it on the change took a tiny bit of the sting out of her humiliation. Only a tiny bit, though. And she was still frustratingly aroused, the need for satisfaction muting her lingering pain. *"Strong feelings."* Understatement of the fucking year.

He'd said to deal with it. She slipped one hand in her tank top while the other unbuttoned her shorts so she could slide her fingers under the waistband of her panties. He'd given her an hour; it would take minutes. She pinched and rolled her nipple and her clit throbbed. In her head, she was still on Sam's lap, grinding against his cock as he lengthened and stiffened underneath her. She'd never given much thought to his cock before, had refused to let her mind go there, but she had felt that ridge of hard flesh under her and she wanted more.

She stroked her clit and shuddered. In her fantasy, Sam stripped her shirt over her head and roughly tore off her bra. Her pinching fingers were his work-roughened ones, his sharp teeth bit and nipped at her skin, sucked her tender, sensitive nipples into his warm, wet mouth. She would feel the scruff of his beard, soft and scratchy at the same time, as he teased her body with his lips and tongue.

Callie pressed two fingers into her pussy and felt her muscles clench as she thumbed her clit and imagined Sam picking her up and carrying her to her bed, throwing her facedown on the mattress and yanking her shorts and panties down her legs. He'd hold her down with one large hand between her shoulders while he dipped the large fingers of the other inside her. He'd be pleased with how wet she was. He'd breathe in the smell of her and lose control. Roughly spread her legs and thrust inside her without hesitation. Fuck her hard and fast, his chest bent over her back, holding her shoulders to pull her against him as he thrust into her.

She slid her fingers free, spreading wetness to her clit. She circled the tight, hard bud with her slippery fingers and pressed against her pubic bone. Her hips jerked with every imagined thrust of Sam's hard cock. He would grunt and growl over her, fucking her hard, making their skin slap together. She'd be spent and sore but it would be worth it. She could almost feel his chest pressed to her back. And when he came, he would bite her shoulder, mark her as his, and the shock and the pain of it would send her spiraling into her own orgasm.

She came for real then, jerking and shuddering on the floor with her hand up her shirt and her shorts half-off. When her racing heart had settled and she could breathe again, she stripped out of her clothes and got back in the shower. Sam might have basically told her to jerk off and pull herself together, but he didn't need to be able to smell the evidence on her.

A thousand cold showers wouldn't be enough to freeze out the feeling of Callie on his lap, nuzzling his neck and grinding on his cock. But it wasn't Callie. Callie had jumped away from him when she realized what she was doing. He remembered what it felt like. The way lust pounded through his veins and the wolf wouldn't take no for an answer, he had to find a release. As a kid, it meant they all did a lot of furious, furtive jerking off, not much different from most teenagers. He had better control of it now. He could run. Hell, he could find someone to fuck. But he never forgot the way it had felt when he first started to shift. Or the way so many of those episodes of overwhelming desire were set off by the same girl who'd just been grinding on his lap.

He'd done the right thing. The wolf and the woman had battled for control behind her blue irises. He would never take advantage of her. He'd done enough to fuck up her life.

He climbed into his truck and headed up to his parents' house, bracing for more of his father's disappointment and anger. The screen door snapped closed behind him when he walked into the kitchen. His father was at the table with his uncles, the three of them looking especially grim, even for them. His mom and aunts were by the sink, looking on with worried faces and clutching cups of coffee.

"What's going on?"

"Sit down, son." Angus pointed at the remaining empty chair and Sam sat. "Do you remember who all was at the party?"

"Kind of. People came in and out. Why?"

"Who saw the accident?"

"I don't know. I don't remember. Bren was there, but I don't know if he saw it or if he heard it and ran. He helped me carry Callie into the house after. What's going on?"

"Patrick Dunphy wants your head, that's what. What I want to know is how he found out about it. Were any of them hanging around?"

"No. God, no. I would remember if any of those assholes showed up."

If it was the right answer or the wrong one, Sam

wasn't sure, but his father's expression darkened considerably. "Tell me about the truck."

"I didn't get a good look at it. It happened too quickly. Older model, black, maybe dark gray."

His father crossed his arms on the table and leaned forward. "Where's Callie now?"

"At her place. She's—" he cleared his throat "—starting to feel it. I left to give her a chance to cool off."

His father looked around the table, met each man's eyes, then over their heads at Sam's mother and Aunts Melissa and Morrigan. "I don't think this was an accident. Dunphy's been looking to shake me from the council for a long time. Provoking my son into changing the girl? I wouldn't put it past him."

Sam looked wildly around the table. "She was dying. I didn't have a choice."

His mom rested her hand on his shoulder. "We know, honey. But they'll say you have no business meddling in the life and death of humans, no matter how much you love her."

He knew it was true, but he wouldn't accept it. They were supposed to be descended from fierce warriors, guardians of the weak and the wounded, protectors who would go to hell and back for their people. What good was the magic in their blood if they couldn't save the people they loved from a senseless accident?

"Dunphy's calling for a hearing in front of the full council. Sam, you are not to let that girl out of your sight. Bring her up to the cabin and stay there. You're going to need her on your side in front of the council. However angry she might be at you for keeping secrets or what you've done, she needs to accept it and she needs to do it quickly, or we stand to lose everything we've done to keep our community safe and peaceful for a hundred years. Got it?"

"Yes, sir."

"Good. Go get her. We'll send someone up to check on you, bring you whatever you need, but you do not leave the cabin."

"Understood." The chair scraped over the old boards as he got to his feet. "I told her to meet me at the Pancake House. We'll eat, then I'll have her pack up some things and we'll head up."

As he walked into the restaurant, Sam had no idea how he was going to survive being alone in a cabin with a newly changed female wolf without violating the promise he'd made to her and himself less than an hour ago. Especially not when it was Callie. Not when she looked like that, slightly flushed and fresh out of the shower, tendrils of still-damp hair escaping the knot on top of her head. Not when she blushed pink to the tips of her ears the moment he sat down across from her in the booth. She'd gotten herself off. And the flush in her cheeks now made him wonder if he'd played a role in her fantasies. His groin tightened.

Their silent communication of scents and heart rates and widening pupils was interrupted by the delivery of a stack of pancakes for her and a cup of coffee for him. He ordered his usual "big bear" breakfast, with a lot of everything, and sipped his coffee, stalling the moment he had to insist that she go up to the cabin alone with him. She shoveled a few bites of pancakes into her mouth, past her perfect rosy lips—he had to stop thinking of her that way. She was his best friend. He had to protect her. From himself, if need be.

"I went to my parents'."

She slowly lowered her forkful of pancakes back to her plate. "And?"

"My father wants us out of town." He dropped his voice and looked around. No one who would pass information back to Dunphy. "We keep a cabin up by one of the old logging settlements. I'm supposed to take you up there as soon as we're done here and stay for a while."

"What? Why? Is that what you normally do when this happens?"

He debated how much to tell her. He didn't want to scare her even more than she already was. But he knew she was hurt by the lifetime of lies he'd told to protect his family's secret. He settled on partial truth and hoped for the best. "My dad wants us both out of the way while he looks into what happened. And it's probably for the best to get you out of town while you're adjusting; there's plenty of space up there and no people."

She leaned in and whispered, "I'm not going to hurt someone, am I?"

Sam wanted to press the crease of worry between her eyebrows with his thumb. "No. It's more likely that a person could hurt you if you lost control." He didn't finish the sentence but Callie nodded and closed her eyes in relief. Of course she was more afraid of what she could do to someone else than what a person who spotted a wolf roaming around Pullman could do to her. "Come on, finish your breakfast and I'll take you back to your place to grab some things."

Chapter Four

She tried to get Sam to stay downstairs while she packed a bag, but he wouldn't let her out of his sight. If he was trying not to scare her, it wasn't working. Something was wrong, no matter how Sam tried to downplay it. She gathered a few changes of clothes into a bag while he waited awkwardly next to her couch, standing nearly on top of the spot where she'd been writhing on the floor fantasizing about him a couple of hours ago.

He drove them up the winding mountain highway, past Farnsworth's Notch, and turned off onto an old access road. "Does the park service know you have a cabin in the middle of the White Mountain National Forest?"

Sam smiled. "We've been here longer than they have. And one of us is always in the local office."

"What about hikers?"

"You'll see."

The road petered out into a barely visible track under closely packed trees. Sam weaved through the dense new growth, running over a sapling or two in the process, and finally parked in a cleverly concealed spot hollowed out from a copse of white birches. A small sign read Trail Closed for Bridge Repairs. Water rushed down the mountain close by.

"Clever."

"This road isn't on any of the trail maps, but we replace the signage every couple of months to be safe. Once in a while, you'll see a question about old logging roads on a hiking forum, but other hikers will usually shut it down, better to stay on known, marked and maintained trails."

"Very clever."

"Eh, it works." He shrugged and slung both of their bags over his shoulder and pulled a cooler out of the truck bed. "Come on, it's up this way."

"I can get my own bag." Callie held out her hand but Sam shook his head and strode up the trail past the closed sign.

"You're still healing, whether you feel it or not."

She followed behind him for a few hundred yards and suddenly a small cabin appeared, tucked under the trees on the banks of the river. It was almost reclaimed by the forest, its dark wood worn and spotted with moss and lichens, shingles curling at the edges; it looked like one good snowfall would collapse it in on itself.

Sam bounded up the steps of the sagging porch and Callie waited to see if it disintegrated under his weight before she joined him at the door. The sturdy lock was the only thing on the place that looked new. Inside, it was surprisingly clean and tidy, right down to the brightly colored crocheted blanket on the single twin camp bed tucked into the far corner.

A small cast-iron woodstove, a few cupboards, and a battered card table and two chairs occupied the rest of the space. Sam busied himself unpacking the contents of a grocery bag into the cupboards while Callie turned herself in circles.

"I'll sleep on the floor," Sam said to the window above the washbasin.

"Huh? It's not that." *It's totally that.* And that a very loud part of her very much wanted to squeeze both of their bodies into that tiny bed. "Bathroom?"

"There's an outhouse about fifty yards that way." He pointed out the window. "And a small pool in the river a little ways upstream for bathing."

Of course. They were in the middle of nowhere, off an unmapped, long-defunct logging road, in a cabin no one was supposed to know about. It was the definition of off the grid. No running water, no electricity. Callie might have grown up in the mountains, but she wasn't much for camping. Day hikes followed by drinking beers around Sam's fire pit were more her speed.

She started to panic. She was trapped in this tiny cabin with nowhere to go and nothing to do but what? Dwell on the fact that everything she knew about her best friend was at least partially untrue and in spite of that she still wanted to climb him like a tree? How could Mr. MacTire have thought they would be safer out here on their own?

Callie slammed out of the cabin and sat down hard on the top step, ready to run down the mountain and hitch her way back into town.

Sam followed more slowly and leaned on the door frame behind her. "Remember I told you we usually start going through this around puberty?"

Callie's face flamed. "Yes."

"Do you remember what it felt like when you were that age?" Sam inched forward.

Oh God, it did sort of feel like she was back in that place where everything felt wrong and it all sucked harder than anything had ever sucked in the history of the world and her moods swung from pole to pole at the drop of a hat. "So, what, I'm going through puberty again?"

"In a way." He sat gingerly next to her, leaving plenty of space between them.

"Is that why you're not supposed to change people without a plan?"

"One of the reasons, yeah."

Callie scooted a couple of inches closer to him. She couldn't help it. Their knees brushed. "I guess I'm glad I'm not dead?" It was almost impossible to wrap her brain around the idea that she could be this, or she could be dead, when she had no memory of almost dying.

Sam snorted. "Oh, that makes me feel much better." He nudged her knee with his, the hair on his legs prickly against her skin. Having him close made her feel calmer, despite the strong urge to rub her nose in his beard.

"What happens now? We stay here, you show me the ropes, then what? How do I even do it? This morning, Bren went 'poof' and there he was."

He shrugged. "There's no good way to explain it. You've already felt it, that overwhelming, almost coming-out-of-your-skin feeling? That's the shift trying to happen without your control. You want to avoid that. But that's the energy you call up when you want to do it."

"And you stay in control, even when you're—" She couldn't bring herself to say the word yet.

"A wolf? You're still aware, yeah, and you control when you shift back." He leaned back on his palms.

"Depending on who you ask, we're descended from legendary warriors the gods imbued with the ability to shift for battle, who stood guard over the wounded and traveled into literal hell to bring back food during famines, or we're descended from clanless boys who raided cattle and spent too much time out in the open, exposed and vulnerable to wayward magic that turned them feral. It wouldn't do you much good in either case if you lost your human consciousness in the process."

"No, I guess it wouldn't."

"Do you want to try it?" He nudged her knee with his again, his expression almost mischievous.

"What, now?"

"That's part of why we're here, so you can learn to shift safely. Come on. It'll feel good to run off some of the nervous energy, I promise."

"What if I get stuck?"

"You won't."

"Promise?"

"I promise, you won't get stuck." He got to his feet and pulled his shirt over his head. "You will need to take off your clothes, though."

"Wait, what?" He'd distracted her with his bare chest.

Sam chuckled. "You should see your face. The clothes don't go with you when you shift. I'll turn around, but you're going to have to get naked. Unless you want to struggle your way out of your underwear when you have no thumbs."

She laughed at the mental image of a wolf stuck in her bra and panties. "Okay. Turn around." Sam turned his back. "You're coming with me, though, right?"

"I'll wait for you to shift and I'll follow, okay?"

"Okay."

Callie shucked her clothes and left them in a neat pile on the steps. Sam's voice behind her told her to call on the restlessness, the desire to run, and let it take over. She remembered her dream of running through the woods, the feel of the dirt under her feet, the smell of pine branches brushing past her face, and she let the urge to run flood her system. She closed her eyes and took a deep breath. Restless energy rolled over her skin in a cold wave, her skin prickling with goose bumps as her shoulders bunched and stretched. Her back arched as the prickling feeling traveled up her skull in pins and needles that made her hair stand on end. Her hands hit the ground with a soft thump and when she opened her eyes, she instinctively knew she had done it.

"Good job."

A voice, her favorite voice, behind her. *Sam, Sam, Sam.* She trotted over and rubbed against his leg, down her spine from nose to tail. His bare leg, all the way up. The first time since they were little kids she saw Sam naked and she wasn't even human.

The next thing she felt was a nose under her chin, a greeting, then a check to her shoulder. His meaning was clear. *Let's go.* She followed. She'd follow him anywhere.

Sam ran ahead. He'd take her to the tree line and back down; exhaustion was good for a wolf. The more tired she was, the more control she could hope to have over the urge to shift. Callie caught up easily and nudged his chin with her nose. She kept pace with him, her body brushing against his as they ran. She was god-damn flirting with him. But it wasn't Callie. Callie had no idea this was courtship behavior, that her wolf was doing her damnedest to provoke the wild, feral part of him into staking a claim on her.

He wouldn't do it. Maybe he needed the exhaustion as much as she did. He sprinted in a final push to a clearing and dropped in a patch of grass under the scrubby pine trees, bent and twisted from the wind howling through the mountains all winter long. He shifted and lay naked and panting in the grass, the air, brighter and crisper up here than down in the valley, drying the sweat from his skin.

Callie dropped next to him and rolled onto her back. Her shift rippled through the grass as her body took shape and settled into place beside him. He turned away from her, allowing her a measure of modesty if she wanted it.

"That was fun."

He smiled to himself. "Good."

"I didn't know it was a race, though." She poked her toes into the back of his calf.

"Callie—"

"I know what she's up to, I'm not stupid. Flirting is kind of universal, I guess."

"It's not that simple."

She groaned. "I know, I'm sorry. You don't have to say it. I'm like a kid sister and you're only here because you're supposed to be watching out for me."

He heard the hurt in her voice, hated rejecting her, hated the voice in his own head crying, *She's ours! She wants us! Take her!* But he let it go. Better for her to be temporarily hurt than be stuck with him for life. She might understand flirting and desire, but she had no idea what it would mean to him, that he would be fighting the voice begging him to claim her, to make her his. It would never be as simple for him as a quick fuck to get it out of their systems.

"Come on, I'll race you down to the cabin." He shifted and waited for her to follow, then ran for his life back down the mountain.

He was on the porch and fully dressed by the time she trotted up the steps. Sam opened the door for her and nodded her into the room. "You can change and get dressed inside. I'll wait out here."

She slunk into the cabin and Sam sat on the steps, praying he would be able to make dinner and put her to bed without a fight. He didn't know how many more times he could push her away before he broke. The door creaked on its spring but he kept his eyes on the water rushing over the stones in front of him.

She sat on the step above him in shorts and a flannel shirt. She leaned back on her hands, thrusting her small breasts up, the two round swells of flesh perched on her rib cage, right at his eye level. "That was not a fair race."

"You weren't that far behind." He stood before he could pull her into his lap and stick his face in her tits, her neck, leave a trail of bite marks on her skin. "I'm going to get a fire going for dinner."

Callie grabbed his arm before he made it two steps. "Wait." He stopped but didn't turn around. Callie stepped in front of him and slipped her hand into his. "I'm sorry I keep throwing myself at you."

"It's okay. You're not yourself." He wanted to hug her, soothe whatever hurt or shame she was feeling, but he pulled his hand from hers instead. "You don't know what you're doing."

"Goddammit, stop talking to me like I'm a child," she growled, and balled her fists. "You said you don't want me to hate you when this is over, but I'm going to fucking hate you right now if you won't stop telling me I'm not myself, like I'm not in my own head. I hear that voice, but it's *my* voice. She's a part of me. And this is never going to be over. Unless there's some miracle cure you haven't told me about, this is it. I'm one of you."

"And I will always be sorry. No one should have to go through this without warning, without a choice."

"Oh my God, that is not my point." She raised her hands like she wanted to push him, but settled for stomping a foot instead.

His own frustration bubbled over to meet hers. "What do you want me to do? Take you to bed only to have you regret it later when you realize it was only because you were desperate and I was convenient?"

"If you don't want me, fucking say it. Don't try to make it sound like you're being all noble and trying to spare our friendship."

She stood there, practically vibrating she was so pissed off, and he couldn't lie to her. "Callie, I have always wanted you. But you don't want me, not really."

She closed her eyes and took a deep breath through lungs that two nights ago had been filling with blood, drowning her from the inside. "You're an idiot. Why did you never make a move? You treated me like your kid sister."

"I had to. It's complicated."

Callie sat back down on the porch. "Un-complicate it."

He sat on the ground across from her, ready to bore her with pack politics until she calmed down. "My family is one of a handful of packs in northern New England, and those families created a council generations ago as

a form of self-governance and protection of our inter-
ests. My dad is on the council because he's the leader
of our family, pack alpha, whatever you want to call it.
I'm expected to take his seat when he retires or dies,
whatever comes first. Probably death."

She didn't laugh at his lame attempt at a joke. "You're
not the oldest, though. What about Ryan? And what
does any of that have to do with me and you?"

"We don't choose succession by age order. Ryan—
Ryan isn't cut out for leadership."

She let out a soft huff. "I see your point."

His older brother shirked responsibility like water
off a duck's back. Ryan was far happier teaching kids
how to snowboard and hitting on their moms at the
lodge over spiked hot chocolates. "Exactly. So it's on
me. And I've always been expected to pair off with a
woman from another pack."

"That's never stopped you from hooking up with
anyone."

"Yeah, hooking up. I've never really dated anyone.
I've never lied about being available long-term. And
you… I never wanted to risk losing you as a friend."
And having to leave her to be with someone for the
sake of clan alliances would have broken him. Could
still break him.

"What if I don't care? Don't I get a say? What if all
I want right now is to get this out of my system? It all
comes back to you thinking you know what's best for
me. Or that I'm going to be some poor, pathetic girl
who falls hopelessly in love with you and you're going
to break my heart."

"That's not what I meant. I never wanted to screw
this up."

"It's pretty fucking screwed up now, don't you think?" She cocked an eyebrow at him. "How much worse can we make it? I want you, you want me." She shrugged. "Let's agree that whatever happens, we were friends first and this was probably inevitable, whether by booze or wolfiness, so why not make the best of it while it lasts?"

She made a deranged kind of sense. Except it was never her heart breaking he was worried about. If they did this, he would never be the same. But when she bit the corner of her lip and offered herself to him, even if it was only temporary, his senses fled. Sam did the only thing he had left to do. He got up, brushed the pine needles and dirt from his pants, hoisted her over his shoulder and took her to bed.

Chapter Five

Callie squealed when he dropped her ass-first onto the bed. The old springs protested loudly as she bounced and she blushed, saw Sam's cheeks go pink, averted her eyes and promptly burst into a fit of nervous giggling.

"We don't have to do this. I can take a walk if you need to relieve some tension." His waggling eyebrows only made her laugh harder.

"Yeah, that worked out real well this morning," she said as she brushed her hair out of her face.

"What did you do after I left?"

Her face flamed. "I imagined something like this."

"Like this how?" He moved in closer to her, framing her body with his, but not touching her yet.

"You, throwing me on a bed."

Sam rubbed her neck with his nose, from her collarbone to the tip of her chin. "We got that far. What else did you picture?"

She bunched her fingers into the rough wool of the blanket. "I didn't get much further. You were rough. I liked it."

Sam nipped her earlobe. "Is that what you want? You want me to be rough?"

"You bit me. It was—" Her voice died in her throat as he bit down where her neck curved to meet her shoulder.

"Like that?"

"Harder. And from behind."

Sam closed his eyes and growled low in the back of his throat. He opened them and his heavy gaze traveled her body, like it was his hands tracing her skin. She squirmed under him, still not touching, something inside her telling her that Sam had to be in control. He pinned her in place when his eyes met hers.

"This is your last chance. If you say no right now, I will walk out of here and take a very long bath in the very cold river and we can pretend this never happened. If you don't, if you say yes, I will strip you naked and fuck you hard until neither of us can move."

She heard his heart thumping, saw the tension in his face and the lines of his body. "Yes. *Please.*"

He groaned and lowered himself onto his elbows, pressing his hips and his chest to hers, his hard cock notched at the apex of her thighs, and for the first time, their lips met. He fit his mouth on hers and cupped her chin in his hands and *kissed* her. He nipped at her bottom lip and she opened her mouth to him, his tongue soothing the bite before he slipped into her mouth and claimed it. A soft hum of satisfaction escaped her throat and he growled back at her.

He pulled back and traced her swollen lips with his thumb, eyes full of fire and possession. *"Callie,"* he whispered, in a voice not entirely his own.

She shivered, arousal and a sliver of fear making her belly clench. Sam lifted a corner of his mouth and sat back on his heels. He pulled his shirt by the neck up and over his head, revealing his muscular chest with its short brown hair that darkened into a line down his belly. Sam had been shirtless in front of her a thousand times, but never like this, never this close and never anticipating the feel of his naked torso against hers. She'd never followed that trail of dark hair to its conclusion, at the base of the cock that was currently straining the zipper of his shorts. She swallowed audibly.

He smirked at her again and leaned forward to put his hands on her belly, inching up the hem of her shirt. Everything about his touch was new but familiar at the same time, and perfect. His work-rough hands scratched the tender skin he exposed as he moved from hip to waist to ribs, bunching the soft flannel up around her breasts. He bent his head and kissed her softly rounded stomach before he bit the crest of her hip and took the tails of her shirt in his hands and wrenched it apart. Snap buttons. No bra.

Callie giggled. "I knew there was a reason I packed this shirt."

Sam answered by biting her nipple and pulling back, making her hiss with pain and pleasure. He cupped her other breast and pinched with his fingers, rolling and pulling on her tender nipple while he let the other one go from between his teeth. Every touch echoed between her legs. She wriggled her hips under him, grinding against his leg, trying to find purchase, friction.

He wrapped an arm around her waist to lift her up and out of her shirt while he bit and sucked at her neck, the hair on his chest tickling her nipples. Callie scratched down his back and gripped his hips, touching him at last; he groaned and bit down harder on her flesh. They would both be marked by the time they were done.

He pushed her onto her back and kissed her, sliding

his hand down the slope of her belly to the button of her shorts. He unfastened it and spread the zipper, dipping his hands down over her panties. She opened to him without being asked, and he rewarded her with a firm swipe of his fingers across her clit.

He drew his hand away and she whimpered in protest. Sam sliding down her body and pulling her shorts off while he pressed his nose to her pussy through her panties produced a different kind of whimper. He teased her, almost naked but for a scrap of pale blue cotton, breathing in the smell of her, tapping her clit with his nose, his tongue, his fingers while she clutched at the blankets and writhed.

"Please, you're killing me."

He bit her thigh, but pulled her panties down. "No turning back," he said as he swept her pussy open with his fingers and groaned.

"No turning back. Please."

He pushed one finger inside, then two, and pressed her clit with his thumb. "What makes you come? Is it this?" He curled his fingers inside her, stretching her, teasing the perfect spot. She moaned in pleasure, but it wouldn't make her come. "Or this?" He sawed his thumb over her clit, every hard brush like a bolt of lightning and she wailed. "This, then." He kept sliding his thumb while he pumped his fingers in and out of her vagina. "I want you to come. Will you come for me?"

She writhed on his hand, panting and groaning, her thighs tensed, her toes pointed, and it ripped through her, leaving her panting and shaking. Sam stopped rubbing her clit and pulled his fingers from inside her. The sight of him licking them clean, eyes closed in pleasure, was almost enough to set her on the way to another orgasm.

"Last chance."

She shook her head. "I want this. Fuck, do I want this."

"Thank God." He lay down next to her and pulled a condom from his pocket before he unbuttoned his shorts and kicked them off.

"Oh, and you happen to have condoms on you?"

"I had every intention of being noble. But I did learn when I was a kid you should always be prepared."

Callie turned on her side and scooted back. She wanted to look at him like he'd looked at her, to touch him, to learn what he liked, to make him come with her hands or her mouth. She reached for him, wanting to take the thick length of his cock in her palm, to feel how hot and hard he was, but he pushed her away and rolled on the condom.

"I want to touch you."

"Later," he growled. "Get on your stomach and spread your legs."

She rolled over and did as she was told. Sam got on his knees behind her and the head of his cock nudged her entrance and thrust forward, bottoming out with one hard push. He rested with his hips against her ass for a few seconds, tipped his body forward, gripped her neck with one hand and her hip with the other, and fucked her. Hard, like he'd promised.

Every thrust dragged her sensitive skin against the rough wool blanket, pressed her into the mattress with the force. Callie clutched the pillow and moaned as Sam fucked into her. In that position, his cock felt huge and hard, filling her pussy like nothing else, stroking that sweet spot inside her with each push, grinding her mound against the bed every time he thrust.

His grip on her neck tightened, his pace quickened, his skin slapped against hers. "Rub your clit. I want to feel you come like this."

She snaked a hand under her belly, pressed two fingers to her clit, and held them there, the force of his strokes and her own wetness providing the rhythm and the slide. She clenched around his cock, and he let go of her neck, swept her hair out of the way, and bit down on her shoulder with a fierce growl. The surprise or the pain or the fact that she was already on the edge made her scream into the pillow as she came hard around him. Sam let go of her skin with his teeth, gave three short, sharp thrusts, and bellowed as he emptied himself.

They collapsed, both panting, the smell of sweat and sex permeating the air. Sated at last, Callie curled into Sam's chest and fell asleep.

She woke up and stretched out on the narrow bed, alone in the gray-blue light before dawn. She'd drifted in and out of sleep since collapsing after Sam fucked her. When she'd startled awake from a nightmare of running, running, running, away from something or someone chasing her through the woods, branches whipping her face, panic making her heart pound in her ears, Sam had soothed her back to sleep with slow kisses and gentle touches. She'd tried to resist his tenderness, but he'd wrung sweet pleasure from her body in the dead of night, until her fear went quiet and she could rest again.

She lay there in the soft sheets they'd tangled around each other and marveled at how content she felt. It was easy, being with Sam. *Like that's how it's supposed to be*. She'd told him he wasn't going to break her heart, but now she wasn't so sure.

She froze when she heard voices outside, then relaxed; it was only Sam and his dad. What his father was doing this far up the mountain at dawn, she didn't know.

"You slept with her."

Callie blushed by herself in the still-dark room. Sam mumbled something on the porch. Mr. MacTire must have been able to smell the sex that still hung heavy in the air. Neither of them had bathed since yesterday, before running in the woods, before the sex and the sleeping together and the making love in the middle of the night.

"Good. You need her on your side."

What the hell? On his side for what? And what did that have to do with sleeping with her?

"Jesus, Dad. It wasn't like that. She was losing control."

"I don't want to know what it was like, son. Do whatever you have to do to keep her here and calm."

"Yeah." Sam's voice was sullen.

Quick feet came up the steps. Callie didn't dare turn over to try to peek through the screen door. She barely breathed, trying to keep the old bedsprings quiet. "Keep her calm and keep your head."

"Yes, sir."

"Good." Booted feet stepped off the porch and crunched through pine needles, farther and farther down the path until she lost the sound of them amid the early-morning stirrings of the forest.

Callie pulled the blanket over her face and screwed her eyes shut, expecting Sam to walk back into the cabin any second and realize she'd heard them. Last night's sweetness soured in her stomach. Something was going on, something had his father worried enough that he'd sent them up here to keep them away from it. Sam knew more than he had told her; she was as certain of that as she was of anything.

The screen door creaked open slowly. Callie tried desperately to slow her breathing and willed her heart to stop pounding so Sam wouldn't know she was awake. He crossed the room and slipped into bed next to her. With an arm around her waist he nuzzled her neck with his nose, like he'd wanted nothing more in life than to wake up next to her.

"You awake?"

Callie felt his smile in the way his beard brushed against her skin. "Mmm-hmm," she mumbled, as if she could pretend she had only just woken up.

"Callie," he whispered and nibbled the spot right behind her ear.

She arched into the bite and hummed. *Does it matter what's happening out there? Does it matter why he's here with you? You've changed, you belong here now.* She had to admit the wolf had a point, even if it was only temporary, this belonging. Temporary was what she'd wanted, demanded from him. To get it out of their systems and go back to being friends. But when Sam trailed nips down her neck like that, she wasn't sure she would ever be able to look at him again without remembering what it felt like to be in his arms in the middle of the night, full of feelings that had nothing to do with temporary.

She rolled over and kissed him to make her brain shut up. She rubbed her nose in his chin, left her own trail of bites down his neck. She wrestled him out of the shirt he'd thrown on to go outside, pulled down his shorts and tossed them over the side of the bed. She ran her hands through the hair on his chest, down over his stomach, and gave a teasing scratch through the hair at the base of his cock, rising rapidly to meet her when she wrapped her hand around it.

He hadn't given her the chance yet, to explore his body, to tease or give pleasure; he'd been too concerned with sating her, calming and soothing her so she wouldn't lose control of the shift. *Like his dad told him to.* She shut the thought out of her mind, stroking his cock, smooth skin covering hard flesh, listening for the hitch in his breath, the beat of his heart, the sound in his throat that would tell her when she'd done it right. A twist of her wrist over the smooth head, sliding her palm through the bead of precome there, made his stomach shudder.

"Fuck, Callie," he groaned and slipped two fingers between her labia, seeking her clit. He teased around the little bundle of nerves, spreading her gathering wetness through her folds, while she kept stroking his cock. "Get on top."

He handed her a condom from the box that had ended up on the floor at the head of the bed and lay down. She couldn't resist the image of him stretched on his back, waiting. She leaned forward and took his cock in her mouth. The smell of him, and of her, of the past twelve hours of sex and sleep, filled her nose as her head dipped down. She swallowed as much of him as she could before she bobbed back up and swiped the flat of her tongue over the crown, teasing like she'd done with her hand. She dipped her tongue into the slit, tasting salt and musk. She bobbed her head back down and up again with a hard suck before he grabbed her arms and pulled her off him.

"Callie," he growled, thunder in his eyes as he held her in place. "Later."

She nodded and he let her go. She sheathed his cock and rose up on her knees. With his hands on her hips, she positioned him and sank down slowly. Her head fell back with the bliss of being filled. No time to think of anything else now, only this, only his big, rough hands on her hips and his cock inside her.

"Grab the headboard."

She tipped her body forward and took hold of the old cast-iron rail. He tightened his grip on her waist and rocked his hips, thrusting up into her from below. Even with her on top, Sam was in control, but why fight him when it felt this good? His strokes were slow and measured, designed to prolong their joining, not to chase an orgasm. She writhed there, strung out between pleasure and completion, while Sam took his own time.

"I don't think I can come like this."

"I don't think I care right now." He found her clit with his thumb and pressed lightly, enough to make her gasp, to make her arousal spool tighter in her belly, to make her muscles clench with it. "Let it feel good."

He kept her hanging there, brushing her clit to bring her closer, but never giving her enough to crest that hill and tumble down the other side. She wriggled in his grip, desperate and whining until he wrapped his arms around her back and pulled her flush to his body. His chest hair tickled her nipples with every sharp, shallow thrust. He wrapped one fist in her hair and pulled, stretching her neck and forcing her back into an arch as he sped up his hips. With her back arched and her

clit pressed into his pubic bone, Callie cried out in relief as she started to come.

Sam groaned as her muscles clenched around him.
He scraped his teeth along her collar bone as he let go
with a low moan. His hips stilled and his cock pulsed
inside her, sending a rippling aftershock of pleasure
shivering over her skin. He held her there, kissing her
sweaty neck, hand still entwined in her hair, and Callie basked in temporary contentment. *This is where you
belong.*

She gingerly rolled off his chest and lay next to him.
"G'morning." She kissed his biceps, and traced his tattoo with her fingers.

"Morning." Sam sat up and got out of bed. He pulled
the condom off and gathered up his clothes. With his
shorts half-on he stopped at the door. "I'm going to start
a fire for breakfast. You need to eat."

Chapter Six

Sam hadn't meant to get back into bed with her, but he hadn't been able to stop himself, seeing her naked body stretched out under the sheets. He couldn't get enough of the feel of her skin, her soft flesh under his hands, the taste of her sweat on his tongue. He was exhausted from staying up all night, alternately watching her sleep and burying himself inside her. In spite of his satiation, his senses had stayed on high alert, listening to every cracking twig, every small night creature that invaded their sphere. He'd long ago lost his head over Callie, but his father was right—his feelings could be a liability.

He'd been stupid to think he could sleep with her in the first place. What was one more lie about not wanting her in the face of all the lies he'd ever told to keep his family's secrets? What was one more lie if it kept them both safe? But he couldn't do it. He couldn't deny that he had always wanted her, had only kept his distance because she wasn't one of them. He couldn't lie to her when she was wound up and vulnerable and every single instinct he possessed, human and otherwise, was begging him to take her. There was only so much he could fight.

Then she'd had to poke at that damn tattoo and remind him of his father's words, his obligations to his clan, his pack.

Sam pulled the grate off the fire pit and dumped in the handful of twigs and bits of kindling he'd been collecting while he stewed. He shook the spiders off the tarp covering the small woodpile and layered a few split logs over the kindling, lit a match, and slowly breathed life into the small fire. His father had delivered a cooler of food with his warning to keep Callie under control.

Callie emerged from inside, stretching and yawning in the same shorts and flannel shirt from yesterday. They'd both packed like it was inevitable. Why else would he bring a box of condoms and she a flannel shirt with snap buttons? He hadn't even realized the shirt snapped until he ripped it open in his haste to bare her torso. Her arms over her head lifted the hem of her shirt, revealing a hint of her soft belly, and Sam had to consciously talk himself out of turning her right back around and throwing her into bed again.

"Hey."

"Hey."

"Is there anything I can do?"

"Not for a few minutes."

She took a seat on one of the logs that ringed the fire, arms crossed and her knees tucked up to her chest. "Did I hear your dad earlier?"

Shit. "He came up to drop off some more food, check on us."

"Sam, what's going on?"

"Nothing." The less she knew, the better. *"Keep her calm. Under control."*

She eyed him dubiously. "Are you sure?"

"Of course." He ducked his head so she couldn't see

him wince with the lie. "Hey, actually, do you mind going inside and grabbing the coffeepot?"

She got up without a word. She knew he was full of shit, but what was he supposed to tell her? Some goon with a grudge against his father might have run her down to get him to do something incredibly stupid? And it had worked. Callie was collateral damage in a long-simmering struggle she didn't know anything about, and Sam faced God-knew-what for his part in it. Knowing that wouldn't help her. She needed time to adjust. To heal. To learn to control the wolf she was stuck with for the rest of her life. Keeping her in the dark would keep her calm. Keeping her calm would keep her safe.

She came back with the pot and a gallon of water and set them down next to him.

"Thanks."

"Sure." She sat on the opposite side of the fire. Maybe it was better this way, to let her put some distance between them. He ignored the voice in his gut insisting he go get her and keep her close. "After we eat, will you show me where the pool is upriver? I must smell rank by now."

In the human world, that was probably true. To Sam, she still smelled amazing. Like sweat and animal and sex, like *his*. "I hadn't noticed." The words slipped out of his mouth before he could remind himself about letting her go. "But yeah, we can go for a swim. I probably don't smell like roses either."

She blushed and mumbled, "I hadn't noticed."

He left her there to go back into the cabin for the food and the ancient cast-iron frying pan that hung next to the door, where it made for a potentially handy weapon as well as a cooking tool. She was quiet while he fried bacon and eggs over the open fire. He fought the screaming need to uncurl her spine and soothe the furrows in her brow. The feral animal inside him wanted to shore up the fragile bond they'd made.

They ate in silence. Sam smothered the fire and rinsed the dishes and the pan. Callie curled herself smaller and smaller, her anxiety tangible in the air. He hated himself for hurting her.

"You ready to go?"

She smiled weakly. "Has it been a full half hour?"

"I think we can risk it."

"Sam?" She looked up at him from her place on the log. "Will you please tell me what's going on? You're being weird."

He sighed and scratched his jaw, prayed a half-truth would satisfy her. "I don't know exactly what's going on either. My dad is worried, but it might be nothing." *But it probably isn't.*

"Look, I get it. You had to lie to me before, because I wasn't one of you, but don't lie to me now. Please."

She was definitely going to hate him for all of this later. "I won't. Let's just get through this, okay?" He could see her anxiety turning restless, the desire to run turning into the need to run away. He had to keep her close. Wolf or no, she could still get lost out here. God help them all if someone else found her.

She unwrapped her arms from her bouncing knees. On her feet, she fidgeted with the hem of her shirt, waiting for something, permission, a cue.

"If you need to shift, do it."

She pulled off her shirt and dropped her shorts to the ground. She stood there naked, her pink-tipped breasts and soft curves golden in the dappled morning sun-light. Sam's cock stirred in his pants at the sight of her, bare and mostly unashamed. "You're getting the hang of this."

She shot him a dirty look and carefully bent forward to pick up her clothes off the ground. "You next."

Sam shucked his clothes and tossed them on the porch with hers. Her eyes on him were like the ghosts of her hands, exploring him under the sheets. The sense memory of her mouth on him sent blood rushing to his cock. She lifted an eyebrow, watching him stiffen, her cheeks pinked, but she didn't hide from the sight of his arousal.

He closed his eyes, summoned the wildness, and found himself on all fours before he could move to take her right there on the ground, rolling around in the pine needles and leaf litter. He turned and took off into the woods. Callie's laugh rang in his ears as she shifted and followed.

They ran, following the river upstream, above a set of falls to where the long-worn granite of the mountain had formed a natural pool. The river itself was swift and cold, even in midsummer, but the pool sat in the sun, warming it slightly above the temperature of the surrounding water. There were others like it sprinkled throughout the forest, and most of them were heavily trafficked swimming holes, but here they had total privacy. She shifted, the change coming more easily every time, and got to her feet.

Sam was lying to her, she was sure of it now. Everything she thought was true, that she'd been absolutely sure of, had been blown to pieces yesterday, and instead of helping her put the pieces back together, her best friend was hiding something from her. Maybe a lot of somethings.

Callie picked her way into the water over the rocks, slippery with silt and algae covering their water-smoothed surfaces. Sam ran in behind her, scrabbling across the rocks, still shifted. He dove into the cold water and dog-paddled around the pool for a minute. He hauled himself out, gave a giant shake that sent droplets flying all over her, still only up to her knees, and shifted back to himself, grinning.

"You're ridiculous."

"It's fun. And the water doesn't feel as cold." Callie couldn't help glancing down to see how cold he was. He cocked an eyebrow, put his hands on his hips and puffed out his chest. "You'll learn soon enough that none of us give a shit that we've all seen each other naked. You see it way too many times to care."

"Yeah, I'm getting that." She eased farther into the water, her nipples tight with cold. *And let's face it, Sam looks like* that *naked.* Sam, goofing around and trying to make her laugh while the world fell apart, while he was supposed to be keeping her calm; of course he was trying to make her laugh. She bristled and waded in deeper, suddenly uncomfortable being bare-ass naked in front of him.

The pool bottomed out at waist-deep, so she dipped her knees to bring the water up to her shoulders and ducked her head backward to wet her hair. Sam watched her from the bank, giving her space. Callie moved carefully to the far edge of the pool, where it was ringed by a group of large rocks jutting up and out of the river. Perfect platforms for lying out in the sun. She'd have to wade through the freezing pool to get back to shore, but she climbed up anyway. The sun-warmed stone felt glorious after the cold water.

Her body relaxed while her mind churned over the conversation she'd overheard earlier, the argument last night that had led to the sex, the way he was clearly hiding something from her now. And in spite of it, she still wanted him. Arousal thrummed through her veins, and the voice in her head was still crowing with delight that she belonged with him. How could she belong with someone who was lying to her?

She'd kept her distance back at the cabin as some sort of last-ditch attempt at self-preservation. She shouldn't get attached. Yet she knew if he climbed up on the rock next to her, she'd be hard-pressed to keep her hands off him. She squeezed her thighs together, thinking of the sight of his cock rising in front of her. Only a few days ago, she'd never allowed herself to think of how glorious Sam's naked body might be; now she knew intimately how good it felt to have him between her thighs. Her clit throbbed in time with her heartbeat, a quickening, and she raised herself up on an elbow and glanced around before she slid her fingers between her labia and closed her eyes.

She stroked her fingers down her slit to dip into her pussy, trying not to think about how full, how possessed, he made her feel when he was inside her. When she'd gotten dressed after he left her that morning, she'd discovered little bite marks all over her body, and she'd liked them. She'd felt the faint bruise he'd left on her

shoulder the first time and she loved it. She was his.
He was hers.

"Callie." Wet hands stroked her, cool droplets from
his hair and beard dotted her skin as he pressed kisses
to her neck. She should push him away, but it felt too
good. She kept her eyes screwed shut and let him kiss
her, touch her, while she kept pumping her own fingers
in and out of herself.

Sam trailed his mouth down to her breasts, took
a nipple into his mouth and sucked. His mouth was
scorching hot after the cold water, his tongue moving in
lazy circles that went straight to her clit. He switched to
the other breast and gently closed his teeth around her
flesh. Callie whimpered and worked her fingers faster,
ground her clit into her palm as she did.

He pressed his body closer to her, his skin still cool
against hers, his cock hard at her hip. Skimming his
hand down her belly, he gently but insistently pushed
her hand away, nudged her legs apart, and got to his
knees between them. He kissed her stomach, her hips,
pushed her knees up and dipped his head to her pussy
and inhaled deeply.

He growled low in his throat and swept the flat of
his tongue through her folds, ending with a short, sharp
suck of her clit. She gasped and he rumbled and used
the tip of his tongue to make tight, hard circles and
pushed two fingers into her. She jerked her hips as he
thrust his fingers, the dual sensations of his hand and
his mouth almost enough to send her over the edge. She
wanted to feel him, all of him. Naked on a rock in the
middle of the river, she wanted him to take her like the
animals they were.

She clutched at his shoulders and pulled him up to

her face. She kissed him and tasted herself on his lips, smelled herself in his beard. She lifted her hips in invitation.

"We shouldn't."

"I don't care. Pull out. I need to feel you." She whined in the back of her throat, a sound as much wolf as woman.

He thrust home and the falls below them caught her scream. The rock dug into her back and her hips but she didn't care. She had to feel this. One more time. Because she couldn't let it happen again.

"Fuck, Callie, you feel good," Sam groaned as he started to move. "I'm not gonna last. What do you need?"

The slide and drag of his cock inside her, the way he filled her and thrust deep into her, made her toes curl and her voice catch in her throat. "Fingers. Clit." He shifted his weight to snake a hand between them and press his thumb to her clit. His fingers fanned out over her hip and squeezed as he started to circle the nerve endings. Callie clenched around him and moaned, "Yeah, like that. Harder."

He fucked her harder, each thrust adding a jolt of pressure where his thumb pressed down on her clit. Her thighs tensed and her toes pointed and pleasure coiled in her belly, until she couldn't hold the tension and let go with a wailing moan as she came. Sam pulled out and stroked his slick cock, the lines of his neck rigid above her. He came with a shout, splashing her belly with hot semen while he wrung himself dry.

Without the distraction of arousal, and with streaks of come drying on her belly, all the hard and sharp places of the rock dug into her flesh, and the sun burned hot on her skin. She sat up gingerly.

"I'm going to rinse off."

She slid down into the pool and underwater before Sam could say anything.

Chapter Seven

Callie was quiet for the rest of the day. There was something final about her silence, like up at the falls was a last hurrah before she pulled away for good. Sam let her be. He didn't sense panic or restlessness in her, only a resigned stillness. She'd said they should make the best of it while it lasted, but he'd thought it would last for more than a day. Being near her was making him itch with the need to touch her, hold her, fix the fucked-up situation he'd gotten her into.

She was tucked into a corner of the bed with a warped and battered paperback that had been in the cabin for God only knew how long when his father appeared out of the forest again. Sam had heard him coming, his senses on high alert for any intrusions into their space, but Callie startled bolt-upright when his boots hit the porch. Sam fought the urge to rub her back until her heart settled.

His father opened the door. "Sam, outside please."

Callie wrapped her arms around her knees and curled into a ball on the creaky bed. Sam couldn't leave her. He wanted to be out of earshot, but the thought of leaving her with no protection made panic spiral in his gut. He looked at her, and she eyed him suspiciously, no doubt hearing his racing heart.

His father sighed. "Fine, you can both hear this. Dunphy's calling an emergency session. You're to report for a hearing on Sunday."

"What? How did he get enough members on that kind of notice?"

"We'll worry about Dunphy's friends in high places when this is over. Right now, he's gotten half the council to believe you attacked Callie without provocation."

Sam's blood froze. This was so much worse than intervening in a human emergency. They'd put him on a steady diet of tranquilizers and constant supervision for the rest of his life for an unprovoked attack. His father would lose his place on the council, his brother or one of his cousins would have to take leadership of their clan. "No. No, Dad, I didn't. She was dying."

His father's temper cracked. "Christ, Sam. You're my son. This is a power play. Callie was nothing but a pawn."

Callie whined from her place in the corner. Without thinking, Sam went to her and pulled her into his shoulder. "What do we do? Bren was there, he saw the shape she was in, even if he didn't see her get hit."

"I know. Did anyone aside from you and Brennan see her in the street, or see you bring her back to the house?"

"I only know Bren was there in the road. I—I did it under the trees at the school. There were only a couple of people left when we brought her back. I took her through the front door so no one would see her. Bren told people she tripped and passed out."

"Why didn't you tell anyone else what happened?"

"There were other people there, humans."

"Why didn't you bring her to me?"

"Because none of us were in any shape to drive." Frustration bubbled up. It felt better to be angry than scared. "Are you interrogating me for a reason?"

"You think you won't be interrogated by the council?" his father asked sharply. "They're looking for any reason they can to turn this on you, and me, and all of us. Dunphy wants control; we can't let that happen."

"I know."

"Callie?"

She pulled out of Sam's arms and cleared her throat. "Mr. MacTire?"

"I need you tell me exactly what you remember."

"I don't remember anything. I was doing shots with Ryan at the campfire, then I woke up in Sam's bed feeling like I'd been hit by a truck. That's it."

"We need you to do better than that," he said pointedly.

"You want me to lie." Her voice was wooden. "You want me to lie so Sam stays out of trouble and you keep your council seat."

"This is more than trouble. How long have you been friends with my son?"

"Since I was five."

"Do you love him?"

Sam glared at his father and held his breath.

"He's my best friend."

A piece of Sam's heart broke and it was his own fault. He was only a temporary solution to the problem of her changing body. He knew that. Hearing her dodge the question still hurt.

"Fine. Do you know what will happen to your best friend if the council finds him guilty of attacking you?"

She raised an eyebrow, ire taking over fear in her, too. "We haven't exactly had time to get into the details of the wolf legal system. Or anything, really." She directed the words at him and Sam winced. "In fact, this is the first I've heard about a hearing or a plot or anyone named Dunphy."

"Callie—" Sam reached for her hand.

"Enough." His father glared at them both. "You can fight about it later. Callie, they will drug and isolate him for the rest of his life. I understand that you're angry about what's happened, but if my son is your best friend, don't let them do this to him."

Callie gripped the thin mattress and closed her eyes. "Fine."

"Thank you." The chair scraped the floor as he got to his feet. "Both of you, stay put and get your stories straight. I have to go track down your cousin."

"What? Where's Bren?"

"I told him to lay low for a few days. He's probably in a hikers' hut somewhere."

The screen door slammed behind him and Sam listened to the crunch of the dirt under his boots going back down the trail. He braced for Callie to turn on him. He could feel the anger radiating off her, but she got up and went outside without a word.

He'd been sure he was doing the right thing, not giving her sketchy details about what might be happening out there. And now this, worse than he'd ever imagined. They didn't think he crossed a line trying to save his friend, they thought he had done it on purpose. That he was so obsessed with Callie he would lose all control.

He would give anything to change that night, to have realized she was too drunk to even walk home. He should have put her over his shoulder and dumped her on the couch when he found her slumped over at the picnic table.

He had to make her believe it.

It had all been a ploy to get her to lie for him. He'd used her. Lied to her about his feelings to keep her pliant and calm. Maybe it was some essential thing about being a wolf she didn't understand, everyone seemed so comfortable with lies and half-truths and omissions. With the need for secrecy gone, all she'd asked for was honesty, and he hadn't even given her that.

Callie paced around the fire pit, the restlessness not giving way to the urge to shift, only a slow burn of anger and frustration and the sick sense that she'd been betrayed by the one person she thought she could always count on. She stiffened at the sound of footsteps.

"I don't want to talk to you right now."

"Callie, please."

She turned on her heel to face him. "I asked you to tell me what was going on and you lied to me."

"I didn't want to scare you when none of us were sure of anything."

"Yeah, I know. I heard your father this morning. 'Keep her here and keep her calm.' Now I know why." He blanched slightly. *Good.*

"You didn't tell me you heard that."

"And you swore you weren't keeping anything from me. Let's do this one more time. What the fuck is going on?"

Sam sat on a log with his head in his hands. "Okay. I'll tell you whatever you want to know."

"Who the hell is Dunphy and why does your dad think he ran me over with a truck?"

"Patrick Dunphy is an asshole from up north who's wanted my dad's seat on the council for years. If he can prove my father is unfit to hold it, like, say, by showing that his son is out of control and a danger to the community, then he can take the seat and gain control of the whole region."

"And that's a bad thing, because…? Do wolves not believe in democracy?"

"No, they don't. And Dunphy is the kind of guy who has his goons hit innocent bystanders with trucks. Not someone you want in charge of the safety and security of our families."

"Why me?"

"Because if you were hurt it was guaranteed I would react."

"Because I'm your best friend."

"Because I've been in love with you my whole life."

No. He couldn't be. He needed something from her, and she wouldn't let him waste away for the rest of his life pumped full of tranquilizers, but he wasn't in love with her. He'd used her. "I'll lie to the council for you, you don't need to pretend. The past couple of days were whatever they were, but you're not in love with me."

Sam took her hands and met her eyes, his eyebrows knotted with earnestness. "I meant it when I said I'd always wanted you."

She wrenched her hands free and kept pacing. "Why didn't you tell me what was happening? Why didn't you tell me about Dunphy or the council or the fact that you were in trouble? Why did you let me think everything was going to be okay?"

"You needed to stay calm so your body can finish healing, so you're in control when you shift. It wouldn't have done you any good to know."

"You don't get to decide that anymore. You don't get to decide what I can and can't handle. Stop treating me like a goddamn child. I'm part of this. And I'm not going to sit around up here with you hiding and pretending everything is going to be fine when it sure as fuck isn't fine."

"Calm down."

"Don't fucking tell me to calm down. I got hit by a truck and your dad just told me I was nothing but a pawn in some fucked-up political bullshit, and you're telling me to calm down? I think I'm flipping out exactly the right amount." The skin on her neck prickled. The wolf wanted out, wanted to forget all of this and run.

"Cal, please. You're losing control."

She growled in frustration and backed toward the edge of the clearing, where the trail led down the mountain and back to the highway. "I can't look at you right now. I'll vouch for you, but I can't be in the same room with you. I have to go."

"You can't."

"What are they going to do? Kidnap me in broad daylight?" She stalked off before he could answer. As soon as the trees and brush closed her out of his view, she started to run.

Running on two feet, she didn't last long, but she couldn't show up naked on the side of the road. She'd hitch back into town, say she got lost and dropped her stuff on the trail because she got too tired to carry it. It happened.

Eventually, she made it back down and skirted through the brush on the side of the road until she got to the parking area at one of the trail heads. A nice middle-aged couple collecting four-thousand-foot peaks dropped her off right across the street from her apartment. Her keys were in Sam's truck, but her neighbor had her spare set. She showered off the dirt and sweat from her impromptu hike and hit a second wind.

It was impossible to get a drink in Pullman without running into half a dozen people she knew, most of whom would immediately call the MacTires, so Callie drove to Chiswick and plunked herself at an unfamiliar bar. She'd scrounged up enough spare tips from around her apartment to buy a burger and a beer, and thanked heaven when the bartender didn't card her. Her wallet was in Sam's truck, too. She could get it back from him at the hearing.

Her anger was starting to burn out by the time her dinner was in front of her. Her thoughts skipped around, replaying scenes from the moment she woke up in Sam's bed to now, sitting in a strange bar, ruminating into her fries. She wanted to hold on to her frustration, but she kept seeing the way he'd looked at her, the complete seriousness in his face when he'd said he'd always wanted her, that he'd been in love with her his whole life. She remembered the way he'd held her in the middle of the night as she struggled out from under her nightmare. The tears he'd shed when he'd told her she almost died. That he'd risked his life to save hers. He was her best friend.

But he'd kept things from her.

Because he had to.

She wanted to talk to him. She'd pay her tab and go to the house. She needed to see him.

A wiry older man sat down next to her. "You look like you've had a rough day, sweetheart. Let me buy you a drink." He gestured to the bartender for another round.

Callie bristled at being called "sweetheart," but she wasn't about to turn down the kindness of strangers when it bought her a drink. "Thank you." She raised her fresh pint and took a sip.

"Name's Pat."

"Callie." She shook his clammy hand and let it go as quickly as politely possible.

"What's wrong? Boy trouble?"

She grimaced. She hadn't asked him to sit next to her and buy her a drink. She hadn't said no, either, but a simple thank-you ought to be enough. "Listen, I appreciate the drink, I really do. But it has been a long couple of days and I'm not feeling like good company right now."

"Aw, come on, cheer up. Whatever he did, he's paying for it now, I'm sure."

Rather than waste a perfectly good beer by throwing it in his face, Callie sucked it down and slammed the empty glass on the bar. "Thanks for the beer, Pat. Now fuck off."

She left a wad of small bills by her plate without waiting for the check and walked out. At the door, she wrapped her hands around her keys with one peeking out from between her knuckles, afraid the creep would follow her. She'd had two beers and plenty to eat and she felt a little woozy, but she was steady enough to drive. Or get out of the parking lot and pull over somewhere else. The voice in her head was telling her to get far, far away. Panic ripped through her at the sound of footsteps behind her. She gripped her keys tighter and glanced behind her. It was only the bartender, coming out for a cigarette. She let out a sigh of relief and told the voice in her head that she was being paranoid and she could shut up now.

Pat stepped in front of her. She tried to throw a punch, but he caught her wrist and squeezed hard. Her fist opened and her keys hit the ground with a clatter. "Now, Callie, that's no way to treat your elders. If that's the way the MacTires are raising you kids, it's no wonder that boy lost his head."

No. No nononono. Patrick Dunphy. She swallowed hard. "It was an accident."

"Are you sure, sweetheart?" He still hadn't let go of her wrist. It felt like it would break if he squeezed any harder.

"He saved my life." The dizziness she'd felt walking outside intensified and made her knees wobble. Panic was the only thing keeping her from passing out. Passing out after two beers and a burger and fries.

"Very well." He let go of her wrist and signaled to someone behind her. The bartender. He'd drugged her beer. Large arms circled her waist. "Put her in the truck."

Those were the last words she heard before the world went dark.

Chapter Eight

Sam watched her go, fighting the urge to run after her, to make her stay, to make her understand. He loved her and she didn't believe it.

But what reason did she have to believe him? He'd lied to her, he'd kept her in the dark, he'd been exactly the asshole she accused him of being. He'd spend the rest of his life making it right. But now, he had to make sure she was safe.

He caught up and followed Callie down the mountain at a discreet distance—someone was going to have to teach her how to pay attention to her surroundings and spot other wolves—and when she was picked up by a pair of friendly middle-aged hikers, he breathed a sigh of relief before he shifted and ran back for his truck.

He drove back into town and parked outside her apartment. He sat across the street, waiting, watching, as she turned lights on, her silhouette in the windows padding from room to room as the afternoon turned slowly to evening. He'd been so scared of losing her that night, it had never occurred to him that he might lose her anyway.

Still, he couldn't regret it. A world where Callie was alive to be furious at him was better than one without her in it at all. Those moments when he thought she would die, the endless waiting for her to wake up after he'd changed her, the past two days alone with her looped through his brain. Nothing would ever compare to the way it had felt to hold her while she slept. To know that she trusted him enough to let go and rest. Trust she felt he didn't deserve. He'd do anything to fix this.

His butt was numb and he was struggling to keep his eyes open as the force of the exhaustion of the past few days hit him. He texted Colin to take watch for him so he could get a few hours of sleep. They couldn't leave her alone. His eyes drifted closed as soon as he put down his phone.

He woke up to Colin shaking his shoulder and shouting. "Sam, wake up! She's gone. Callie's car is gone."

He told himself she'd probably gone to get something to eat. "Call Ryan, tell him to start calling bartenders. She can't have gone far."

The need to shift, to scent her out, follow her, *find* her flooded his system. He gripped the steering wheel, knuckles white, fingernails digging into his palms. She was gone and it was all his fault.

In the few minutes he'd been asleep, Callie had disappeared. No one had seen her leave town, no one knew where she went. When she didn't come back after closing time, they went into panic mode.

Sam had been spiraling through a series of worst-case scenarios for hours, each one worse than the last—car accident, shifted and lost or hurt or both in the forest, Dunphy. He couldn't tell if the sick feeling in his gut was plain fear or intuition. He wanted to ignore it, but his father hadn't been able to track down Bren either.

"Where is she?" Sam ran his fingers through his hair and pulled, a better alternative than punching a wall, but a lot less satisfying.

"We'll find her, Sam." His mother handed him a cup of coffee and forced him into a chair at her kitchen table.

He was running on little sleep and adrenaline, he couldn't sit still. It had to be Dunphy. His father was on the phone with the council, reporting Callie and Bren missing. Either Dunphy was utterly confident of his support on the council, or he was utterly stupid. The only two people who could speak for Sam and they suddenly went missing within a day of the hearing? Only an idiot or someone who'd been generously bribed would believe that was a coincidence. Sam prayed Dunphy didn't have that kind of money.

His father hung up the phone, looking grim. "They're still calling the hearing."

"What about Callie? Even if they want to see you kicked out of your seat and whatever they'll do to me, are they going to let a newly changed wolf roam free in the meantime?"

"They're 'looking into it.' Dubois knows more than he's saying."

"And Bren?"

"A grown wolf disappears for a few days? 'Not their concern.'"

"Fuck."

"What the hell were you thinking, letting her leave?"

"What was I supposed to do? Chain her to the stove?"

"You were supposed to keep her safe!" his father yelled.

His mom stepped between them before they could attempt to strangle each other. "Stop it, both of you. Callie and Brennan don't have time for this."

"I can't lose her, Dad. I know I fucked up, but I can't lose her." The only thing keeping him from running out into the woods to try to find her was the careful control he'd learned from the man standing across from him.

"I know. She's one of ours, always has been. We'll find her and bring her home."

His brother slammed into the kitchen looking more than a little wild around the edges. He'd been driving around for hours, looking for her car, calling every bartender and waitress he knew between Pullman and the Canadian border. The MacTires would have known if she'd been seen anywhere in town and they had friends to the south.

"She was in Chiswick. I found her car." Ryan tossed Callie's spare set of keys on the table. "They left those behind. No other signs of a fight, but that doesn't mean anything; she might not have been conscious enough to struggle."

"What are you talking about?"

"If there had been some kind of fight in a bar in Chiswick on a random Friday in July, we would have heard about it. And the bartender is Dunphy's cousin. He probably drugged her."

"I swear to God, when I find that rat-faced little motherfucker, I'm going to wring his neck."

His father was already murmuring into the phone, updating the council on Callie's car being found with the keys on the ground, outside a bar run by one of Dunphy's goons.

Ryan accepted a steaming mug from their mom and

unfurled a local map on the table. "I'll be next in line, Sammy. And you can kick my ass when we're done."

"What are you talking about?"

"I was the idiot sharing a bottle with her until she blacked out. If I hadn't—I'm sorry. It's my fault. I should have cut her off." His brother didn't wear guilt well, he looked miserable sitting there, waiting for Sam to condemn him for what they'd all been doing that night.

"Help me bring her home and we'll call it even." He clapped him on the shoulder and cleared his throat. "Do we have any idea where he might have taken her?"

His father walked back into the room. "Durand. He's got a place on the old hotel land. Hugh Sutton came around when I told him Ryan found her keys and his nephew has been missing for two days."

"What about Dubois?"

"Too far in Dunphy's pocket. The last thing we need is for him to move her before we can get there. We leave in a half hour. Sutton is leaving Vermont now, he'll meet us there."

Sam and Ryan raced back into town to round up Colin and whatever weapons they could, then rode back to their parents' in grim silence with a trunk full of hunting rifles and bear mace. Mace or a bullet wouldn't put down a wolf for long, but it would have to be enough to get in and get Callie out. His father and his uncles were assembled outside the house, and for once, Sam believed the legends that said they were descended from warriors, gifted by the gods with strength and determination in battle.

"Sam." His father pulled him aside. "Are you prepared for this?"

"You're not leaving me here."

"You haven't slept in days and you're so full of caffeine and adrenaline you're shaking."

"You can't leave me behind, she's my—I love her."

"I know. She's yours. Has been since you were seven years old." He breathed a heavy sigh. "Let's go get her."

Sam nodded once and got in the truck. He'd bring her home or die trying.

Callie woke up with her head pounding. It should have been impossible for her to feel worse than the morning she'd woken up after being literally hit by a truck, but her head hurt like it was trapped in a vice and her eyeballs were being squeezed out of their sockets with every throb of her pulse. She rolled to sitting on the packed dirt floor and opened her eyes warily. A shaft of dim light made its way through a grimy window on the other side of the room. She wasn't alone.

He sat with his back to the wall, knees up, hands in his lap, with his head tipped back and his eyes closed. His breathing was deep and even; she couldn't tell if he was asleep.

"Bren?"

His eyes popped open. "Callie?" He rushed to her side. "I wasn't sure you were going to wake up. They must have given you enough to take down a fucking elephant."

"Where the hell are we?"

"No idea. They shot me with a fucking tranq dart while I was hiking out on Wednesday. I didn't come around until I was already here. They dropped you sometime last night."

"Fuck."

"Yep."

How could she have been so stupid? How could she have doubted Sam? Whatever lies he'd been forced to tell to protect his family, he never would have intentionally hurt her. Ever. Yes, his protective streak and keeping things from her because he didn't think she could handle it was frustrating as all hell, but what had she done? She'd gone rushing into danger in a snit when he'd told her what was happening. She should never have left the cabin. She definitely should never have left town, where everyone knew her, where there would always be someone who would keep her safe and out of the hands of creepy old men who had no problem almost killing her in order to what? Get a seat at the table with the other wolf clans?

"I don't get it. Why? I know they came after me to get to Sam, but why?" If she could focus on untangling whatever twisted reasoning Dunphy had for this, she didn't have to think about how she was trapped in a basement and had no idea what they were going to do with her.

"I don't know. He wants that council seat, badly, he always has. He thinks Angus is soft, that we shouldn't have to live in secrecy, play by human rules, but he's never done anything about it, just grumbled about us being a superior race. Someone smarter than he is has to be pulling the strings."

"He wants to start some sort of race war between wolves and humans?"

"I don't know. There aren't enough of us left for that."

"Not now. But if it doesn't take much to make more…"

"Then he'll have a small army of unstable, newly changed wolves."

"Whose aggression he can use." Callie shivered at the thought of a ragtag bunch of young men, newly changed, feeling all the hair-trigger anger and frustration and sexual need of puberty all over again, being set loose on the towns and villages she'd grown up in. Add the giant chip on the shoulder some of them had from living in a land ruled by the almighty tourist dollar now that logging and the paper mills were long gone— It would be mayhem. "How do we get out of here? Can we shift? Aren't we stronger that way?"

"Even if we could break down the door, they can shift, too. And they have guns and enough large-animal sedatives to take down a zoo. We'd both end up dead that way."

"There has to be a way. We can take them by surprise."

"They've probably been listening to this entire conversation, there will be no surprises."

"No. There has to be some way to get ourselves out of here. I'm not waiting around for whatever that—" she pitched her voice louder "—*fucking asshole* is going to do to me."

"I know." Bren dropped his voice to barely a whisper. "But you're not going to go barreling up the stairs. You'll get yourself killed. We have to be smarter than they are. Which shouldn't be that hard, especially with two of us."

"They're probably going to kill me anyway." Or force her to—She couldn't let her mind go there. She'd never be able to get herself out of the ball of sick horror she'd be if she did. "I might as well die on my own terms."

"The council will know you're missing by now; no one will believe it's a coincidence. They'll come looking for you."

"They'll probably kill me and dump my body somewhere to make it look like I ran off and fell off a cliff or something."

The door from upstairs opened. "Well, well. Thank you, sweetheart. That isn't a bad idea."

Callie backed against the wall, as far from the stairs as she could get in the tiny room. Bren sat where he was and kept his eyes on the floor. Her stomach roiled and she fought the urge to shift and lunge for Dunphy's throat. She'd never get out of her clothes in time. And Bren was right. Two men followed Dunphy down the stairs with guns at the ready. She wouldn't make it two steps before one of them shot her.

Dunphy stepped closer to her and she wanted to shrink into the wall, but she forced herself to stay upright, defiant. He gripped her jaw in one hand, pressing her cheeks painfully into her teeth, like she was a rebellious toddler. She trained her eyes on the ceiling, anything not to look into Dunphy's eyes, the cold, slippery, pale brown of the silt-covered rocks in the frigid mountain rivers.

"Look at me, sweetheart," he crooned and squeezed her face harder.

She met his gaze. "I am not your sweetheart."

He turned his head and said to the men at the bottom of the stairs, "I like this one, she's got spunk." He sniffed her and Callie's stomach roiled. Sam was the only one she ever wanted to know her that intimately. "Yes, Callie, you could be quite useful. If you behave. If you don't…" He shrugged. "Well, the council might find your body dead and broken somewhere. Such a shame for a girl with so much—" he paused and flicked the corner of his thin mouth "—potential, to have an accident like that."

Her skin crawled. She wanted to close her eyes and shut out the sickeningly avid look on his face. She would die first. She belonged to Sam, he'd marked her, claimed her. "What are you going to do to me? Why is Bren here?"

He let go of her face and stepped back. Callie took a deep breath to steady herself now that she had room to do so without her chest brushing his.

"The boy's hearing will go on as scheduled. Neither of you will be there to support him, of course." He carefully brushed a lock of hair off her forehead. She couldn't help her cringe. "You were so angry, Callie, when you left him. He'd betrayed you, lied to you, forced you to become one of us. You lost control and took off running. Got turned around in the woods, poor thing. We found you, patched you up, took you in. You won't go back to him, not after the way he used you so you would cover up for his lack of control. The boy's obsessed, dangerous, it would be foolish."

He knew. He'd been watching them somehow. Callie didn't think she could want to crawl out of her skin and disappear any more than she already did. Finally, he turned to Bren.

"As for you, Brennan, always the second fiddle. You couldn't live with yourself if you let him get away with it. You saw what he did. How he plied her with alcohol, then brutally attacked her. You tried to intervene, but it was too late. You feared for your own life if you didn't play along, so when your uncle told you to disappear for a few days? You did as you were told."

It almost made sense, if he planned on keeping them both in this basement for the rest of their lives or killing them both. "And what happens when you trot both of us out to prove there was no foul play? What's to stop either of us from telling the council what you did?"

"Angus MacTire's seat will be mine. You'll be reporting these supposed transgressions to me."

"And the others?"

"Now, Callie, sweetheart, you've been through so much. No one blames you if you're a little confused." His voice was soft and slimy, like a caress from one of his clammy fingers. "And you," he said sharply to Bren, "you might try to get back into the family's good graces after betraying your cousin. But as a young man of upstanding morals, you could be rewarded here."

Bren growled in the back of his throat, his muscles tensed, but he didn't move. "Never. Shoot me, throw me off a cliff and get it over with. I will never be one of you."

"Suit yourself."

They trooped up the steps. The solid wood door came to rest in the frame with a heavy thump, the locks turned and clicked, and feet creaked over the old boards above them. She slumped onto the floor and pressed her palms to her eyes to stem the burning sensation. She swallowed the lump in her throat. She was going to die in this basement and have her body thrown into the forest, maybe never to be found. But she wasn't going to sit there and cry about it.

Bren scooted next to her and took her hand. "He's

coming. You have to hold it together until he does. We're getting out of here."

"What if that's what they want? We can't let them walk into a trap," Callie whispered as quietly as she could.

Bren looked around. "I could probably boost you through the window, but I don't think I'll fit. You'd have to go alone."

"Then I'm not going through the window."

"It might be the only way out. You could find your way back to Sam and help them figure out how to get in here."

"No. I won't leave you behind. I don't want to know what they would do to you for helping me escape. And Sam would never forgive me if I got you killed." He probably would never forgive her for getting herself kidnapped in the first place, but she didn't say it out loud. He would come to her rescue, put himself in danger for her, because she'd been too stubborn and stupid to believe him when he'd said he loved her. She couldn't let him risk his life for her again. She went to the steps and began feeling for loose planks. "We're getting out of here. I don't care if I have to beat Dunphy to death with a board to do it. This one's wobbly, get the other end."

Chapter Nine

"What's our plan?" Ryan asked from the backseat as the SUV bumped and rattled along the road riddled with potholes and last winter's frost heaves.

Sam was only half listening, every muscle in his body tense with the need to *go get her* and never, ever let her out of his sight again. Or at least until they got back to some semblance of normal together. *Please, God, together.*

"Sutton will go in first, see if Dunphy can be reasoned with," his father answered. Sam and Ryan both snorted. "I know, but it will give us the lay of the land. And if by some chance it works, we can get them both out without a shot fired."

"And when that doesn't work?"

"We'll know what he's got for numbers and weapons and go in prepared." His father's mouth was set in a grim line, his eyes on the road.

They fell quiet as they drove into the village. Dunphy's hideout was tucked up into the forest above the site of a defunct hotel. The only tourists who came through here now were serious hikers, and the population had dwindled severely with the fall of the logging industry. All of which made it perfect for someone like Dunphy. Half the locals were probably related to the fucker.

They met Sutton at the sole gas station and followed him up and out of town. Sam held his breath the whole time, expecting Dunphy's goons to come out of the trees at any second, but it remained eerily quiet. Sutton signaled for them to stop their trucks while they were still out of earshot of the house, and opened his door. Sam and his father followed suit.

"I'll go ahead—hopefully they don't know we're coming. If I don't make it back down in an hour, assume they're extremely hostile."

His father nodded and they got back into their cars. Sam watched Sutton's truck trundle up the hill with a sick feeling in his gut. If he didn't come back down, with or without Callie, they were going in blind. There was no way they could send a scout, even on foot, without risking one of Dunphy's goons hearing or smelling him. Their only choice would be to go in armed to the teeth, and hope for the best. He couldn't wait for the council to act. Callie had already been stuck with the weaselly motherfucker for hours. Sam didn't want to imagine what they might have done to her. And Bren.

The helpless waiting was killing him. "I need some air." He reached for the handle and his father locked the doors.

"Roll down a window."

"I can't sit here." His legs were jiggling, his skin was too tight, and if he ran his hands through his hair one more time he was going to pull out hanks of it.

His father nodded at the windshield. Sutton was coming back down, alone. They all piled out of their cars and huddled by the grille of Sutton's truck.

"He says he doesn't have them."

"Bullshit."

"I know. I had to let him think a verbal denial would be the end of it. They're in there. I could smell them."

"Where? What do we do?"

Sutton held up his palms. His father put a hand on Sam's biceps. "Easy, son. How many guards?"

"It's a single room with two men on Dunphy, two by what I'm fairly certain is the door to the root cellar, one on the porch, another on a window well, maybe more in the woods, all armed for an elephant hunt."

His father nodded. "If he's got someone on the door and on the window well, they're in the root cellar." He turned to face the rest of them. "Which means we have to get into the house."

"Let's go." No amount of careful planning was going to get them out of what they had to do. His father's large hand gripped the back of his neck, hard. No one had done that to him since he was a little kid.

"No. You go in there half-cocked, you'll get yourself killed."

Sam rubbed the back of his neck when his father let go, chastened but still itchy to get moving and do something. The longer they waited and planned, the more damage Dunphy could do to Callie. They assessed their weapons, added Sutton's guns and stash of veterinary sedatives—"Large animal vet." and he shrugged—to the tally, and his father assigned them positions.

"Sam, we'll cover you. Get to the door and get them out. Don't engage unless you have to on the way in, do whatever you have to do on the way out. Incapacitate if you can, kill shot if you have no choice. We're not trying to start a war here." He nodded once and gestured for the others to move up the hill. He held Sam back with a hand on his arm. "Get your head on straight, son."

Sam closed his eyes and took a deep breath. He pictured Callie, brazenly dropping her clothes for a run up to the swimming hole, the way she'd tasted fresh from the water and spread out on the sun-warmed rock. "I'm bringing her home, Dad."

"Good. Let's go."

They stalked through the woods, scenting the air. Sam blessed the thick carpet of pine needles that muffled their steps. The house came into view at the center of a small clearing, all quiet. Sutton silently pointed out the two guarding the outside; they hadn't encountered any others. They should have been on high alert after Sutton's unexpected visit, but the one was leaning against the porch with a rifle slung over his shoulder and the other paced around the window well kicking grass like a kid who got lost on the soccer field. Criminal masterminds they weren't.

Dunphy wasn't bright enough for any of this. He was nothing more than a small-time thug who liked to complain about his father's assimilationist agenda. Someone else was behind this sudden switch from idle grumbling to action. All the more reason to get Callie and Bren out of there as quickly as possible.

The seven of them gathered around the edge of the clearing. The second a shot was fired, all hell would break loose. Getting close enough to use a needle full of horse tranquilizers was trickier, but stealthier. They all froze, waiting for the perfect moment for Colin and Ryan to move in.

"I'm taking a piss," the window well goon yelled and shuffled off toward where Ryan hid in the trees.

Ryan moved before the guy even had a chance to get his pants down. He covered the goon's mouth with one hand and jammed the needle into his neck with the other. As soon as Ryan had him on the ground, their father signaled the others to make their moves. Ryan pocketed the empty needle and moved across the clearing, crouching low in the high grass. He and Colin took out the porch goon with a well-placed punch from one side and a needle from the other. It would have been comical if Callie wasn't in the house.

Sam's father squeezed his shoulder once. "Follow once we're inside. Get them out, get them down the hill, then take the truck and go."

Sam nodded. His only job, his only focus, was getting Callie and Bren.

With the outside guards taken out, the other six crept onto the porch, led by Sutton. As soon as he opened the door, chaos erupted and Sam sprinted for it, gun drawn.

He flew into the house and skidded to a halt at the door to the root cellar, gunshots ringing in his ears in the tight space. Flooded with adrenaline, he used the butt of his gun to break the padlock and flipped the deadbolts. His feet pounded down the steps, narrowly avoiding missing treads.

Callie and Bren launched themselves from the far corner, armed with a couple of wooden boards. Callie dropped the plank midswing, eyes wide and unbelieving. He couldn't stop to soothe her. He'd spend the rest of their lives making this up to her, but they had to move.

He handed them both a gun and grabbed Callie by the shoulders as gently as he could. "Stay close behind me, between me and Bren. As soon as we hit the door, *run*. Use this if you have to, but we'll be covering you. Get across the yard and down the hill as quickly as possible. That's all you have to do." She nodded dumbly. He took her hand and led her upstairs, where it was still chaos. Callie blinked. They couldn't stop. "Callie, *run*," he yelled and tugged on her hand.

Shaken into action, she ran with him through the front door, off the porch and into the woods. Every time she stumbled over a root, he felt a jolt of terror that it would be the slip that cost them their lead. He couldn't be sure one of them hadn't followed. Didn't stop to look as they flew around the trees, his sole focus on getting them to the truck and as far away from this godforsaken hill as possible.

He picked up Callie and threw her into the cab, too desperate to get her out of there to trust her to climb in on her own. Bren threw himself into the back and Sam threw the truck in Reverse. He waited until they passed out of the village to breathe a sigh of relief. Callie sat next to him, looking thoroughly shell-shocked.

"Sam?" she asked in a small voice.

"You're safe. I've got you."

"Can we pull over? I think I need to throw up."

Sam pulled over onto the narrow shoulder and got out with her. He rubbed her back while she heaved over the guardrail and Bren watched the road from the driver's seat.

After a few minutes, Callie straightened and threw herself into his chest. "I'm so fucking sorry," she wailed. "I should never have left. I shouldn't have doubted you. I should have listened." She dissolved into tears, clutching his shirt.

He held her and stroked her tangled hair. "I'm sorry,

too. I should have told you from the beginning. I should have trusted you. I gave you every reason to doubt me."

"No." She cupped his face in her hands. "You've been my best friend since I was five. You've never lied to me about anything you didn't feel you had to. You were trying to keep me safe. And I'm an asshole who put everyone in danger and I love you and you came for me and I'm scared you'll hate me forever for making you come for me and—"

He pulled her to his chest and kissed the top of her head. "Callie, I love you. I will always, always come for you. Now let's go home."

They climbed into the backseat, where Callie rested her head on his shoulder and promptly fell asleep.

She woke up as they pulled into the driveway at Sam's parents' house. His mom and aunts ran out to meet the car as it rolled to a stop. Bren held his mother while she sobbed and clutched at his shoulders. Sam gingerly set Callie on her feet before he wrapped his arms around his mom. Callie stepped back and leaned against the door of the truck. Melissa and Brigid and Morri had risked their husbands, brothers and sons, and it was all her fault.

Brigid let go of her son and held her arms out. "Callie, come here." Callie came forward from behind Sam, Brigid pulled her into a bear hug, and Callie's chin wobbled. "It's okay, sweetie. You're home." Brigid stroked her back. "Let's get you inside, okay? By the time you take a shower and a nap, the others will be back."

"They called?" Sam asked.

Brigid nodded and let go, and Callie sagged with relief against Sam's solid chest. "They've got some cleaning up to do, but they're all coming home."

"Dunphy?"

"Will be bitching about the bullet in his hide for a couple of days," Brigid answered with a smile.

"What happens to him then?" Callie clenched her fists. She wanted that weasel to pay.

"Hugh rallied the council. He'll be dealt with, I promise you," Melissa answered with a fierce look that said if the council didn't take care of it, the family would.

"Everybody inside, come on. Sam, help Callie to the shower. I'll get her some pajamas and you can put her in your bed." She cupped Callie's cheeks in her warm, soft hands. "You need some rest. We all do."

They trundled into the house as one and Sam took her upstairs to the bathroom. As the adrenaline started to leave her body, she was overcome with a level of exhaustion she'd never felt. She could barely muster the energy to pull her shirt over her head. Sam turned as if he was going to leave her alone to shower.

"Don't go." She didn't trust herself to stay on her feet and she didn't want to be alone.

"Wasn't going to." He handed her a towel and a fresh toothbrush from the closet and started the water. "I wasn't planning on letting you out of my sight for at least six months, maybe a year." He started to shuck his own clothes. "Go on, I'll be right behind you."

She brushed her teeth, then stepped into the shower, feeling the fear seep out of her system with the dirt and sweat the hot water carried down the drain. She was with Sam. She was safe. Everyone would come home and Dunphy would be forced to answer for what he'd done. She stood under the stream with her eyes closed, not moving to pick up the shampoo or soap, though she desperately needed both.

The curtain twitched and Sam joined her. He kissed her between the eyes, spun her around slowly and washed her hair. She leaned against his chest and let him scrub her scalp with his strong fingers, groaning with pleasure and exhaustion. He rinsed her hair clean and soaped her body, gently massaging as he went, Callie feeling like she was going to melt into a puddle at any moment. Then he gave himself a quick rinse and toweled her off.

Sam helped her dress in her borrowed pajamas and put her in his childhood bed, bundled with blankets. She was cold in spite of it being July. Sam put on an old T-shirt and pair of shorts he found in a drawer.

"Scoot over." He got into the narrow bed next to her and pulled her against him to spoon, blankets and all. She breathed a sigh of relief. "Callie, I'm not leaving you, I promise."

"What happens now?"

"You get some sleep."

She nudged him with her blanket-padded elbow. "You know what I mean."

He kissed the crown of her head. "I know." He squeezed her once. "The problem is I don't know what happens now. Dunphy gets dealt with, but I have a feeling he's not the end of it."

"So does Bren."

"So we try to figure out what the hell is going on, and get back to something resembling normal."

"I don't think there's such a thing as normal anymore."

He sighed. "You're probably right." He kissed her

behind her ear. "Then I guess we decide what's normal, now."

Callie wiggled in the blankets until she faced him. "This. I want this to be normal. Not the being in your parents' house part, but this, you and me, together—"

He cut her off. "You babble when you're nervous."

"I know."

"Callie, I love you. I belong to you, I always have. I'm not leaving unless you kick me out."

Her mind settled. "I belong to you, too. She's been trying to tell me that all along."

Sam lifted her chin and kissed her, gentle and slow, a comfort instead of an invitation for more. "I know. Mine, too. Now get some sleep."

Chapter Ten

Six months later...

Sam hadn't been kidding about the not-letting-her-out-of-his-sight thing. He'd moved out of the bachelor house and into her apartment within a month of the accident. Conveniently, she already worked for Melissa, so someone from the pack had eyes on her almost all the time. Before the change, she would have balked; after everything that had happened, it was reassuring, knowing one of the pack was never far away. She was family now, of course they protected her.

She'd spent months jumping at every stranger who walked through the door of the coffee shop, and was plagued with nightmares of their run down the mountain away from Dunphy's homestead, chased by a pack of wolves they could barely keep ahead of. Callie would wake up panting and sweating, right at the point when sharp teeth closed on her ankle and dragged her down. But the longer Dunphy and his cronies stayed quiet, her terror consumed her less. No one thought it would last forever, but the winter season kept everyone too busy to scheme for the time being. Whatever they were plotting next, Callie would be prepared.

Callie and Sam spent as many of their days off as they could together up at the cabin, cuddling and talking, making love, and shifting for the fun of running through the woods together. Every day she spent up there, she gained more control of the shift, learned to work with the voice inside her, to trust her and the sharpened senses that had come with her. She'd never let herself be taken by surprise by a couple of wolves again.

The first truly frigid night in January found them curled together under a pile of blankets in front of the woodstove. They'd spent the afternoon chasing each other through the woods, rolling around in the freshly fallen snow because it felt good, coming inside by twilight. Sam stoked the fire and pulled the blankets onto the floor.

He laid her down and rolled the two of them up like a burrito, laughing and kissing her neck. Callie sighed and stretched into his questing hands as they traveled over her body, his touch even more arousing now with familiarity and hours of exploration. They'd spent days learning all the ways they could bring each other pleasure with hands and mouths and his cock buried deep inside her. Sam slid inside her now, fucked her with a slow and steady rhythm. The fire spread its heat to the air in the room while Sam warmed her from the inside, their sweaty limbs tangled and their chests pressed together, as close as she had ever been to another person.

He brushed her clit with his thumb and bit her neck, where it sloped into her shoulder, marking her again as his. Callie cried out as she came with Sam's teeth on her skin and his cock thrusting deep inside her. The clench of her muscles as the orgasm rolled through her brought him over the edge, his groan muffled by her shoulder as he thrust hard and let go.

He held her in a sated heap under the blankets, planting small kisses on her neck. "I love you."

"Says the guy who just had an orgasm."

He rolled her onto her back and pinned her underneath him. She giggled too wildly to put up much of a fight as he wrestled her arms above her head. "I love you," he growled.

"I know. I love you, too." She shivered and her nipples tightened with her chest exposed to the open air of the room, where it was still too cold to be naked and sweaty.

"Marry me, Callie."

"What?"

"Marry me. Please."

"Sam—"

"It doesn't have to be now, or even soon, but someday."

"You babble when you're nervous." She wiggled her arms free and put them around his neck, pulled him down to kiss him. "I love you, of course I'll marry you."

"You will?"

"Yes." She kissed him again, the voice in her head content. Sam was her best friend, her partner, her family, her lover. She belonged here. She always would.

* * * * *

Acknowledgments

First, a huge thanks to Angela James and everyone at Carina Press for the opportunity to put this story in your hands. Another major thanks is due to Deb Nemeth for guiding me through the editing process.

To Team Lu for being the most absurdly supportive set of coworkers anyone has ever had. And for only laughing a little bit when you found out what I was writing.

To Karin, for being the first set of eyes to ever see anything I write and for being my best friend.

To my family, for listening to the stories I've been making up since I learned how to talk. Sorry, not sorry.

To Brady, who can't read this because he's a dog, for not whining too much while Mama tried to write. And for the times you whined so much and made me go outside with you. You were right, my fuzzy friend, it was a perfect day.

And last, but most important, to my husband, who only kind of batted an eye when I told him I wanted to quit my job and write romance novels. You are my best friend, my partner, my family, my love. I could not have done this without you.

About the Author

Sionna Fox has been writing stories her whole life. Her first book was about dinosaurs, and according to her mother, it was adorable. She was late to the romance game, but hasn't looked back since picking up the habit and firmly believes romance novels can save your life. She lives in New England with her very patient husband and a very put-upon dog.

You can find her procrastinating on Twitter (Twitter.com/sionnafox), posting pictures of her dog on Instagram (Instagram.com/sionnafox) and on Facebook (Facebook.com/sionnafox). She's also been known to fangirl about books on her website (sionnafox.com).

DRAWN TO THE WOLVES

Shari Mikel

**Also available from Shari Mikels
and Carina Press**

Christmas Curveball

To my husband: my rock, my partner, my muse.

Chapter One

The next time someone told her that finding something would be as easy as pie, Kate Ballard was going to have to clarify with the person exactly what kind of pie it was. Especially if that person was her best friend. Kate's version of an easy pie usually included the words *no-bake* in the title. On the opposite end of the spectrum, her bestie managed to whip up apple pies with lattice top crusts like nobody's business.

Which was probably why it'd taken Kate forever to decipher Cindy's directions on how to get to the Brighton Hotel in Whiskey Grove, Tennessee, population 1168 according to a sign on the way into town. Of course, with a town that small, Kate would've thought she'd be able to find one simple hotel with a wonderful reputation fairly easily.

And now she just hoped that the pot hole she'd hit because she'd been paying attention to street signs instead of road conditions hadn't done too much damage to the underneath of her car.

But she was here now and she could already see why Cindy wanted her to stay here. The sign in front read *Brighton Hotel: Established 1857*. The building itself looked like an old Victorian home turned into a bed-

and-breakfast. The clapboard siding was painted a pale baby girl pink, and the shutters and trim were all white. It looked like a little girl's dream dollhouse. The front porch wrapped around all three sides for as far as Kate could see, and there were multi-person swings at each of the corners. The rest of the space was taken up with rocking chairs and even a couple two-person benches.

The parking area in front was all gravel, and from what Kate could tell, there was open field immediately surrounding the hotel itself, but then that area was surrounded by woods all around.

She reached behind her and grabbed her purse and duffel bag before exiting her car. The screen door at the front of the hotel swung open and Kate was greeted by a woman, probably in her late fifties.

"You must be Kate," she said with a huge smile, while drying her hands on an apron.

"I am."

"We've been expecting you. I'm Mrs. Brighton. Your friend Cindy called and wondered if you'd made it yet. She couldn't get a hold of you on your cell phone. I told her you were probably just enjoying the scenery."

Close enough to the truth, although Kate probably wouldn't go so far as to say enjoying. She would, however, love to go back out around town and take in the quaint sights of such a small, but old town with its cute main square and older buildings and facades.

"Yeah, it took me a little bit longer than she said it would." Kate reached into her pocket and checked her cell phone. Yep. *No Service*. Oh well.

"Well come on in, child. I hope traffic wasn't so horrible coming up from Atlanta."

Kate followed the woman inside and felt nothing but

warmth and welcoming from Mrs. Brighton. She also saw nothing of what she was expecting from the decor. She'd expected old-timey couches and lamps, lots of fussy knickknacks and pictures of people she wouldn't know. Instead, on the left was a dining area set up with smallish round tables covered in white table cloths and four chairs around each. Rectangular tables with their covers folded on top lined the room. Except for one. On it were two multi-tier displays of cookies and fruit, along with what looked like coffee, iced tea and water.

"I see you eyeing the goodies table. Come on over and have some. That's why they're there."

Kate headed straight for the iced tea and a chocolate chip cookie. The cookie was just a bit crispy on the outside but then soft and gooey on the inside. Perfection.

Mrs. Brighton was looking at her and Kate felt concern hit her. She realized she must have chocolate on her lips or chin. Her rule was to lick off the chocolate, but that was probably considered rude right now. She quickly grabbed a napkin and swiped her mouth.

"You haven't said a word since you got in here. Are you all right?"

Oh. Non-chocolate-related concern. "Yes. Sorry. I'm fine. Traffic wasn't horrible. I hate to admit this, but my biggest problem was getting lost right here in town. Cindy said it'd be easy for me to find this place, but it wasn't. At least not with all the landmarks she gave me. Is the 'Pay and Pump' what used to be the 'Gulp and Chug'?"

Mrs. Brighton let out a huge laugh and slapped her thigh. "Yes. Oh my. We were the brunt of too many jokes in these parts, even amongst ourselves. There was such huge controversy when the new owners wanted to change the name." She shook her head but still had a huge grin. "I'm glad you're fine. I was starting to get concerned. Cindy likes to talk and I couldn't imagine her having a friend who was so quiet as you."

"Well, if you know Cindy that well, you'd know that sometimes it's easier just to nod and listen than to try to get a word in edgewise."

"Now if that ain't the truth." Mrs. Brighton reached for Kate's duffel bag. "Here. Let me take this for you and show you up to your room. Mr. Brighton was out fiddling in the garden last time I saw him, but he should be back in soon. We've had a couple storms come through here and the last one was pretty fierce. His tomato vines got knocked over and he has to try to stake them back up."

"I'm good, thanks. I can carry my bag." Kate followed her up the large curving staircase in the foyer, and made a mental note to check out the rest of the house. It looked like the room across from the dining area was actually a modern sitting room. She got a brief glance of a large screen TV and some couches. Both rooms had large fireplaces that practically faced each other across the foyer.

"By the way, I saw that there are woods surrounding the hotel. Are there paths that I can explore? I don't want to get lost, but I'd love to look for some wildlife to sketch."

"There's lots of woods and lots of paths to follow. There are even some open meadows and such along the way." They got to a room situated along the back of the house, and Mrs. Brighton stopped with her hand on the knob and the key in the lock. "Now, I doubt you'll go out so far, but about a mile toward the north, there's some private property and the owners don't like trespassing. At all. But they've got signs posted throughout so you'll know when you've hit their property line."

"Sounds good."

Mrs. Brighton showed her into her room. It held both a double and a twin bed. The colors were done in light purples and teal blues with some greens mixed in, and Kate found the entire color scheme for the room incredibly soothing.

Exactly what she needed after ten years of being a sketch artist with the Atlanta PD. Ten stressful years of feeling, perceiving every victim's emotions and some criminals' inherent evil.

Kate knew she was unusual in this respect, and she'd always chalked it up to an advanced sixth sense. But it wore on her and she needed out.

"This is beautiful, Mrs. Brighton."

She gave Kate a broad smile. "Thank you, child."

The one part of her gift Kate truly enjoyed was experiencing the positive emotions from others, like Mrs. Brighton's pleasure at the compliment.

She wasn't sure how long she'd be able to stay, but this was a good first step in leaving her old life behind and beginning a new one. One where she could focus on drawing for the enjoyment of it and not drawing because it was desperately needed by so many people for so many reasons.

"The bathroom is back there in the corner. Unfortunately, this room got one of the tiny bathrooms, but hopefully all this light coming in from these windows will make up for it."

The lighting and view were amazing. The outside wall was all windows, overlooking a huge field and surrounding woods covering the side of the mountain that Whiskey Grove was at the base of.

"It looks great. Thank you for your consideration."

"Do you need any help getting settled in?"

"Not right now. I want to head out and explore some before it gets too dark. I've been sitting too long in my car today and I'd love to get out for a walk. I just need to change into some more comfortable clothes before I head out."

Mrs. Brighton pointed out the windows. "You have a few hours before it'll start getting dark enough amongst the trees that you won't be able to see any of those critters you're wanting to sketch. I'll pop into the kitchen and grab a water bottle for you to take with you. Come meet me downstairs when you're ready to go."

"Perfect. Thanks so much."

Kate took the key from Mrs. Brighton's proffered hand, and turned to her duffel bag once she was alone in her room. She dug into her stack of Atlanta Police Department T-shirts she'd brought with her and pulled out one of the long-sleeved, but thinner shirts. Seemed like it would be perfect for the cooler temperatures in the shady trees.

She snatched up her cross-body tote with her sketchbook and pencil case inside, and popped her wallet, car keys and phone in her bag as if on automatic. It was her normal gear for all jobs she went on, whether out in the field at crime scenes where she had to sketch a recreation or layout, or at a precinct where she sketched suspect descriptions.

Kate retraced Mrs. Brighton's steps back downstairs.

"Here's that bottle of water for ya." She met Kate in the foyer between the stairs and the front door. "You can go out the back door, through the back porch, and be on your way for exploring before any more of the afternoon gets away from ya."

"Thanks again, Mrs. Brighton."

"My pleasure, child. Now go enjoy yourself. But don't go getting yourself lost. I don't want to have to send out a search party for you this evening."

"I'll try not to." Kate didn't bother explaining that she'd grown up playing in woods and had learned at an early age how to figure out which direction was what and which way was home.

She set out along the most northern path, hoping it would give her more opportunities to see and sketch animals she didn't get to usually see back home.

Except it wasn't her home anymore. She'd sold her little house and put all of her stuff in storage. That life was through and this was her opportunity to start anew, doing what she'd always loved doing.

She dragged her thoughts back from her previous job and focused on a chipmunk scurrying along the forest floor. It had an acorn in its paws that rivaled the size of its face. Kate sat on the ground, trying hard to make as little noise as possible, and began drawing. A couple rabbits gathered across the way, and they looked as if they were carrying on a silent meeting. She imagined they were plotting a takeover of the rodent world and added them to her picture. When she was through sketching the scene, she got up and continued along the path.

Mrs. Brighton had been right. It wasn't too long before Kate came upon a meadow that was covered in tall grasses. Grasses that partially hid a couple deer grazing in the waning daylight hours.

Kate didn't try sitting this time. She remained standing, and did the best she could balancing her sketchbook on her arm while she captured the image of the deer, one taller than the other, eating their late afternoon meal. They didn't completely ignore her, each one taking its turn looking at her, letting her know they knew she was there, but she guessed she was far enough away that they didn't view her as too much of a threat.

A noise like what she'd expect to hear in a tropical rainforest came from the trees. No. It came from the sky. The deer shot off into the woods like arrows, and Kate stared at an incredible bird of prey. The wingspan was huge, the body brown and the head white. But the noise it was making was like that of a tropical bird, not a screech like she'd expect from a...bald eagle?

It made a turn over the trees and she was in danger of losing sight of it. Instinct had her running after it. If it really was an eagle, she wanted a closer look. She wanted to see it better so she could draw it. And she also wanted to tell her brain she wasn't crazy, because there was no way she would've ever expected that chattering noise from such a majestic bird.

As she ran, she managed to avoid large limbs, but the smaller twigs slapped against her. She ducked her face a few times to keep from getting scratched, but all the while, her focus remained on following the bird circling and soaring high above. There were fresh limbs down along the forest floor that she leaped over as if she were in PE class, and even a very large tree she used as a vault to catapult herself over and keep going.

Her lungs burned, her legs threatened to give out, and she began hoping for another open meadow or field of some sort that she could use to not only slow down or stop, but get a final long glimpse of the only possible eagle she'd ever seen, because she wasn't going to last much longer. She'd left whatever paths had been worn down by hikers throughout the years, and the uneven forest floor combined with her gymnastics and running were taxing every tiny muscle in her body to the point she wanted to collapse.

The sound of rushing water came to her over her own gasping breaths just as the trees opened up to a river bank. She skidded to a halt down the incline, barely keeping her precarious balance. She gingerly stood and beat the dirt from her hands off on her jeans, then tried to wipe that dirt off as much as possible. As she worked on getting rid of the dirt on her art bag, the hairs on the back of her neck stood on end, and everything inside her froze.

She carefully, slowly raised her head and met the eyes of a man who held a rifle against his shoulder, pointed in her direction. He stood across from her on the other side of the narrow river, up on the bank, looking down at her.

His rifle was aimed slightly off to her right, back toward the direction she came from, which left her the options of going into the river or ducking into the line of fire. Or, what she did, remain in place.

His medium brown hair stood every which way, giving off a "bed head" vibe, and his scraggly beard rounded out his unkempt facial features.

The waves of menace pouring out of him flooded her system.

"You're in my woods, and I don't take kindly to trespassers being on my property." His orange, brown and tan flannel shirttails flapped easily in the light breeze.

She opened her mouth to say something, to try to diffuse the situation, but stopped as two wolves exited the forest behind him. And then nonchalantly flanked him.

She might've squeaked had her inability to breathe not tried to choke her.

Those weren't *just* wolves. She knew what *typical* wolves were.

A childhood friend wanting to play with the "big doggies" had turned into a life-changing tragedy as Kate watched her friend get mauled by those dogs-that-were-really-wolves. Her friend survived, barely, but was never the same afterward, and Kate had learned exactly what wolves looked like that day.

These weren't the same as from her childhood.

No.

These were man-size wolves.

Their huge heads, easily two if not three times the size of a human's, reached the man's shoulder, and their thick, furry bodies stretched out for many feet behind them.

Kate couldn't begin to grasp how long they were. Six feet? Seven feet? Eight feet long? More?

Fuuu—

And the man looking down at her stood between them, staying at ease, not recoiling. He continued glaring at her instead of the wolves, like it was a perfectly natural thing to stand between two vicious monsters. As if they were pets he could control without a collar or leash in sight. Was he out of his mind?

He tugged at the dingy brown T-shirt worn beneath his flannel shirt and tucked into his loose-fitting, faded jeans held up by a rope tied at the waist. "Well? What do you have to say for yourself?"

Her mind began panicking, wanting to crumble in on itself.

What could she possibly say to keep the crazy man calm and not shooting at her?

"Hi. Um, I'm a little lost," she said, trying to keep things light.

Both wolves bared their teeth and growled while lowering into a crouch.

Oh shit.

Wolves. Wolves, wolves.

Even though she now faced only two compared to the four that had bitten and chewed and pulled on her friend, each one of these wolves was easily equivalent to two or three of the wolves her friend had faced as a child.

She was going to die.

Chapter Two

Anxiety hit Callan Mohan out of nowhere, and yet was subtle, as if the pathway wasn't familiar or was unsure of itself. He reached out, tried to find the source, but the path wasn't established and therefore he was blocked from being able to follow it. He kept the channel fully open on his end, hoping whoever it was attempted to reach out again, and next time he'd be able to grab the thread.

He focused on his sister and her portion of the update meeting for how far along they were in being ready to open their lodges as a vacation destination. She'd been working on putting in place an advertising campaign and had been adamant about calling them all together today.

"The cabins themselves are ready to go. We have staff lined up and some of the younger wolves will be helping out until we're booked enough that we can afford to hire full-time human staff and not have to worry about letting them go due to low revenue coming in. However, when I was putting together the pictures for the pamphlet layouts, it hit me that there's something missing that we've overlooked. Something huge."

Carleigh displayed an oversize collage of several pictures she'd obviously taken in one or two lodges, then looked around the room at each of them as if waiting for someone to venture a guess. Nothing but silence greeted her from each person gathered at the table.

Callan sighed. "Just tell us, Car. We've obviously missed it, so we're not even going to bother trying to guess."

She stuck her bottom lip out slightly, as if thinking about pouting, but pulled it back in and shook her head instead. She sucked in a huge breath before launching into her revelation at the assembled group. "Pictures! Decorations on the walls! We have nothing in the lodges except bare wood everywhere." She looked exasperated with the whole lot of them.

"Yep, you're right," Connor, their brother, answered her, all calm and smooth, not giving in to her need to stir everyone to action.

"But we need to do something about this. The walls look incomplete. They're bare. Ugly. Hideous—"

"Now, Car—" Callan said.

"Fine. Not hideous."

"Nor ugly," Connor said.

"Nor ugly. But they're bare, which is almost as bad as ugly, so we've got to get on this right away." Carleigh put her hands on her hips.

Another wave of anxiety hit, this one stronger. The feeling came and went quickly, and Callan was so busy blocking the signals from going out to his pack, that he didn't get the chance to grab hold of the thread to follow it. He also hadn't covered up his reaction in time to hide it from his second in command.

Everything okay? Grayson asked.

A concerning mystery. Callan refocused on what his sister was saying.

Nice try, Gray said. *What's going on? What do I need to know?*

That's just it. I don't know what's going on yet. It feels like someone is in trouble, but I don't know who.

I'm going to do a few check-ins.

Fine.

Carleigh held up the mock-ups. "At the very least, we need artwork, pictures on the walls. I don't care what we put up there. I don't care if we frame cheap posters from Walmart. We need at least one large picture in the main room of each cabin, and we need at least one smaller picture in the bedroom of each cabin. I don't care if every single one of them is the same right now. I just need something done so I can retake these pictures before I put out brochures and flesh out the website."

Callan would've usually thought the anxiety was coming from his sister, but he was used to her code-red dramas and they never hit him like this. He was one hundred percent certain of that when the anxiety switched to fear and hit him hard. Hard enough for him to suck in a breath. Hard enough that he could feel the tension ratcheting up in the room because they could feel the fear coming from him.

And it wasn't just the fear coming through to him. No. It was his own fear for her. Because he now had hold of the thread. The thread that was now cemented into a bond, the strongest type of pathway possible.

Callan needed to do things orderly first, because he had no idea who she was nor where she was except that she was close. So he'd have to start from the top.

"We need to shift this meeting from artwork on walls

to locations of people. Someone's in trouble nearby and I need to find her."

"Her?" The question echoed around the room, both out loud as well as in his mind, but Carleigh was the loudest. "How do you know it's a her?"

"I just do. Gray. What's going on at the plant? Any trouble reported in any parts of the distillery or the warehouse?"

Grayson looked up from his phone. "None. At least nothing that Kelli is reporting. What are you feeling?"

Callan had already done a quick mental check-in with several pack members working at their whiskey and moonshine plant to see if anyone knew of any problems or trouble that might be happening, but the responses had all been negative. Everything was fine from that direction. "Fear coming from someone." And as long as there was no trouble at the plant, he could rule out his idiot cousin. Probably.

Gray had his phone out, typing out orders left and right, Callan was sure. "What do you need us to do?"

The fear he'd been feeling turned to terror. A silent, wordless scream forced Callan to one knee and he choked off the pack bond completely. He hadn't been fast enough for the people trapped in the meeting space with him, and when he looked up, he faced a room full of wolves who hadn't been able to control their shift. They smelled the terror emanating from their alpha and they'd shifted to protect him.

Now he needed to find his mate to protect her before it was too late.

He rose to his feet and leaned on the table with his knuckles. The wolves in front of him were pack. Family. And they were barely managing to stay in one place waiting for him to speak. The instincts triggering the shift resulted in an excess of restless energy and an abundance of tension, causing them to quiver. They were willing to take on the world to protect their alpha from whatever had caused him to reek of fear.

Grayson tilted his head and gave Callan a don't-b.s.-me look.

"I have—"

The conference room phone rang and they all jumped. It never rang. The only person who had the number was Callan's assistant and she never interrupted him.

"Yes, Ginger?"

"Mrs. Brighton is on the phone. She has a guest who went for a walk in the forested area behind the hotel."

Callan wanted to interrupt and ask what this had to do with him, but something inside him clicked into place and he remained silent. Grayson let out a low whine, but cut it off quickly when Callan gave him the stink eye. "Put her on."

The call switched through. "Mrs. B?"

"I'm sorry to bother you, but last night's storms must've knocked down the trail signs as well as the *No Trespassing* signs for your cousin's property."

Callan got a sick feeling in his stomach. Maybe his idiot cousin *was* responsible for the trouble today. "Go on."

"Mr. Brighton was out working in the garden and then decided to clean up some of the trail debris when he saw the girl take off running. She of course outran him, but when he got to where he knows your cousin's land begins, he stopped. He's certain she kept on going, but we know we can't step foot on there, not even to help out one of our customers. Mr. Brighton thought he heard another sound and he hurried back here as fast as he could to have me call you."

"What's her name?" Callan barely kept his cool.

"Kate Ballard."

Kate.

"We'll be right there." Callan hung up and looked at his wolves. "Gray, I need you to pull yourself together enough to change back once we've left. Then I need you to take my truck down to the Brighton Hotel."

Grayson whined. Callan would get an earful later about his own safety as well as his decision to leave his number two behind. But this was important and Gray would understand everything soon enough.

"Once you get there, meet the rest of them—" Callan glanced around the room "—behind the hotel. I want you to stay in human form as long as possible. Carleigh, I want you to wait for Grayson at the tree line behind the hotel. Everyone else can spread out along the property line. I'm not quite sure what I'm walking into, but I know Kate Ballard is important. Got it? Let's go."

Callan knew his family would be right behind him as he ran for the front of their house. The house had been their family home and they'd turned it into the pack house when their parents had given up alpha status to allow their mom to recuperate from a serious illness in private.

He shifted with a swiftness that gave lie to the calmness he was trying to project in what for him was the greatest emergency of his life. His mate was frightened and on his cousin's property. Property that no one was allowed on, and if they did wander onto it, his cousin was more apt to shoot first than to ask questions at all.

The terror she'd been sending through their bond was now at a controlled level. Back down to fear rather than mind-numbing, vomit-worthy terror. Why? Was she fading? It took every bit of his strength just to keep his footing as he tried to puzzle it out and run full-out down the mountain toward the small town at the base. Luckily, he'd been running these same paths ever since he was a child, both as a pup and as a boy. He knew where the rocks to avoid were, and he knew where the footholds that would give him the most traction were laid out.

As long as she continued sending some amount of fear along their mental pathway, she was alive, and Callan would have to hold on to that.

I need you to hang on for me. Do whatever it takes.

He was going to have to kill his cousin.

And it certainly wouldn't be the first time that a pack war began over a situation with a mate.

The man let the rifle droop slightly, which caused his flannel shirt to catch on one wolf's fur. The movement revealed a huge rip in his jeans where the end of the pocket poked straight through, matching the rips at both the knees. "Now, now, fellas. The lady says she's a little lost out here in our woods." He sneered at Kate. He even sneered at her in the emotions she picked up from him.

Of greater concern to her was the fact that no one else was out here with them except for the wolves, and he was talking to them like they were pets. Like most people spoke to their cats and dogs.

He shrugged. "I don't know, Billy. She's a might pretty thing. You think we can keep her? You think she'd even stay with us? She seems a little dumb, not speaking to us much. But she's not tried running from y'all yet. I wonder if that means she knows anything or not. She's definitely not from around here."

Okaaay. Who the hell was Billy? Was this guy talking to himself? Some invisible person? He still looked straight at her. None of this made sense. And he wanted to keep her? What kind of talk was that?

"Who are you talking to?" She hadn't meant to say anything. She hadn't meant to engage the crazy, but sometimes her mouth did things before her brain gave it permission.

He re-aimed the rifle, this time directly at her. "Don't you never mind. You're the one in the wrong and you need to hush."

"Hushing."

His face reddened. "You're just like every other female. Gotta get the last word—"

"Bobby, I think that's enough." From upriver, another man approached along the river bank, on the same side as rifle guy. Human and wolves, all, turned toward him at his words.

The sound of his voice held a note of authority, but the note was off-pitch just enough that Kate barely held her flinch in. It was like listening to a familiar tune played on the bells, but one of the bells had a dent or ding in it, causing it to no longer ring true to the pitch it was meant to be.

That was how this man's voice hit her—as if he were almost complete, almost who he was supposed to be, except there was something wrong with him. Something wrong with his authority.

"But, JT. She's on our land. Running around like she owns it." Rifle dude—Bobby—was looking at the newcomer but hadn't dropped his rifle.

Also, the wolf closest to her was back to staring at her instead of the new guy—JT.

Never in Kate's life had she thought there'd ever be a threat to her worse than a pack of wolves, but she tore her gaze from the two monsters and their master across the river, and turned her eyes just enough so that she could focus on this new possible threat.

JT took measured steps, coming ever closer. "And what did she have to say for herself?"

"I said I was lost." She shouldn't be in trouble just for getting carried away trying to chase an eagle. *Said every victim in a horror or slasher movie ever.*

The wolves growled at her again and Bobby refocused on her. "I told you to shut your mouth. She can't do that, JT, can she? She can't go running around in our woods. You've said so."

JT, in his dark blue, almost black, denim jeans and tucked-in flannel shirt, hadn't looked away from her since he'd first arrived that she could tell. He, too, didn't seem fazed by the man-size wolves.

His deep black hair shone in the late afternoon sun as he shook his head. "Nope. You're right. She can't."

"Well, so me and the boys was patrolling and were just now trying to figure out what we was going to do with her."

Kate tried to keep up. She still had no clue who Billy was. God. Could she really have landed in backwoods Appalachia? This kind of stuff didn't really exist, did it?

JT still didn't take his eyes off her. "Let's clarify one point, Bobby. It's my land. My property. You're supposed to patrol it. You've done your job and caught a trespasser. Let me do my job and find out why she's here." Every word was spoken calmly and with control.

And yet, that dissonance in his voice continued to clash against her senses.

In the movies, it was always the one who spoke softly and carefully who was the most dangerous. She believed that about JT. Not only did he own all this land that she was on without permission, but he easily spoke to—and rebuked—a crazy man flanked by two huge wolves.

JT walked a few steps closer to her. He was still farther away from her than Bobby and the wolves, but JT was on her level at the river bank, not up on the hill looking down at her. "Tell me. You got lost. What were you doing that got you lost and had you missing all of the many *No Trespassing* signs we have posted."

Kate tried to get a read on him, but all she got back was *cold*. Everything coming off of him was just…cold. It wasn't that there was nothing. It was like he was ice. "I was chasing an eagle."

He gave the slightest nod, except…it was diagonal. Not a yes, not a no.

A noise to Kate's left grabbed her attention.

The wolves were on the move, making their way down the steep incline.

"An eagle," JT said.

Kate whipped her eyes right in time to see JT traveling down river again, closing the gap between them while advancing toward the approaching wolves. He casually waved his hand at the wolves, pointing toward them and then behind him, and they altered their path, ending up directly behind JT.

Oh, God. She was going to be sick.

JT was definitely the most dangerous of all the creatures, especially if he could command those monsters to do whatever he wanted them to do.

Those weren't normal wolves, and this wasn't a normal situation. She was even more concerned that there was no way she could get out of this alive, or at the very least, unharmed.

JT and his wolves stopped their journey directly across the river from Kate. His appearance was average enough, what with his red, black and white plaid flannel shirt, but even that conflicted with the spring growth on the trees and the pollen in the air. It reminded her of winter. Once again...cold.

Going by looks alone, though, was always a dangerous thing. Didn't "they" always say most serial killers looked "normal"?

Besides, she was in the backwoods, alone, with no cell service. The only thing keeping her from completely collapsing was the expanse of water between her and the wolves, though were wolves water-averse?

All she needed now was the negligee and high heels and she'd be ready for her audition in any teen horror flick.

And gee, for some reason, that line of thinking didn't ease her mind at all. No, all it did was increase her anxiety to stomach-churning levels.

JT stepped closer to the river's edge. "What's going on in that pretty little head of yours? Because you're awfully quiet over there."

Kate wanted to back away, but glanced up to see the rifle still pointed directly at her. Instead, she righted her art bag as surreptitiously as she could to her side and not in the way of her arms or legs needing to move.

White-hot rage replaced the cold she'd been picking up from JT. Growls made up the accompanying soundtrack. And Bobby's steady stream of annoyance changed to anger with an undercurrent of fear. "What the hell is Atlanta PD doing up here so far north? You don't belong here," JT said.

Her damn T-shirt.

"No. I'm not—you don't understand."

"I understand you're wearing something that marks you as being an Atlanta Police Officer and I want to know what you're doing here and what's in that bag of yours."

Shit.

She'd never given a single thought to how her life might be in danger because the only workout clothes she now owned happened to all have Atlanta PD on them.

It was then she realized that the only things moving on her were her brain and her heart. Oh, and maybe her lungs, but she couldn't guarantee that. Those puppies kept freezing on her like she didn't need to bother with breathing all that often.

JT ran two steps and leaped onto a rock on his side of the river. The rock was jagged on top and yet he easily kept his balance.

She was helpless, couldn't even run away, and her brain was screaming in terror when she wished it was her voice. The experience brought to mind *The Scream* by Edvard Munch, and she projected that helplessness the only way she knew how, she screamed for help mentally.

It wouldn't do her any good, but there'd been this voice in her dreams that would comfort her on nights she'd been anxious or scared or had a harrying experience at work. And more than anything, she wanted the comfort and strength that voice always brought to her through her subconscious. For almost twenty years, she'd accepted that voice as a secret companion, and if she were going to die here and now, then she wanted to hear that soothing voice inside her head one more time.

"That's a neat little trick you've got there. Who're you trying to communicate with?" JT tilted his head and the wolves lowered their heads and whined.

Huh? "What do you mean?" Kate wished she knew how to mentally send the sound of a dog whistle to the canines just to take them out of the picture.

JT narrowed his eyes. "You're communicating with someone. Or trying to. Something's happening."

Hoping and wishing she could certainly wouldn't make it so. But how could he know…? "I truly have no idea what you're talking about." Everything inside her was starting to fall apart, and she was beginning to lose the strength to stand much longer.

"I don't believe you."

Kate.

That voice.

Her protector's voice.

The one that cradled her like a full-body down pillow and wrapped around her senses like a silk sheet.

JT jumped to another rock, on *her* side of the river. One Kate could barely make out because the top skimmed the surface of the water.

She'd *never* heard that voice during her waking hours. It had only ever come to her in dreams. But dammit, that voice? That voice was worth living for and finding. There was no fucking way she was going to let herself die on the side of a mountain.

"I'm getting tired of asking these same questions over and over and getting non-answers from you."

Now that he was closer, Kate could see the knife handle sticking up out of JT's boot. "I'm sorry you don't like my answers, but they're all I've got."

JT jumped to her side of the river then, once again defying what should've been natural laws of physics and motion and what the average person could do.

Kate forced herself not to flinch. To stay as still as possible.

"Thing is, I'm looking at you from the Atlanta PD, wanting to know why it is that a cop from down there would be up here on my land."

"I'm not a cop," Kate said.

JT ignored her response. "And we ask you how you come to ignore all of my *No Trespassing* signs, and you tell us you were chasing an eagle and got lost."

"I was. I wanted to sketch it." She wasn't helpless. Not completely. Terrified beyond anything, yes. But she wasn't a ten-year-old girl facing down animals. Kate was in her thirties and she'd been trained in self-defense as a requirement for her job.

Now she just had to convince her body to act on what her mind wanted it to do.

Yeah. That.

I need you to hang on for me. Do whatever it takes.

"Then I asked you who you're trying to communicate with and you pretend like you're stupid. That pisses me off the most, see, because I can feel the energy, so I know something's happening."

Kate called on one of her skills from her time in high school marching band—use of peripheral vision without moving the eyeballs—and took in her immediate surroundings to try to determine what she might use to defend herself. To use as a weapon.

She opened her hands out in front of her to show

she wasn't a threat. "I went for a walk. I work out in Atlanta PD T-shirts. I saw an eagle. I wanted to sketch it. I hoped it would land so I could see that. I didn't see any *No Trespassing* signs. I'm sorry."

A huge stick lay to her left, almost like a small log, but she couldn't tell from her position if it was stuck in the mud and river silt. A stick to her right lay on top of a pile of leaves. It was longer, but much thinner and wouldn't help her out. Of course, if she couldn't dislodge the larger one, it wouldn't do her any good, either.

"I don't like it when people lie to me. We've got signs posted everywhere. You would've had to trip over one in the direction you came from." JT stalked closer to her. "And I noticed you didn't deny the communication this time."

I'm almost there.

Here here? At this river, *here*? How?

Kate needed to keep him speaking instead of acting. "I don't know what to say or how to react to someone accusing me of talking to people with my mind. I'm sorry, but it just sounds really bizarre."

She wanted a simple existence.

She'd thought she'd deserved that at this point.

"Don't patronize me, little girl. I'm the last person you want to cross right now," JT said.

Kate once again evaluated her options, quickly discarding the idea that she might be able to get to any kind of weapon and use it in time.

Plan B it was then. One of her self-defense instructors liked to explain that a knee was only supposed to bend in one direction. If it was forced to bend in any other direction, it would only fold that way once, leaving your attacker whimpering on the ground. Kate wasn't going to assume that JT's knee was normal since nothing else about the situation or any of his physical feats had been normal so far, but knees still had to be weak on everyone. Right?

"I get that. I do. And I'm not trying—"

JT took two steps back, peering over his left shoulder into the trees that dotted the riverbank.

Kate spared a glance to her left, and the wolves, too, were focused on the trees on her side of the river. Bobby swung his rifle and had it aimed that same direction instead of at her.

Several seconds later, Kate finally heard footsteps approaching at a fast clip, although she couldn't see who it was.

"What are you doing here?" JT asked, crossing his arms at the chest. The white-hot rage he'd been steadily streaming at her now turned into hatred.

"JT." The man sounded like the voice in her head, but the trees and hill muffled him.

Maybe she was just projecting hope onto some poor, unsuspecting sap.

"Cousin," JT spat with disgust.

Sooo, the newcomer was a good thing. The enemy of her enemy was her friend, and all that.

Leaves rustled above and to her right, and even though to this point she hadn't taken her eyes off JT, everything in her, every instinct, every curiosity, compelled her to turn her head.

He wore medium blue jeans and a light green Henley T-shirt that hugged his muscular chest. The sleeves of his T-shirt were pushed up to reveal muscular forearms while his arms dangled casually at his sides.

His strong, defined jaw squared off before reaching

the white-blond hair covering his head. A couple shocks of dark brown hair sat high on his head, as if they were reverse gray patches.

Despite the animosity directed at him from JT, this man's face and emotions radiated warmth, even happiness. Comfort began to drown out the negative emotions that had bombarded her since this whole ordeal began.

And, oh, his eyes. His eyes bore into her, creating a connection that spanned not just the small distance between them, but the energy fields that surrounded them.

Gravity tilted. Vertigo threatened. And then everything in Kate's world righted itself.

"Kate. Mrs. Brighton said you got lost. She sent me out to come find you." *I need you to nod yes, even if you're not.* "Are you okay?"

She jerked her head once in some semblance of a yes.

JT widened his stance and kept his arms crossed. "What do you think you're doing? You know this woman? How?" He narrowed his eyes into a glare. "And what are you doing with a cop?"

"Yeah, what're you doing with a cop?" Bobby asked.

Great. He'd made his way down to the river bank and stood directly across from her on the other side of the river. Much, much closer than he had been.

The new guy made his way down the hill, easily navigating tree roots and the like, all while focusing on JT with a few glances at Kate mixed in.

"I'm helping Katie back up the hill and escorting her back to the Brighton Hotel, where she's staying as a guest. On vacation. What does it look like I'm doing?" *I'm assuming you're here on vacation.*

Katie? Really? That had been way easier than it

should've been, the whole talking to someone else in her head.

He smiled at her. *Seems right.*

I don't think so. By the way, what's your name?

Callan.

Thanks for the rescue, Callan.

Looked like you were doing fine all on your own.

JT bent and pulled the knife from his boot but held it at his side, then got in Callan's face just as he was passing. "I don't know what kind of bullshit you're trying to pull by bringing the law around here, but I don't like it, and I will make you pay."

Callan remained calm.

Kate waited for fear to leak through his emotions to her, but all she got was Zen-like peace.

I'm a sketch artist. Or used to be. That's it.

"Sometimes, my dear cousin, people happen to get lost in the woods. And sometimes those people happen to have worked in the law enforcement field at one point. That doesn't mean that they currently do. Nor does it mean that they're out to get you." Callan turned his back on JT and walked straight to her. The moment he touched her arm, his energy nearly knocked her over as electric tingles flowed from the point of contact throughout her body.

He turned back to his cousin. "Sometimes, JT, your paranoia is just paranoia." His voice was just as soothing out loud as it was in her head.

Kate tried lifting her foot, but her shoe was stuck in the river mud as if it were concrete holding her in place.

Callan wrapped his arm around her waist and gently lifted her straight out of the sludge.

Her brain barely worked enough to scrunch up her

toes so she could hold on to her shoes. The second, possibly even more important thought was, *Oh God, his arm is around my waist.* Although she wasn't sure it was quite so coherent as it went on track repeat the entire time Callan dragged her up the river bank.

"Hey," JT called out behind them. "You and your pack and your family and your friends and everyone else you know need to stay off my land."

Callan looked over his shoulder. "And you need to make sure that your signs are well maintained, especially after we've had storms in the area."

JT's warning tickled the edges of Kate's mind. It wasn't quite right. But she'd been through too much, and she was at the end of being able to process anything other than Callan's touch. Her adrenaline crashed and there was nothing she could do about it. She was just so freaking sleepy. Her feet were too heavy and she stubbed her toe against a tree root. She tripped.

Callan caught her, his one arm staying at her back and the other swooping under her legs. "I've got you."

Kate breathed in his clean, woodsy scent. It, combined with his protective hold, embodied feelings of home.

He put his lips close to her ear. "You look like you need some rest."

She laid her head on his shoulder and gave herself over to some welcome sleep.

Chapter Three

Callan took the Brighton Hotel's back porch steps three
at a time, dropped Kate's muddy shoes at the top of the
porch and passed through the screen door to have them
met by Mrs. B.

"Oh, child! What on earth happened to you?"

"She's fine, Mrs. B," Callan said.

Kate quietly groaned.

"Some animals scared her nearly to death and her
legs are quite a bit shaky. I figured it was easier for me
to carry her back here."

Luckily, Kate's face was turned toward him and she
missed the look Mrs. B gave him. A look that managed
to combine "I know how far you carried her and that's not
normal" with "I think you liked having her in your arms."

Callan gave her a casual shrug.

"Take her on into the sitting room and I'll make you
both some iced tea. I've still got a few cookies left, although no chocolate chip cookies. She seemed to really like those earlier. I'd have to bake another batch—"

"Tea and whatever cookies you have left will be
fine." Callan carried Kate into the sitting room, dropped
the bag she'd been carrying next to the coffee table, then
settled on a love seat with her still in his arms, on his

lap. If she insisted on sitting on her own, that was fine, but she'd still be next to him.

Mrs. B returned with two glasses of iced tea and a plate of cookies. She gave him an arched eyebrow but didn't say anything about Kate being on his lap. "This is the last of the cookies. I need to finish doing clean-up in the kitchen, but I can get you anything else if you need it."

"We'll be fine, Mrs. B. Thank you."

After she left, he turned Kate so he could see her face better. "Let's get a little bit of food in you before the adrenaline crash happens."

"S'already happened," she said. "I just want t'sleep forever."

"Yeah, I bet. Let's have you eat something anyway." He helped her sit up straighter, and when she didn't try to move off his lap—probably because Mrs. B had put the tray down on the corner closest to where he was sitting—he took that as a small victory.

"Fine." She picked up a cookie. "Ugh. Oatmeal raisin. I know people love oatmeal raisin cookies, but I just don't. I think they're out to get you, all looking like chocolate chip cookies, the raisins pretending to be yummy chocolate, but then pow, you're eating something somewhat healthy that's masquerading as a cookie."

Callan threw back his head and laughed so hard that he knew he was shaking poor Kate. So much so that she slid the tray down the coffee table so that it was closer to the other cushion and she moved off his lap.

"Hmph." She scrunched up her face and threw him a side-eye.

That just made him laugh even harder. For a woman who'd been terrified to the point of being frozen in her tracks, she had a very strong opinion about oatmeal raisin cookies.

She began lifting the glass of tea to her lips. "Don't make me spill this tea all over Mrs. Brighton's nice couch and floor. I'll be very mad at you."

He *was* still jiggling the cushions with his laughter, so he instead focused on her lips as the glass hit them. Her very full, very soft looking lips. When he'd first seen her, she'd been pale and her lips almost ghost white, but they'd regained some color and were now a pale rose. He bet they'd darken to full rose if he kissed her.

And he'd be more concerned about the track his mind was taking if she were still pale and hadn't just ranted about the evils of oatmeal raisin cookies.

Callan reached for the other glass of iced tea and he was greeted with yet another side-eye. "What? I just carried you over many miles of mountainous terrain. I'm thirsty."

"You can go ask Mrs. Brighton for some water. Hello, dealing with an adrenaline crash here. I need the caffeine and sugar in my system."

He took the glass of tea anyway and heard a mock gasp of outrage. He could tell it wasn't real, because even though she might not know they were mates and had a connection, he did, and right now there was not a single emotion aimed toward him that came close to anger or outrage. All he was getting from her was… well, not those. Definitely not those. He was going to have to teach his Katie how to shield her emotions, because she was broadcasting all sorts of things to him she probably didn't want him to know.

Like just how much—

She pretended to slap at him. "I can't believe you just stole my iced tea."

"Fairly certain that since there are two people in here and there are two glasses, Mrs. B meant for us both to get a glass."

"How rude. Her name is Mrs. Brighton."

"Yes, it is. And I've called her Mrs. B all my life. I'm not going to change now just because an oatmeal raisin cookie ranting woman says I need to."

Her eyes widened and her small smile turned into a huge grin. She dazzled him with the brilliance of the gesture. Her whole face lit up and her eyes twinkled with her humor.

Kate ate a few bites of the cookie. "I just don't like being fooled into thinking I'm getting one thing when really I'm being forced to eat something healthy. It's wrong and deceivious."

"Deceivious?"

"Absolutely."

Callan let the silence fall for a bit while the sky grew darker outside. Mrs. B called out her good-nights to them, saying she needed to get up before the sun the next morning to prepare breakfast for the guests. Eventually, Kate's breathing evened out and her head slowly slid to rest against his arm. He didn't dare move that side of his body. It felt too good having her, in effect, snuggled up against him, her left side almost completely touching his right, her cheek against his arm, her breath blowing across his biceps.

He'd already removed his phone from his pocket earlier and now he typed on it with just his left thumb and contacted Connor.

At b and b. K is resting. Haven't gotten story. Won't be home for supper.

It wasn't long before Callan got a response.

Duh. Car and I kinda figured out the supper thing when you didn't make it home in time for it.

Whatever. He contacted Gray next.

JT isn't usually so close to b and b. Is usually much closer to my uncle's property. Any way we can find out something?

The response was immediate.

I'm already working on that. Patrols say he's been down there more recently. We don't know why. I can try a drone, but they make noise and he has guns. You might want to make plans to visit your uncle sometime soon. None of us have seen him in a while and JT is popping up more often in town and such instead.

Will do.

Callan thought about his uncle and how much he missed the fun-loving version of the guy from his childhood. The one who'd looked at all of life as a game rather than a competition. Back before he and Callan's dad had their parting of ways over the way to do business properly and the way to handle the government. Something Callan and JT were somehow still fighting over, although Callan had no reason to fight, nor did he want to.

He shook his head and felt the gorgeous woman beside him stir.

"Hello, Sleeping Beauty. I didn't mean to disturb you."

"No, I'm fine." She stretched, and Callan admired every inch of her body she put on display. He'd feel bad ogling her only if he got caught.

"You sure you're fine?"

"Yep."

"Are you up for telling me what happened?"

She sighed. "I could use some food first."

"Then let's go raid Mrs. B's kitchen, unless you're up for going out."

"I'm so not."

Kate accepted the feelings of peace and comfort that flooded her system now. She needed them to help gain distance from and perspective of the afternoon's events. He probably didn't know how much he was helping her, so she was going to soak it up while she could.

Callan took her hand and led her back to the kitchen, going straight to the fridge.

"It's like you know exactly what you're doing back here," she said.

He winked at her and she wanted to freeze the moment in time. His eyes were beautiful, kind of a pale hazel brown, almost gold.

"I might've worked here as a teenager for a year or two or three. I had to make beds, clean bathrooms and take breakfasts up to guests who wanted their breakfasts in their rooms instead of coming downstairs to eat."

Kate pulled her attention from his eyes and leaned around him to peer into the fridge. "What's there to eat?" And then she spotted it front and center. "Oh my

God. Are those ready-to-bake chocolate chip cookies? I thought she made her own. Like from scratch."

"She does, but I bet she keeps these for emergencies. Also, it's awfully convenient that they're right here, easy for us to find." He pulled them out and tossed the package on the counter. "Let's turn on the oven and get washed up."

"Are you sure we won't get in trouble?"

"Positive. Now the longer you yap, the longer it's going to take to get cookies baked."

Kate scoffed. "You don't even know me. I don't yap."

He gave her a look she ignored while washing her hands. He then pulled out a cookie sheet from one of the cabinets and popped open the package of cookie dough. Kate helped him place the pre-cut cookies on the baking pan and then they just had to wait for the oven.

Callan leaned against one of the counters, his hands folded low across his stomach, his legs stretched out, one crossed over the other at the ankle. He was much taller and bigger than she'd initially realized. Sitting next to him, standing beside him hadn't had quite the same effect as standing across from him, taking in all of him in one long view.

"Can you talk about what happened while we wait for the baking to happen?" A small furrow sat between his brows and his tone was soft, caring.

She didn't want to talk about it, but since he was her rescuer and she'd just napped on him, she owed him that. Besides, his voice still soothed her. It wrapped around her and refreshed her. She'd initially thought that maybe it was just the idea that there was someone who'd help her when she couldn't help herself, but it was more than that. His voice was familiar. It was the one from her dreams. And that just didn't make any sense at all since she'd never met Callan before today. "I guess so. Especially since there's not all that much to tell."

The oven beeped, and Callan moved to put the cookie sheet in before Kate realized that meant the oven was already at temperature. Her brain was elsewhere. Obviously.

A stainless-steel prep table took up the area that most people associated with a kitchen island, and there were four stools stacked in a corner. Callan grabbed two of the stools and slid them up to the table, motioning for her to join him.

His smile was reassuring. "Okay, I'm ready to listen."

"Well," she said and shrugged, "I guess it's really pretty simple. I went for a walk in the woods and got caught up sketching different animals. I walked up on some deer grazing in an open meadow of tall grasses. I was completely and totally focused on them, trying to capture what I could see of their markings, when I heard what sounded like a monkey or a tropical bird approaching." She shook her head. "It so wasn't."

"An eagle?"

"Yup. An eagle. I thought they'd have screeches or something sinister like hawks. But it had a brown body and a white head and what sounded like the voice of a tropical bird chattering away. The deer took off into the woods at a ninety-degree angle from where the eagle was coming from. I watched as the eagle made a turn and then I took off in the direction it was going. It was all happening so quickly, and I wanted to see if it really was an eagle."

She let out a gusty sigh. "I took off running in the trees, not paying the least bit of attention as to where I was going. All I cared about was keeping up with the few little glimpses I got of that majestic bird of prey. And boy was it ever majestic. But its call is puny if it really was an eagle. I'd made a mental note at the time that I wanted to look that detail up when I could get cell service."

Kate drummed her fingers on the table.

Callan reached over and took her hand. "Go on."

"Looking back now, I do recall there being a chain with a sign face down that I jumped over near a tree I used as a vault. So yes, I'm sure it was one of those *No Trespassing* signs Mrs. Brighton warned me about, and it sucks that all of this was my own damn fault."

Incredulity crossed his face. "What I want to know is how on earth you were able to run for so long?"

"Eh. I did a lot of sitting at my job, like most people do, so running is my exercise of choice. I enter 5ks and 10ks fairly often."

"Came in handy."

She nodded. "At least until the crash hit."

Silence fell between them, but she continued feeling that same sense of comfort, although it was stronger than what she usually picked up from people. She didn't understand it, but she wasn't going to question it. After the day she'd had, letting Callan soothe her, however he was doing it, just felt right.

The timer went off and she jumped. Her nose had already told her brain that the cookies had to be done, but luckily Callan knew not to just follow his nose. He grabbed a cooling rack and a potholder, and there they were, warm gooey chocolate chip cookies, ready for her to burn her tongue on.

He gave her a pretend glare. "Don't even think about it."

"How can you possibly know what I'm thinking?"

"You look like a starving woman getting ready to

dive in. Give them two minutes on here and then we'll move them off. In the meantime, we can get something to drink."

"We need milk."

"Milk?"

"Of course. Milk and cookies. It's the perfect meal. You have your dairy food group, your proteins—"

"I don't think you get to count dairy as a protein," he said.

"Sure you do. You also have your breads, your fats and your chocolates."

Callan did a spit take into his sleeve. "I'm sorry, what? Since when is chocolate a food group?"

"Since forever. Ask any woman."

"What about fruits and veggies?"

She shook her head. "You don't need those food groups this late at night. The chocolate takes care of them."

Callan looked in the fridge. "You're in luck. Mrs. B has milk."

"You should have some, too."

He gave her the most put-upon look ever, but poured two glasses of milk. He then moved the cookies to a large plate and set it before her. "Ready for you to burn your tongue on."

"Just what I was thinking. Perfect timing."

"And you wondered if I could read your mind."

"Mmm." Kate couldn't answer him because she had a delicious, piping-hot cookie burning her mouth and was attempting to put out the fire with the cold milk. She was in heaven.

When she eventually came up for air, after five or six cookies—she'd lost count—she noticed Callan staring at her with a peculiar look on his face. "What? Do I have chocolate all over my face?"

"As a matter of fact, you do."

She tried licking her lips, but he reached over and swiped his thumb along the corner of her mouth then down along her chin. He looked at the chocolate for a few seconds then reached for a paper towel.

"No!" How dare he? "You don't go wiping chocolate off on paper towels or napkins. That's sacrilege. You're supposed to lick it off."

He raised both eyebrows at her.

"Well you do. And if you don't want it, then I'll have it back. It's my chocolate."

It wasn't until Callan's thumb was pressed against her lower lip that Kate's brain finally caught up with her diarrhea of the mouth. She'd just offered to lick chocolate off his thumb. Possibly one of the more intimate gestures, and she'd only just met him a few hours ago. Oh lord, what was she thinking?

She wasn't. Hence diarrhea of the mouth.

Kate looked into Callan's dilated eyes as she quickly, but with enough force to get all of the chocolate off in one swipe, licked his thumb then pulled away.

Except he didn't go anywhere. Instead, he took that same thumb and ran it along the other corner of her mouth and along that side of her chin. And this time, he brought the bit of chocolate to his own lips and ran his tongue along it.

Oh. My. God. He was tasting her and the chocolate. It was almost like a kiss.

Well then.

Chapter Four

Callan broke eye contact and finally reached for a paper towel. "By the way, my cousin is an idiot."

Kate was confused. "Your cousin?"

"JT. The one who brought his guard animals with him to confront you."

"Ah. Yes." She remembered hearing JT refer to Callan as "cousin." "But those weren't just any ol' animals. Those were wolves."

His gaze sharpened on her. Those pale hazel-brown eyes turned more gold, and he leaned forward. "What makes you say that?"

"I know the difference between dogs and wolves. And those were wolves."

"What caused you to know the difference?"

"There was an incident."

"Tell me about it?" His face was open and he reached toward her to tuck a stray hair behind her ear.

She crossed her arms. "I don't really want to. I don't like talking about it."

"But it's what caused you to become so terrified of wolves, yes?"

"Yes." She nodded.

He uncrossed her arms and took her hands in his.

"You were a frozen block of ice when I came upon you this afternoon."

"Fine." Kate glanced around the kitchen. "Mrs. Brighton doesn't keep alcohol stocked around here, does she?"

"Probably not for guests. We can go shopping for some whiskey moonshine if you'd like."

That was a shocking proposition. She refocused on him. "I thought moonshine was illegal."

"Only if you aren't willing to pay the government the taxes you owe on your profits."

"Oh."

He lifted one hand to her cheek and cradled it. The palm of his hand and tips of his fingers were calloused. "You were saying…"

"I wasn't, but here goes nothing."

Callan slid his hand down her jaw and retook her hands in his.

His touch ignited her and consoled her all at once, and she felt better already for it. "My best friend and I were around ten years old at the time. I remember the summer clearly." The trees surrounding the overlook, the beautiful scenery could do nothing to erase the nightmarish images from coming back to her as if they had happened yesterday. "Our town was growing quickly. I remember my parents having conversations amongst themselves and saying things like the town council only seeing dollar signs in front of their eyes. I now know that my parents meant tax dollars coming in from new housing developments and bringing in new businesses, but at the time, I had no idea what they were talking about.

"All I knew was that a bunch of the play areas my

friends and I would go to for playing kickball or kick the can or stuff like that during the summer were no longer available or no longer safe for us to play at. There was a ton of construction all around and my friend, Ellie, wanted to find a new wooded area in order to build a fort slash dollhouse."

Callan squeezed her hands and reassured her with his smile. She gave him a small smile. At least she hoped it was a small smile. It might've been a grimace.

"At the time, we hadn't known that all that construction was also pushing wolves out of the area and into the increasingly smaller and smaller wooded areas available surrounding our town. I know that now, logically, and I remember hearing that afterward."

"Afterward?"

"Ellie thought they were just 'big doggies.' Her words." Kate shook her head. "But something inside me told me to stay back. To stay away." She couldn't describe the attack. She didn't want to relive those moments through the spoken word. "She lived, Ellie did, but huge sections of her body were mangled. A friend of ours had stopped by my house looking for us to play with. My mom had told him we were out looking for a place for a new fort, and he found us because he heard our screams. He was on his bike." Kate shook her head again but the image wouldn't leave. "I don't know how Ellie managed to make it home. Adrenaline can override a ton of the body's signals, I know that for a fact. Because there were parts of her that didn't look human when she got on William's bike, and yet she rode it home. He and his bike saved her life. There was no way I could've carried her home and she certainly couldn't've walked home."

Kate closed her eyes and drew in a deep breath of chocolate-chip-cookie-scented clean mountain air. "Ellie was never the same again. As far as I know, she never rode a bike again. I think she eventually walked, but her parents moved the family away from our town and we never kept in touch like I should've tried." She opened her eyes again and looked into Callan's. "To this day, I don't know why that pack of wolves attacked her so ferociously and they left me alone. I wish I knew. At one point, there was so much blame going around from her parents, they even accused me of causing the attack since I came out of it without a scratch. But the blaming me bit didn't last long because William stuck up for me saying that I wasn't as close to the animals, yet I was there screaming my fool head off."

"He said that?" Callan asked with a slight smirk.

"Maybe not the 'fool head' part. But it became easier for her parents to blame the town council and the developers and everyone else, which is why they finally moved."

"Sounds like they wouldn't have appreciated you trying to keep in touch with their daughter anyway."

Kate shrugged one shoulder, as if it hadn't hurt as much as it did. "Possibly not, but she'd been my friend and I'd witnessed her go through something traumatic that changed her life in every fundamental way possible. I was there. I should've at least tried to contact her when we were older."

"You know you can still try."

"Yeah, I know."

"I can see how that incident would make you terrified of dogs. And of course, wolves."

She pulled her hands out of his and hugged herself,

wrapping her arms around her waist. "Yeah, there's not much I can do about that. But the funny thing is, it was soon after that that I began dreaming about this one wolf."

Callan sat up straighter, his focus even more intense, even though she hadn't thought that was possible. "This one wolf? What wolf is that?"

"This is going to sound so stupid."

"Go on. My family has always believed in the power of dreams."

Kate let out a long, slow breath. "I've been dreaming about this one wolf for almost twenty years. It's almost all white except for these dark brown points on its ears and at the top of its head. Almost like the markings of a Siberian husky. But it's most definitely a wolf. After Ellie, well, I know what wolves look like. Anyway, it also has these golden yellow eyes. At least that's what they look like in my dreams."

"Have you dreamed of any other wolves? Maybe any of the wolves that attacked your friend?"

"Nope. None of them. Just the one."

Callan recaptured her hands. "I saw the sketchbook in your bag while I was carrying you."

"You with the carrying thing again."

He gave her a look of mock disbelief. "Of course. I'm not going to let that go."

She made a rude noise, which Callan proceeded to ignore.

"Anyway, the sketchbook. Do you happen to have any pictures of this wolf you've dreamed about?"

"Not in that book. That one's brand-new. I bought it for this trip specifically. But I do have some pictures scanned in on my tablet as well as just drawn on my tablet. It's up in my room." Kate hesitated. "I could bring it down here. Or..." She stopped again. "You could come upstairs with me and I could show you all of my sketches."

Callan tilted his head. "You sure?"

No matter how she answered, Callan wasn't going to let anything go too far.

"Yes, I'm sure." She said the words carefully, but that only reinforced his decision to make sure they didn't do anything tonight. She'd gone through a traumatic event and was still dealing with the emotional ramifications of that. He didn't want her to regret any of her time with him at any point.

Especially after hearing how terrified she was of wolves. Because of course his mate would be terrified of the very thing he was. That's the way life worked out for him.

No, he hoped to snag her with her feelings for him all on their own, with no outside influencing events in the way.

She took his hand and led him back through the house to the foyer. After popping into the sitting area to grab her bag, she then led him upstairs to her room, and paused outside the door.

"Now—"

"We're not going to do anything but take a look at the drawings you want to show me. That's it. In fact, if you want, you can just get your tablet and we can go back downstairs to take a look at your sketches in the sitting room."

She exhaled. "No, it'll be fine." She smiled at him.

"I don't know why I trust you, but thank you for what you just said."

"I mean it."

"Somehow I know that."

He saw that her room was still designated as the parents and one kid room, and her bags were on the smaller bed.

"I haven't had a chance to unpack yet. Obviously. My plan had been to get my walk in and get some sketching done before it got too dark. Of course we know how that went."

"Did you get any sketching done?"

"Actually I did."

"Then part of it went right."

She reached into her bag and pulled out a sketchbook, smaller but thicker than the one she'd been carrying. "Here. You can take a look through this first. I need to change out of these clothes so I don't get dirt on Mrs. Brighton's bedspreads or that beautiful chair." She pointed to the one chair in the room, upholstered to match the colors of the room. "I'll be right out." She got some clothes from her duffel bag and disappeared into the small bathroom.

Callan tried not to think about Kate in the bathroom changing clothes. Because at some point, changing clothes meant she'd have to be some portion of naked and he very much wanted to see that. But he'd promised her they wouldn't do anything and he'd promised himself he wouldn't betray her trust—because that was going to be all too easy to do later on when she found out what he was—so he forced his mind from his mate in the bathroom back to why she'd brought him up here in the first place.

He sat on the edge of the bed and focused on the sketchbook she'd put in his hands. He began flipping through it and the talent shining forth from the pages floored him. Each page came to life, whether it was people at parks, on their own or with their pets, or animals in city settings. And then he came upon the pictures of the wolf. Many pages of them.

She'd drawn it just as she'd described, like an arctic wolf, but with brown points along its ears and on the top of its head. Its eyes didn't have any color in the pencil drawing, but the irises were definitely lighter than some of the surrounding shading.

Callan continued flipping through the pages, studying each of her wolf drawings. The thing he most noticed was that none of the pictures showed the wolf as being vicious. Teeth weren't displayed and it wasn't snarling. In each picture the wolf had an almost friendly countenance, and that's not what Callan had expected. Especially not from her description of today's incident plus her childhood trauma.

There were other drawings in the sketchbook of just nature scenes, with no animals and no people in them at all. Which gave Callan an excellent idea. That meeting with his sister this afternoon—had it really only been this afternoon?—where she wanted artwork for each of the guest cabins, and now having met Kate and seen her sketches. Kate drew magnificent pieces of art and he wanted her to draw for him. All he had to do was convince her.

Callan looked up as Kate came out of the bathroom. He hadn't thought it was possible, but somehow she was even more beautiful than before. To him, she was stunning. She'd cleaned up, put on a different Atlanta PD

T-shirt, and her hair was pulled back in a long, sleek ponytail. She looked angelic to him. Part of that might have also been because the light from the bathroom was shining behind her.

"So, what do you think?"

About how she looked? No. That couldn't be right. "About what?"

"About my sketches, of course."

Duh. "I think you are an amazing artist. You said you used to be a sketch artist. What do you do now?"

"Ah. I was a sketch artist for the past ten years for the Atlanta PD, but I just recently put in my resignation."

"That explains all of the T-shirts. But remarkably, doesn't answer my question."

She stuck her tongue out at him. "I'll get to that. But yeah, I pretty much stocked up on PD gear for my work-outs and casual clothes. They were cheap and easy to wash and wear. I should probably invest in some differ-ent clothes now…or at least some cover-ups."

Callan pulled her a bit closer, not wanting her beyond arm's length away. "Go on with your story."

"My best friend, Cindy, put me in touch with a few professors she works with at a research university out-side of Atlanta. A couple are interested in my sketching abilities. They have grants available to them in different areas at different times of the school year. One particu-lar professor wants me to do some scientific sketching for a specific research paper he is working on."

"Wow. Okay. So what are you doing up here?"

"Oh. I haven't had a vacation in a while, and Cindy recommended that I come to this area to rest and relax. Wait 'til I talk to her. I guess she's from this area, but she certainly didn't mention wolves and crazy people."

She shook her head. "The fact that I'll be doing some scientific sketching on different animals had me wanting to take my vacation near some wilderness anyway. Up here in the mountains gives me a lot more nature to be able to sketch than staying in the Atlanta area. Since I also grew up playing around wooded areas when I was a kid, I *thought* this might be a good escape. Boy, was I wrong."

"You do realize there are dogs everywhere, all over the country, no matter where you go, right?"

"I do realize that, I'm not stupid. But I also know that those weren't just dogs. Those were oversize pet wolves of some sort. Also, that one guy was absolutely insane. He was talking to the wolves as if one of them was actually going to answer him. That's crazy."

"Most people would say that the fact I could reach out to you mind to mind was crazy."

"That's okay. I would tend to agree with them on that. I can't seem to do that again so I think it was a fluke. Something that happened during the heightened emotional and highly tense situation."

"You do, huh? Have you not ever heard of telepathy?"

"Of course I have. But usually it's just crazy people who actually believe that stuff is real or claim that they can do it."

"So you're counting yourself as crazy."

"Absolutely. In fact, tomorrow, I probably won't believe it even happened."

Callan didn't know what to make of that, so he let it go. He wanted to get back to the task at hand. He had what he hoped was plenty of time to convince Kate that magic and other unexplained phenomena really did exist. "I have a business proposition for you."

She looked at him with one arched brow.

"My—" Callan didn't want to say pack "—family and I are in the process of trying to turn our many old lodges and cabins into guest lodges and cabins. We're hoping to start up an all-inclusive adventure vacation resort. The meeting I was in when Mrs. B called me—"

"I'm so sorry about that."

Callan wasn't sorry. At least not over the part about getting to meet her. He was sorry she had to go through the trauma of facing wolves that brought to mind her childhood nightmare as well as sorry that she had to deal with JT and his idiot friends. "It was my sister telling all of us that we needed artwork on the walls of these cabins and lodges, because the walls are hideously bare. At least according to her they are. After looking through your sketchbook—"

"You haven't even seen my electronic portfolio yet."

"I would like for you to consider doing the artwork for our cabins."

Kate couldn't believe her ears. "The artwork."

"Yes."

"For cabins."

"Yes."

"How many cabins are we talking about here?" she asked.

He shifted on the tiny bed, his stature making the bed look even smaller than it already was. "We currently have fifteen ready for check-in as soon as we start taking reservations. We need to make sure there are several things in place first before we take that first call, but we have at least ten other lodges that need fixing up that can be added to the resort."

"Fifteen sketches due right away."

"Well, technically, I think my sister wants there to be at least two pieces of art in each cabin. She wants one in the main room and one in the bedroom."

Kate shrugged and threw her hands out wide. "Of course she does. Thirty pieces."

"Yep."

"And you're not talking simple little small pieces either, are you?"

Callan shook his head and settled further back on the bed. "Well, no, probably not. They'd need to be twenty-four by thirty at the least for the main room. Maybe eighteen by twenty-four for the bedroom."

"Any particular requests for subject matter?"

"Does this mean you'll do it?" Excitement shone all over his face, as well as permeated her sixth sense.

"Subject matter?"

"Just what you have here in your sketchbook. You already draw exactly what I'm looking for."

"What about what your sister is looking for?"

"Eh, she came to us about the artwork problem, but didn't present any solutions. I have a solution."

"I haven't said yes."

"But you will."

Kate rolled her eyes. "You're awfully cocky."

"And I don't think you want to turn this down. Not based on all of these drawings. And like you said, I haven't even seen your electronic portfolio. But if you'd like, we can send that to my sister."

"What about wolves?"

Callan furrowed his brow and looked puzzled. "What about them?" An undercurrent of nervousness seeped in.

"What about them as subject matter for some of the pictures?"

His nervousness waned. "That should be fine. But maybe not that same wolf over and over."

"Hmm. No, probably not. What about the wolves in the area?"

His expression went blank and the nervousness was back. "What about them?"

"Aren't they a danger to any of your guests?"

"That's one of the things we need to work on getting in place. We're working on security and safety."

"Okay." Kate let the topic go for now. She was too excited about the idea that someone might actually want to pay her for her work. And not just her work to get the bad guys, but her work as an artist, and as someone who loves to draw nature and people enjoying it. "I want to see the cabins before I commit to anything."

"That sounds fair enough. But it's too late tonight and you've gone through enough today. You should get a good night's sleep and I'll come pick you up in the morning."

Here was her chance to start living the life she wanted by making her own choices and not just letting things happen to her. She could let Callan leave and wait to see him in the morning, or she could say what she really wanted and take the risk that he might want that, too. "I know you don't have a change of clothes with you, but I really don't want to sleep alone tonight."

"Kate."

"At least, not alone in this room. We don't have to do anything and we can still get some sleep, but there are two beds and I just don't want to be by myself. I'd like for you to stay if that won't cause you too many problems."

Callan gave her a wicked grin, one that shot sparks all throughout her body. "It just so happens, I do have a change of clothes in my truck, which happens to be parked outside. If you'll let me have the room key so I can get back in the house, I'll run outside and get them."

Kate immediately went to where she'd set down the key. "Are you sure?"

"I was going to ask you the same thing."

"I'm very sure that I don't want to be by myself."

"Then I'll be right back." He jogged out of the room.

Kate moved her bags from off the single bed and stuffed them in the drawers of the dresser. She'd already washed up and changed clothes, even though she was still just wearing regular clothes. But since he would be, too, she figured she'd stay in what she was wearing to help out with the not-going-to-do-anything-tonight decree. She pulled the pillow from underneath the covers on the twin bed and settled at the foot of it.

Callan re-entered the room just as she was sitting again. He headed straight for her and stopped abruptly. "This is your room. Why are you on the small bed?"

"Oh, maybe because you're a giant and you need a giant's bed to sleep on."

"I think I'm too tired to argue with you about that tonight."

"Good, then it's all settled."

He disappeared into the bathroom and Kate lay down. She turned on the night light at the base of the bedside lamp and turned out the main light. She yawned and could barely keep her eyes open while she waited for Callan to return so she could turn out the light.

The next morning, she vaguely recalled three things: Callan turning out the light, telling her "good night," and kissing her on her temple. She much more clearly recalled dreaming about wolves. Lots of wolves. Wolves fighting wolves.

And her white wolf led the group that her dreams said were the good guys.

Awesome.

Chapter Five

After breakfast and lots of interesting looks from Mrs. Brighton, Kate got to shower in peace while Mr. Brighton found some chores for Callan to help him with.

It was during her shower that she remembered some of her other dreams from the previous night. Dreams where the voice that had comforted her for years was in fact Callan's voice. Confirmation of what she'd thought she'd figured out the previous evening. Having his voice come to her during her shower, though, only served to turn her on and make her want...things done to her. But she ignored all those feelings because she was supposed to be taking a fast shower.

Afterward, she met Callan downstairs and he drove them north, up a winding road that had her sliding in her seat, alternating between leaning against the door and leaning toward him. Unfortunately for her, every time she leaned toward him, he was leaning away from her toward his own door.

She'd had way too many dreams and not enough sleep last night. As a result, she had no mental defenses against the onslaught of naughty pictures her mind kept coming up with as she watched his strong arms and hands grip and control the steering wheel. Or come closer to her as he changed gears.

He'd carried her with those arms yesterday. And now she was obsessed with his forearms and...fingers. Now that she knew he had calloused hands, she wondered what they'd feel like against other parts of her body other than her hands and face.

She'd no longer been paying any attention to where they were going or the scenery or anything until he pulled the truck to a stop. Finally prying her eyes away from him, she took in her surroundings.

"Oh, it's beautiful." The villa looked just like a miniature log cabin, complete with a steeply sloping A-line roof. It had a little porch that was part of the roof protection and extended from one side of the roof line to the other. There was a chair on either side of the front door, along with a window on each side sporting a planter box. Off in one corner sat a wood box. "Wow. Are all of the cabins like this?"

"No, each one has a slightly different roof line or different amenities. This one has everything on the main floor, with a reading nook in the loft up there." He pointed to the lone second story window.

"It's incredible and I can't wait to see them all."

"All of them? That'll take all day."

Kate clapped her hands together. "You could point me in the correct direction and I could go wandering."

"I'm not letting you out of my sight. Come on. Let's start by giving you a tour of just this one."

He opened the door for her and placed his hand on her lower back, letting her enter the cabin first. It was just as she'd imagined it would be. The layout had everything someone needed, all there, all in one room.

Kate spun around and quickly saw what Callan's sister was talking about. The only thing on the walls were windows, the fireplace, the TV of course and the items associated with the kitchen. There were no decorations anywhere.

"Do you see why my sister said these walls are sad and empty?"

"Definitely." Her voice came out in barely a whisper.

Callan encompassed a large portion of the room with a sweep of his arm. "I now know someone who can fill these walls with beautiful drawings. Nature scenes of all sorts."

Kate continued with her tour, this time taking the opportunity to absorb the details of where everything was.

The kitchen was to her right along the wall, with a four-top table placed central. Beyond the kitchen was a door that Kate assumed was the bathroom. Along the back wall sat a large four-poster bed. And on the left wall sat a fireplace. A large screen TV hung low on the wall between the fireplace and the bed. And the center of the room held a long puffy couch, matching chair and a coffee table to pull it all together.

She turned back toward the bed and realized she'd not been keeping up with where Callan had disappeared to. At least not until he came up behind her, his breath hot along her neck, giving her chills as the sensations she'd been ignoring zinged through her.

"Your artwork will look amazing in here."

How close were his lips to her neck? Was he going to kiss her? She wanted him to. God, did she want him to. She'd only met him yesterday and she wanted him to—

"So will you say yes?"

"Yes." She let the word last for much longer than it

should have. And then some part of her brain kicked in. She turned to face him. Probably a huge mistake since just looking at him made her brain cells want to mis-fire again. She shook her head. "What on earth have I just agreed to?"

"To put your artwork in all of our guest cabins." Callan gave her a wicked smile, like he could read her mind. "Why, what were *you* agreeing to?"

"That. Definitely that." What was it about this man that had her wanting to jump his bones?

Really. His voice was already an old friend to her. It was in her head, soothing her, wrapping around her and caressing her as if it were his hands on her.

"Uh-huh." And with that he dipped his head and took her lips in what started as a gentle kiss. But thankfully it didn't stay gentle for long. He nipped at her lips, then ran his tongue along the seam of her mouth. The thrill of being able to taste him had her opening to him while reaching behind him and fisting his shirt in her hands.

His tongue slid along hers, each stroke generating tingles in her clit. It'd been far too long since she'd been with someone, so she was already moving to create fric-tion against the seam of her jeans, knowing it would provide her some much-needed sweet relief.

Her nipples beaded against her bra, and she pulled Callan in closer so she could use his nearness to provide that extra pressure she needed to help get off.

Callan practically growled. Seriously, honest-to-god, growled. "I can smell your arousal. You don't need to dry hump me, love. I'll help you come."

Kate should've been embarrassed, and she knew she would be later, but by then she was almost mindless with need. It was as if she could feel not only her need but Callan's as well. As if hers was magnifying his, which was magnifying hers and so on. Which was an absolutely insane theory, but that's what happened when she was going bonkers with needing to come. Needing to feel his mouth on her. Anywhere. Everywhere. She didn't care where. She just *needed*.

He used his lips and teeth along her jawline and neck, working his way down her throat while he popped open the button and zipper of her jeans. When he licked a path down her chest to the swell of her breast, she held his head there, her hands closing in on his hair with a tight grip. He bit and sucked hard, forcing her hips forward toward him. The hand he slid down the front of her panties bumped her clit and she gasped in a breath.

She wasn't going to make it much longer. The feelings were too intense. Too overwhelming. They were everything.

He stroked a finger along her opening. Then a second. "So, so wet, Katie, love," he murmured against her breast. He slid two fingers into her channel, placed his thumb on her clit and had moved his head enough that he took her nipple between his teeth through her shirt and bra, and bit down. She came with a scream.

Part of her brain told her that she needed to be quiet, that she had no idea how many people were around and how many people might barge in thinking she was in trouble. But another part of her didn't care. The sensations. The ultimate, intense pleasure coursed through her and she never wanted it to end.

Eventually it did start to wane—it had to—and she came back down to earth, but the aftershocks running through her told her she wanted to go again. Now.

Good lord. Who was she?

And who was Callan that he'd done this to her?

All she felt was overwhelming happiness from him and because of that, she couldn't even muster up enough strength to be embarrassed yet.

"Wow."

"Yeah, wow. Are you ready for round two?"

Oh my God. "Ummm. But you haven't had round one yet yourself."

"Trust me, I almost did. And watching you? Well, let's just say I'll enjoy having you in my arms when you fall apart next time."

"Where's that going to be?" Kate was thinking maybe his place, but her eyes also wandered to the very prominent bed not five feet away.

"There's good." Callan picked her up and placed her on the bed, her feet and calves dangling off the edge.

"But this room is ready for guests. It'll need to be cleaned again." Even *she* could hear the merely token protest in her voice.

"Which is why we pay several local teenagers to do just that. It'll be fine."

He made quick work of getting rid of her jeans, shoes and socks so that the bottom half of her was laid bare to him. "I'm partially naked and you're not at all. There's something wrong with this picture." A lot wrong, because she could tell he was strong and she wanted to see that body he was hiding underneath all those clothes.

"When I get naked, I'm going to want to be inside of you immediately."

"Not seeing the problem here."

"I want to feast on you first."

"Oh. Well, okay then."

He slid his hands underneath her hips and moved

her until her butt was at the edge of the mattress. He knelt before her and blew on her curls. "So very wet and ready for me."

"Of course I'm ready for you. I already told you that."

His answer was a slow glide of his tongue along her slit. "You taste delicious," he said against her most intimate parts.

Kate's back bowed as he pressed his tongue against her clit and sucked it into his mouth. The quick and light lashes of his tongue combined with the steady suction of his mouth had her ready to lose her damn mind. Every once in a while, he'd throw in a graze of his teeth against her swollen sex organ and she wanted to explode. She squirmed in his hold, but couldn't figure out whether she was trying to get away or trying to get closer.

When he dipped his tongue in deeper, she had her answer. She wanted him as close as she could get him.

"I don't want to come again unless you're inside me."

Callan lifted his head, stretched up and kissed her again. "Okay. You win."

He crawled off her and made quick work of disappearing his clothes.

She'd already known he was tall and had to have been built like a tank, but she didn't think a literal tank was as close to the mark as it was. He was solid, with a broad chest and arms that she could probably lick for days. Kate knew she was an arm person. What she hadn't known was just how much of an arm person she really was. Damn, he had the full package.

His chest was covered with the same white-blond hair that made up most of the hair on his head. It traveled along his stomach to meet a slightly darker shade of hair that made up the nest surrounding the base of his erection. His erection that currently stood straight and tall. For her.

And she'd had enough of the eye candy portion for now. She could have another dose later.

"You all done?"

"Just for this little bit. I plan on ogling you more later."

"Good to know."

"Um. What about a condom?"

"Oh. Hold on. There might be one in my wallet."

Kate shook her head. "Never mind. I snuck one from Mrs. Brighton. It's in the outside pocket of my purse."

"Really, now. I'm not sure I want to know how that conversation went."

"She keeps a supply for her guests. Just get the damn thing and let's get busy."

Maybe it was because she was picking up on Callan's feelings for her as well, but she'd never before in her life wanted sex with someone so much.

Wanting him to have as much room as possible on the bed, she turned so she was laid out lengthwise. When he returned to her, he'd already rolled on the condom.

He dipped his tongue between her lips and kissed her deeply. She felt a hunger for him and from him that showed in his intensity.

"I want inside you. Am I allowed in now?"

"Absolutely." She spread open her legs and he pushed in maybe an inch before withdrawing and pressing in again. Each time he pushed in, he bumped her clit and sparks went off inside her.

Once he was fully seated, he stopped, rested his forehead on hers, had their noses touching.

"Please move. Please," she whispered.

"I will. I just… I want to savor how you feel wrapped around me. You're so hot and tight. You're already squeezing me hard and I know I'm going to shoot off like a rocket. I just want to let this moment sink in."

Kate wrapped her hand around his neck and brought his lips to hers. He took control immediately and deepened the kiss. She rocked her hips and he moved, matching her rhythm.

All the emotions flooding her, the physical feelings, had Kate coming in no time flat. Her scream was swallowed by Callan and he joined her with a groan.

Rather than collapsing on top of her, he rolled to the side and dragged her with him.

"I wish you'd gotten more than one condom from Mrs. B."

"I guess we need to hit a drug store in town."

"And I'll make a health checkup appointment so you can feel safe."

Chapter Six

A week later, Callan and Kate had spent as much time together as they could without keeping each other from getting their work done. Although Callan had to admit, he was way behind in getting updates from several areas, as well as getting things done that he'd been tasked to do. Even things he'd given himself to do.

That afternoon, Kate had been exhausted, and he teased her only a little for getting old and not having the stamina of a young person anymore when he kept her up each night having his wicked way with her. So he'd left her at the B and B and came back up the mountain to have a meeting with Carleigh and Conner.

Chris and Grayson were doing a final run through of some security items Gray had on one of his many lists that he was constantly checking and rechecking.

Heh. Next Christmas, Callan was going to make Grayson go as Santa Claus for the pups. Callan wondered how many of the pack would get that it all had to do with the lists.

Carleigh held up a thin stack of large papers. "Kate whipped up some quickie drawings for me to be able to use, not only for promotional materials, but as she called them, a temporary place holder. She said once she's had time to do proper pieces, then members of the family could take the original ones and use them as toilet paper for all she cared."

Callan was distracted by Carleigh mentioning Kate and quickie in the same sentence. He adjusted his position in his chair. "Toilet paper?" He rolled his eyes. "What is that woman thinking?"

Carleigh snickered. "No idea. I assured her that nothing she came up with could possibly be used as that. The more interesting thing to me, though, is that she still thinks all of us on this mountain are family. Not pack." She leveled a glare at Callan. "She still doesn't know, does she."

It wasn't a question. It was an accusation.

"I can't go into the reasons. It's her story to tell and it's incredibly personal, but she's scared of wolves."

Connor asked, "How could she possibly be scared of wolves? It's not like they're hanging out on every street corner."

Callan raised his eyebrow.

"Fine. Around here they are, but we're different."

Callan shook his head. "I told you, it's her story to tell. The point is, I just haven't figured out a way to spring 'Hey, you know those creatures who scare you to death? Well, I am one' on her yet. I know. Crazy."

"Dayum. Sorry, big brother." Carleigh walked around the table and hugged him.

Callan accepted her hug then shrugged. "I'll figure something out. Meanwhile, I'd still love to know what JT is up to before we officially open."

Connor smirked at their sister. "Hey, Car. Didn't one of the brothers have a crush on you? Or was it their friend? Why don't you offer—?"

Carleigh threw her notebook straight at Connor's head. If he didn't have the reflexes of a wolf, the spiral binding might've poked out his eye.

"Let me make sure you've got this straight in that pea-brained head of yours. I don't care how badly you want to know what JT is up to. I will *never*, and I mean *never*, contact any of the three crazies he hangs out with. Got it?"

Callan sat up straight. "I certainly have it. Connor? Any confusion on the subject?"

Connor threw his hands up in front of him. "Nope. Crystal clear over here."

Car growled at them both. "Good."

A car came up the drive. It was Kate's car. Huh.

"I thought you said she was staying in town to get a nap," Carleigh said.

"That's what she said she was going to do."

"If you count stopping off at the distillery, we've been together a couple hours already," Connor said.

"Whoa." Callan hadn't registered the time passing by so fast. He made his way to the door. "Looks like she has another drawing for us."

Kate hadn't had an afternoon nap in forever, so needing one today was unusual enough. Although maybe not completely unusual given her extracurricular activities over the past week. And her dreams had always been weird so she'd just taken them for granted.

Picking up on people's feelings was a quirky gift. Not a gift she talked about with anyone, but a gift nonetheless. The fact that she could pick up on Callan's feelings as if he were telling them to her, well, that was strange, but she figured it was all part of the connection they had.

Which took her back to her dreams. She'd learned not to talk much about them. Cindy had figured out a long time ago that the wolf she drew and painted and drew again, over and over and over, was one from her dreams. But ever since Kate arrived in Whiskey Grove, her dreams had been getting more and more bizarre.

The one she had this afternoon while she was napping was so outlandish that she'd had to draw the picture immediately upon waking.

She gathered up her purse and the quick sketch she'd done, and was greeted at the front door of the house by Callan. His siblings were close behind.

"Hey, what are you doing here? I thought I was picking you up a little later so we could have dinner in town? Did you sleep okay?"

"That's actually why I'm here. I had probably my most bizarro dream yet, and this time, it was about your cousin and his wolves. But he had three wolves with him this time. And...well, I didn't understand all of it. Here." She handed over her drawing.

"What's this?" Connor asked.

Kate liked Connor. She hadn't gotten a chance to spend much time around him, but what little bit she had, she really liked. He acted the way she always imagined a protective older brother might act toward her.

"This is where my dream took place. I didn't recognize any bit of it, but this craggy rock looked distinctive so I knew I needed to capture it."

"That's Devil's Tower," Carleigh said. "It's just on the other side of this mountain."

Callan pulled her to him. "What else can you tell me about this picture?"

"Well, I dreamed your cousin was just there, at that rock."

"Devil's Tower."

"Yeah, and he was with these three wolves here in the picture. They weren't very distinctive, not like how I could see his facial features."

"What do you mean?" Callan asked.

"This was a dream, right? Everything was distorted. It was like I was only able to get part of the image into focus, as if I was looking through a decorative glass door. Part of the glass is perfectly clear so you can see exactly what there is to see outside. But then they frost other parts or put other effects in the glass, and when you look out those sections, the images that you see are distorted."

"Ooohhh. That's really interesting." Callan hugged her close, but she could feel the tension increasing amongst the three of them, even though their expressions never changed. "Go on."

"So it was as if I were able to look out this one piece of clear, circular glass to see your cousin's face, but the rest of the image was distorted by frosted glass."

"Got it." Connor nodded.

"Okay, so what does all this mean?" Carleigh asked.

"Well, so the Devil's Tower rock was right behind your cousin so it was part of the clear-as-day picture. The wolves in the picture were part of the frosted portion. I couldn't get a lot of features from them, although I'd swear two of the three were from that incident by the river." Kate couldn't help but shudder, thinking of what had happened and what could have happened had Callan not shown up.

"Katie, love, we're waiting for the bizarro part."

Kate wasn't going to tell Callan any time soon that she'd stopped minding him calling her "Katie." She wasn't sure how long she'd let him go on thinking she was annoyed.

"The bizarro part was that he, JT, your cousin, dropped down out of the clear portion of the picture, almost like he was on all four limbs, and…"

Out the back windows, something moved. There was Grayson. She'd seen him around Callan multiple times. His security chief, right-hand man, go-to guy, etc. He was walking with a wolf. Talking to it, as if it could understand him.

Callan and his siblings turned toward the back, probably to find out what had captured her attention so wholly.

Callan yelled, "No!"

Too late. The wolf shifted into Chris, Callan's best friend, and rushed into the house behind Grayson.

Kate's eyes didn't want to tell her brain what they saw, and her brain didn't want to tell her heart what it knew.

Chris had been a wolf and now was a fully-clothed human being. As if he hadn't just been a four-legged monster.

How many of them were there? Were they all like that? Were they all monsters? Kate's brain snapped and she began screaming. No words, just a constant scream that would kill her throat for days if not weeks, but she didn't care. And wasn't that a preposterous and random thought to have in the middle of a freak-out?

Kate.

No. She wanted out of there, but there were too many monsters between her and the exits. And as everyone knew, monsters were strong. Scary strong.

Like, strong enough to carry her for more than a mile through the woods.

JT had said to Callan, *You and your pack and your family and your friends and everyone else you know need to stay off my land.*

Pack.

Of course. A wolf pack. They weren't family. They were a pack of wolves.

Katie, love.

She continued screaming.

Callan stood before her and transformed into the white wolf with the brown markings on his ears and the top of his head that she'd been drawing for more than two decades.

He'd transformed into her white wolf. The only wolf she'd ever trusted because it hadn't been real.

Except it was. He was.

She stopped screaming.

Callan's wolf had eyes of slightly brighter gold than Callan did. He held her gaze as he sat on the floor, and continued holding it as he folded his limbs and went down to his belly.

Callan's voice and his wolf had been in Kate's dreams since she was a child. She believed in the power of dreams. She believed things happened for a reason.

She was meant to meet him. She'd already fallen for him and they barely knew each other.

How was she ever going to get over this? How was

she going to work through getting to know this family of monsters? Was it even possible?

But if it was meant to be, she had to at least try.

"I guess we need to talk." Her throat *did* hurt, randomness for the win, and her voice was raspy. "But first I need some water."

"I can get you that." Carleigh was already moving toward the kitchen.

"I also have a best friend to fire." Kate pulled out her phone, forgetting that she probably wouldn't have cell service. "Although finding a new cell provider should probably be a top priority for me at some point this week."

"What did you mean by having a best friend to fire?" Connor asked.

Callan remained on the floor, staring up at her with golden eyes.

"My former best friend, Cindy, grew up in Whiskey Grove. She's seen my drawings of, well, him." Kate pointed at Callan. "And she's had to have known about the wolves in this area. She also knows how I feel about wolves." She looked down at the white wolf. "Present company excluded. My guess is she put two and two together after her last trip home, she figured out who he was, and, therefore, my trip here was highly encouraged." Kate took the glass of water from Carleigh. "Hence, I have a best friend to fire."

Chapter Seven

Weeks had passed since Kate's huge freak-out. The cool spring days in the mountains had turned into warm summer days. The professor was thrilled with the drawings she'd done for his research paper, and he now awaited news of it being published in the nature journal he'd submitted it to. The grant she'd done some drawings for had run out, but she'd received word that they'd been approved for a new grant to begin in July and they wanted Kate on board with the continuation of the project.

She'd traveled to the university in Carrollton, just outside Atlanta, a few times to attend meetings, and she knew Callan had worried and wondered if Kate would even return to him those first couple times. But she'd returned. She hadn't been able to leave him. Not when he'd been so caring and patient with her, truly wanting to give her as much time as she needed to get used to his wolf, to get used to being so near such a large creature.

Kate had given Callan permission to pass her story along to everyone else, just so she wouldn't have to tell it over and over again. It'd helped. The other...pack members—because that's what they were—stayed away from her for the most part when they were wolves. She was still able to observe them interacting with each other, wolf to human, wolf to wolf, but she didn't have to be in their space, up close and personal. That was the most important thing.

The only exception being Callan, of course.

For the most part, she'd done okay. He'd gone slowly with her, many times just curling up on the floor, trying to look as innocent and unassuming as possible. Like anyone could mistake him for being unassuming. He was a presence and a force to be reckoned with as a human. That didn't change when his wolf came out.

Overall, it'd been way easier than she'd ever imagined. She guessed that's what she got for having dreamed about that wolf night after night for a couple decades. And drawing him over and over countless times.

Some part of her brain was very happy to accept him. He was familiar to her. He got inside her. He soothed her.

The part of her that balked at even acknowledging such creatures existed was shrinking by the day. Enough so that she was willing to try an exercise Callan had been wanting to attempt for a while now.

After putting away her tablet, Kate popped into Callan's office. "Hey, you. Whatcha doin'?"

Callan leaned back in his office chair. "Hey, yourself. I just got off the phone with my parents and they're looking forward to meeting you."

Kate swallowed hard. "Meeting me?" She wasn't so sure she was up for meeting Callan's parents yet.

"They want to talk to you about all the things that make you special."

She definitely didn't like the sound of that. "You mean grill me."

He leaped from his chair and was by her side, pulling her into his arms within a second. "Heck, no. Special, as in, your gift, and why you might've escaped unharmed from the childhood incident. Things like that. They think they might have some explanations for you."

"Oh my God."

"Yeah, it's a good thing. We'll fly out to Arizona as soon as our schedules allow it. Does that sound good?"

Explanations were always a good thing. "Definitely."

Callan nudged her. "So what did you want to talk to me about?"

"Oh. So I was thinking I'd like to go on that hike with you…and Chris and Grayson."

His eyes widened to saucers. "Whoa. Are you sure?"

"I'm sure, and don't ask me anymore because all I'll do is change my mind."

"Yes, ma'am. Let's go get our hiking shoes on and we'll meet them at the base of the easiest trail."

He shut down his computer and grabbed her hand on their way to his cabin.

That was the other thing she wanted to talk to him about, but she didn't want to do it in front of his brother and best friend. She had her own cabin but spent all of her nights with him. The only thing her cabin was good for was clothes storage and a quiet place for her to work uninterrupted. And even then, more and more of her clothes were making their way to Callan's place and staying there. So basically her cabin was her office space.

She definitely needed to talk to him about his place becoming their place and turning her cabin into either her office or finding some office space of her own somewhere. But that also meant that she needed to stop thinking about his cabin as *his* and instead as *theirs*.

"You got awfully quiet all of a sudden. What's up? Are you having second thoughts?"

"Hmm?" Second thoughts? "Oh. The hike. No. I was actually thinking about the fact that my hiking boots are at your cabin and not mine. Along with most of my current season's clothes."

"Is that a problem?"

"That's just it. I don't think it is a problem. I was just giving myself a pep talk about broaching the topic with you. Maybe calling your place ours sometime soon. But I don't want to encroach on your bachelorhood. I know how guys can get."

Callan stopped and pulled her in close. "I'd thought that you taking the step to go on a hike with some wolves fairly close by was probably the happiest I could be today. I was wrong. Having you want to move in with me and take a chance on us, even knowing what I am, what my family is, definitely makes me shout-from-the-mountain-top happier."

He wrapped his hands behind her neck and head, and took her mouth in a hard kiss. His tongue demanded entrance and Kate didn't try to deny him. All of the feelings of rightness, of how perfect they felt together hadn't been one-sided. She'd been picking up his emotions all along and hadn't distinguished them from her own.

Just as she was ready to start running her hands up his stomach and chest, he pulled away. "Don't go pouting at me. It's all I can do not to take you back to our cabin and ravage you, but you said you were willing to try a hike with Chris and Gray, and they're already waiting for us."

"How do you know? You haven't even called them?"

Callan tapped his finger against his temple.

"I forgot the telepathy thing isn't just a you and me thing. You do realize none of this is normal, right? Not normal in the least little bit."

"It's all normal for me."

"Which goes to show just how much is wrong with you."

Callan grabbed her and flipped her over his shoulder in a fireman's carry.

Kate squealed but toned the noise down immediately. People and creatures with super sensitive hearing around and all that. Instead, she kicked her legs and beat her fists on his back. "Put me down, you animal." She almost said literally, but bit it back in time.

He squeezed her legs tighter, making it hard for her to move them at all, and her fists didn't seem to faze him one bit. When he did finally put her down, it was with a plop on the small front porch of his cabin. "There you go. Now you can get your hiking boots on without any more distractions, and I will let them know that you're the holdup."

"Butthead."

"Yep."

Kate stopped giving him a hard time and headed inside. Three minutes later, a quick change of clothes and a trip to the bathroom had her ready to go.

"All set?"

And then it hit her what she'd agreed to do. She hesitated in answering but knew Callan would keep her safe. If Chris and Grayson lost control of their wolves, Cal-

Ian would protect her. She knew this deep down inside. "As ready as I'll ever be, I guess."

"Let's do it."

They made good time jogging down, then slightly across the hill that separated the cabin from the start of the trail. As promised, Chris and Grayson were waiting patiently for them. Both were half sitting, half lying at the trail head, looking bored out of their minds. That was funny to Kate and she started giggling.

"What?" Callan asked.

Chris's and Grayson's wolves slowly stood and stretched. Chris's wolf let out a huge yawn.

She laughed even harder.

"I'm happy to hear you laughing so hard, especially in the presence of wolves, but if you don't tell me what has you so tickled, I'm going to start tickling you so I'll know for certain why you're laughing."

"No! You wouldn't dare." Kate sucked in air. "It's just that their wolves are pretending to be bored to tears and I—"

"Katie, love?"

"What?"

"It's not their wolves. It's them. They're not two separate entities."

"I...know."

"Do you?"

She hesitated. "I'm trying to know."

"That's not Chris's wolf. That's not Gray's wolf. That's Chris and Gray. They're just in wolf form right now. Got it?"

"I think so."

"I'm sorry I stopped your laughter. That was rather

enjoyable, and I'm getting the mental stink-eye from both of the guard dogs over there."

Gray growled and Kate jumped nearly ten feet out of her skin.

"He's playing, Katie, love. He's playing. He forgot that he needs to only play in a lighthearted way around you and not push it too far. It's okay. He just wanted to let me know what he thought of me calling him a guard dog. It's fine."

She put her fist to her chest, making sure her heart was still where it was supposed to be and hadn't leaped out to make its escape. When she couldn't find any noticeable holes, she figured she could start breathing again.

"Okay. I'm okay. Or, I'll be okay. Grayson, don't you ever do that again. At least not any time soon. I mean it. I can't handle it."

Grayson's wolf…er, Grayson dipped his head to her.

She figured she couldn't hold their horsing around against him. "I'm okay. I'm sure of it. Let's get going."

As promised, Chris and Grayson remained in front of Callan and Kate throughout the hike so she could always know where they were. Even when they ran off to give her some space—both physical and emotional—they remained within eyesight.

While they hiked, Callan continued working on exercises with Kate to help her build her shields, empathic as well as mental. He wasn't as familiar with her empathic abilities, but the exercises he gave her seemed to work. She practiced on him, which was harder because of their bond, but it worked great when she practiced on their companion wolves.

Once they reached the top of one of the trails planned

for the resort's medium hiking adventure choice, it was later than they'd planned.

Callan held out the bottle of water for her to have some. "Do you mind if the guys change back so they can drink water with us? Or are you going to make them go scrounging around for a water source?"

"They can change." Kate had been getting used to Callan doing the shifting thing. Sort of. She had to get used to seeing others change, too.

Before she could think twice, Chris and Grayson appeared as humans before her. "Wow."

"I really am sorry I scared you earlier." Grayson still had his head dipped down.

"It's okay, Grayson. I know you were playing around with Callan. I'll get used to all this. I will."

"We need to get back down to base before it gets too dark up here," Chris said.

Callan elbowed Chris. "Look at you. Already using the terminology and everything. Base."

"Shut up. We're running back. See if you and your eagle chasing girlfriend can keep up."

"Hey! I resemble that remark." Kate hiked more now than she ran so she was looking forward to a friendly challenge.

Although she rethought that challenge when Chris and Grayson changed back into their wolves, no, shifted into their wolf forms, on-the-fly as they ran.

"We better get going." Callan grabbed her hand and they took off after them.

Kate ran as hard as she could, but she was no match for any of them. She felt nothing but relief when they finally made it back to the bottom of the trail.

And her lungs hated her. Big time.

She leaned over and rested her hands on her knees while she gasped in oxygen.

"You okay? It might be better if you stood up straight—"

"Hush," she rasped out. She loved Callan, but he— Wait. What?

She looked up at him and was in no way blocking her feelings for him because he flooded their link with those same feelings in return.

"Good night, guys," she called out to the wolves still hanging around, and she grabbed Callan's hand.

Callan looked over his shoulder and saw his two friends following them.

"You heard the woman, good night."

The problem was that he and Kate both were giving off the scent of arousal, and those two jerks were trying to be pains in the ass.

Get lost, ya mangy mutts.

Their laughter in his head meant that not only were they being difficult on purpose, but they were going to continue doing so.

He swept Kate up into his arms and took off at a dead run to his cabin. The element of surprise and the added speed from being an alpha were the only things that allowed human him to get inside his house, with the door closed and locked, before one of the wolves made it inside. He would've hated to have had to hurt one of them.

Laughter echoed in his head as they took off to their own homes.

But now, now he had Katie all to himself.

She slapped his shoulder. "Where are you taking me? Put me down."

He set her down in the master bathroom. "We're sweaty and we need a shower. I'm just expediting the process."

"Mmm-hmm." Her T-shirt clung to her curves, her sweat having soaked it through until it hugged her all over. As he stared, her nipples beaded and her breathing picked up. He stripped his shirt off over his head.

Her eyes dilated as they focused on his chest.

He dropped his shirt to the floor then gave a quick flex of his pecs.

Katie snorted. She tugged at her shirt.

Callan slid his hands up her sides, along her rib cage until he snagged the edge of her top, pulled it off and dropped it on top of his. "I'm thankful every day you came into my life."

She shivered and he ran his hands along her back until he came to her bra clasp. He unhooked it with one quick twist then slowly guided the straps down her arms. When the cups finally fell away, he sank to his knees and took each of her breasts in his hands, preparing them for his mouth.

"I'm all sweaty. You said so yourself."

"I don't care." He swiped his tongue across one nipple while he ran his thumb across the other. Then he switched sides.

Katie dropped her head back and moaned. God he loved that sound.

Callan switched sides again, this time sucking the nipple between his teeth and biting just hard enough for her to jerk her hips toward him. With his hand on her other breast, he rolled her nipple between his thumb and forefinger, tighter and tighter until he pinched together hard at the same time he bit down on her other nipple.

She cried out and jerked her hips forward rhythmically. He matched her rhythm with the timing of his pinches and bites.

"Oh my God. You've got to stop. I want you in me. Now." She pushed his head away and began stripping the rest of her clothes off.

Before Callan could think clearly, Katie was naked, in the shower, with the water already streaming down her body. "I thought you wanted me in you."

"I do. Now. Get naked and get in here."

"Bossy."

"You know it."

He did as his woman said and got naked, then joined her in the shower. "Your nipples are incredibly red."

"They're quite sensitive."

"Good." He spun her around so her front pressed against the cold tile wall.

"Oh!"

"Maybe that'll help some with that sensitivity."

"I don't think it will." She pushed back with her hips, but he gave no quarter, and all that did was rub her ass against his cock.

He took both of her arms and placed them raised on the wall, curved above her head. Putting his lips next to her ear, he whispered, "Leave them there."

When he was met with only a whimper, he knelt behind her and spread his hands across her ass cheeks. He followed her curves around to her hips and angled her pelvis slightly so that he had better access to her pussy.

Gently he pushed her legs apart with his torso, forcing her feet to span the width of the shower. He ran a finger through her curls and slickness greeted him.

"Love, you're soaking wet down here."

"I'm in a shower. Of course I'm soaking wet."

He sank his teeth into the succulent flesh of her booty.

"Ow!"

"Naughty woman. Maybe I should stop now since you're only wet because you're in a shower?"

"God no. You'd better keep going."

"That's what I thought." Callan licked the spot where he'd bitten her while gliding his hand up the inside of her leg. She shivered beneath his touch.

When he neared the junction of her thighs, he switched to the other leg, once again starting at her ankle.

"Please."

When he reached her slick curls this time, he gathered up some of her arousal and spread it around her pussy lips, barely grazing her clit as he circled. Katie's hips jerked and he bit her ass, this time on the other cheek, and not quite so hard, wanting it to be for pleasure instead of punishment.

He slid two fingers inside her, scooped up some more of her juices and applied them directly to her clit. Capturing it between his fingers, he squeezed with enough pressure to make her squirm, but not enough yet to make her orgasm.

"Dammit. I need to come. Either you can do it, or I will."

Callan brushed her clit then slid his fingers between her lips and up the crease of her ass as he stood.

He reached around her, worked his fingers between

the tile and her nipples, and pinched them while pressing her to the wall.

She shoved back against him, but he used his upper body to keep her in place. He bent his knees so he could line his erection up with her opening. He rubbed the tip forward and back along her swollen labia, enjoying her moans as he hit her clit each time.

"Quit playing around and just take me already."

He pulled back and plunged to the hilt in one stroke. Katie cried out.

He wrapped one arm around her hip and pressed his thumb against her hypersensitive clit. Entangling her hair in the fingers of his other hand, he gently pulled her head back until more of her neck was exposed to him. He ran his tongue along the water that dripped down her jaw to follow her neckline, then timed his bite to coincide with another plunge.

Applying steady pressure with his thumb, he sank into her again and again while sucking on the tender spot just below her ear as she squeezed his length and came around him for what seemed like minutes. When it felt like her orgasm let up some, he took her hips in his hands and pumped into her a final few times before letting himself fall over that edge with her.

"Dayum."

He had to agree.

Chapter Eight

Kate couldn't believe how well the distillery blended with the surrounding scenery. Part of the building disappeared into the rock of the mountain itself. And the rest of it used the trees surrounding it as camouflage.

"Wow." She made the word into three syllables.

"Yeah?"

"One would almost think y'all were trying to hide from the law up here with this setup."

"Keep in mind, we once were. When my dad decided to stop hiding and go legit, we were able to expand and ended up selling more than we ever imagined we could."

"Aren't you worried about the trees coming down on the roof and damaging everything?"

"The mountain protects us from the west, which is the direction most storm systems come at us from. We also have some protection from the south in case we get storms that way as well. Other than that, we have some roof re-enforcements that we can deploy during major storms, including ice and snow storms, so we won't have trouble. We've tried to think of everything. Kevin went to NCSU for his engineering degree and I trust him to keep our livelihood protected with his innovations."

"Wow."

"You said that once already."

"Yeah, yeah, I know." The pride Callan felt for one of his extended family members was impressive. The complete trust and delegation of responsibility for this particular area was remarkable.

Callan swung his arm out to encompass the whole plant. "We're hoping to incorporate the distillery as part of both the backpacking tour as well as the scenic tour. We know the golf carts can make it along the road. We've already tested that out, and we're hoping if all goes well, we can add a few more carts to our fleet before too long."

"Your fleet, eh." She elbowed him in the ribs. "Sounds all fancy and junk."

He scoffed. "Well, it's not the Biltmore House and their winery, but we're hoping to do okay. In fact, from the very beginning when their winery opened up, they've had a tasting room at the end of the tour. You can sample different Biltmore wines and pick the ones you want to purchase to take home with you. We want to add something small like that to our tour of the distillery."

"All you'll be doing is getting the tour members drunk on whiskey moonshine so they'll fork out money for more."

"Why, Katie Ballard. That sounds like a very deceivious business plan. Also a good one."

She grabbed his hand. "Mmm-hmm. That's what I thought."

The front of the building could've been the frontage to almost any kind of small business, certainly not a distillery that was supporting a pack family of a couple hundred. And not just supporting but allowing them to thrive.

"On top of the drawings you're doing and have done for the lodges, I'd love for you to check out the tasting area and see if you can class up the space with some of your artwork."

"You know I'd love to."

"I was hoping you'd say that." He squeezed her hand and the electricity that always surrounded them bounced around in the area of her heart a few times.

"Come on. I'll take you in through the warehouse first. I want you to see where we package up the Whiskey Shine bottles."

"I've been wondering about that anyway. I was wondering how you get big trucks all the way up this mountain."

"We don't. I'll show you how we've figured out transportation."

Callan put his hand low on Kate's back and the thrill of possession zinged through her. Not that he owned her. No. It was more just the feeling of someone saying, "She's mine, guys. Back off." Or, "I want to show the world that I claim her for myself." She wanted to say the same things about him, but something was holding her back and she wasn't sure what it was.

It certainly wasn't their chemistry. He lit up her lady parts like no one ever had. It wasn't that she didn't like him. Everything about him screamed responsible adult. He was a caring leader who took care of the people he was responsible for. She'd listened in while he weighed the different options brought to him before he made a decision everyone followed without argument.

Kate didn't have time to try to figure out the mystery

any longer. Callan was introducing her to the woman behind the front desk.

"Katie, love. This is Cassie. She runs this place with an iron fist. Cassie, this is my Kate."

Cassie stood and offered her hand. "It's nice to finally meet you, Kate. I've heard a lot about you already." Her grip was firm, but not overly so.

"I just bet you have. I can only imagine what all you've heard."

"All of it good. I promise. We just hope you won't let this rapscallion corrupt you too badly."

"Ignore everything Cassie says."

"I thought you said she runs this place with an iron fist. And if I'm going to be doing some artwork for the—"

"Ignore her anyway."

Cassie let out a hearty laugh indicating the two shared a great relationship. Cassie winked at her. "Let me know whatever you need when the time comes and I'll make sure everything is set up for you."

"Thanks. It was great meeting you."

Callan laid his hand low on Kate's back again and led her down a hallway to the left. "Stay away from her. I'm sure I can find someone else for you to work with," he said loudly.

Cassie's laughter followed them down the corridor.

Along the way to the warehouse, Callan pointed out different areas of the distillery that he found interesting. He pointed out rooms and viewing locations that were on the tour and private spots that they'd installed extra security for.

When they finally reached the entrance to the warehouse, Kate was already amazed by all she'd seen. "I want to say 'wow' again."

"Not original enough. You need to come up with a new word."

"Whoa?"

"Doesn't convey the same sense of positive wonderment."

"Golly."

"Really?"

"Whoopee!"

"Never mind. You can repeat 'wow' as many times as you like."

"Wow. Thank you!" She leaned up and gave him a smacking kiss on the lips. "Now please continue the tour, kind sir."

"We're coming from the offices side, whereas the door to and from the break room is the usual interior entrance. So this door here doesn't get used much at all. All of the walls and doors between the warehouse and offices are soundproofed so the office areas can remain as quiet as possible. I tend to not use that break room entrance and have found this door blocked with boxes before. That was interesting. I scared the crap out of one poor guy that day. He was beginning to believe in ghosts. Heh."

Kate snort-laughed.

Callan opened the heavy door, and just as he'd predicted, pallets of boxes mostly blocked the entrance. And those boxes were moving.

Callan seethed. Bobby and Billy, his and JT's cousins many times removed, were opening boxes like there was no tomorrow. They wore the black pants, shirt and hat uniform of the warehouse workers, but their faces were turned toward the wall. In fact, that looked like the only thing they were hiding—their faces. Certainly not their actions. But why in the hell had no one stopped them from opening all those boxes?

Squeezing her hand, Callan sent as much love and warmth as he could to Kate through their bond while sounding a mental alarm to Grayson and Chris. He trusted them to alert warehouse security and staff.

Bobby's and Billy's complete focus on the task at hand, along with the warehouse noise, made Callan's appearance a surprise. And not a nice one for them.

Callan's chest grumbled as he growled, "What the fuck are you two doing?"

Not only did Bobby and Billy freeze, but activity across the warehouse stopped, too. Except for Kelli, the warehouse manager, and security, who were all heading straight toward them.

Bobby and Billy tossed open boxes into the middle of the space around them. Bottles slid out, breaking glass and spilling whiskey everywhere.

The fire hazard didn't escape Callan's notice. Because he was looking for it, he was already mid-leap by the time Billy pulled his lighter from his pocket. Without regret, Callan broke Billy's fingers while removing the lighter. Billy was a wolf. He'd heal. And Callan wasn't going to let his entire pack's livelihood burn up because of this asshole.

Billy's howl of pain preceded him shifting, and his brother Bobby followed suit. With Callan between them, the brothers bared their teeth and growled at a steady hum.

That was fine by Callan since they wouldn't be able

to flick a lighter with their paws. He couldn't afford to take his attention away from them, so he closed himself off from the rest of his pack except for emergency messages. The only bond he kept fully open was the one to Kate. Knowing her status at all times was like breathing for him.

A couple security guards remained in human form while another shifted. Grayson and Chris showed up, both in wolf form, as Callan figured they would be.

He had four people in human form, five counting Kate, plus three wolves surrounding the troublemakers. It should've been enough, but these two could be desperate enough to try something else.

Finding out what they were up to was a priority, because the two of them weren't in his warehouse just to open boxes and dump the contents. Set the warehouse on fire? Maybe. But the idiots would've been caught in that blaze, too. And beyond that, they never went anywhere without JT, so where was he? "You know, I bet we could get some of those crates that humans buy for training their pet dogs, and we could put y'all in there until you decide you want to tell us what you were up to."

They shot away, on opposite sides, but both headed toward the exit bay door. Gray and Chris gave chase, but with security coming from the opposite direction, the brothers were going to escape. Callan shut down all pack pathways, even the one with Kate, to concentrate on bringing the intruders down. The mental energy required for controlling a non-pack member was immense, but he slowed them enough that Grayson and Chris had subdued them.

Unease prickled Callan through the mate bond, followed by a fear that he hoped he'd never experience again. Because if he was experiencing it, that meant Kate was experiencing it. And if Kate was experiencing it, something was going wrong that he couldn't see.

Maintaining his mental hold on the intruders, he glanced at her, but hadn't expected to see her staring away from him, down an aisle between a whole bunch of pallets.

"Now, now, boys." JT's voice preceded him as he exited the boxes, passing directly in front of Kate and throwing a smirk at her, then Callan.

JT swaggered over to the action. "I don't think we need to be quite so dramatic and extreme in our threats here."

"What are you and your pets doing here, JT?" It gave him chills to think how close JT had been allowed to get to Kate again.

"I'm here because these two wandered off from our stroll. They obviously decided to cause a bit of mischief. Sorry about that. I can't help that they find your product so much more inferior than ours and decided it needed to be destroyed. Too bad they couldn't get rid of more and save your customers from paying so much money for government swill."

Callan took a calming breath. "You know how you've told me on numerous occasions that your policy is to act now and think later?"

"Sort of, though that's not my creed. It's shoot first and ask questions later."

Callan nodded. "Exactly. Neither you, nor Billy, nor Bobby had better show up on any of our property ever again. Because if any of you step foot near this warehouse again, you'll run smack dab into your own policy."

JT walked over to Bobby and Billy. "You can release your hold on them and we'll leave peaceably. Come on, boys. Let's go."

Callan released the brothers. His shoulders dropped as the mental tension eased.

Despite being escorted out by two wolves and a guard in human form, the brother wolves still managed to jump up and knock over a pallet of boxes. Growling wolves chased them the rest of the way out.

Kelli gave orders to clean up the mess.

Callan reestablished pack communication and turned to Kate, except she was gone. The link with Kate popped back into place, and he could tell that she was still close, but not as close as she had been. Her fear still came through their bond, but it was controlled now. Maybe because of the shielding lessons he'd given her. Maybe she was subconsciously protecting him from the full weight of it.

Which kinda pissed him off, because he didn't want her protecting him. He should've been protecting her. And he'd done such a bang-up job of that. Which also pissed him off.

Crap. He felt something else from her, too. Determination, maybe?

Callan needed to ensure the safety of his pack, because no matter what else happened, he had to take care of them. They were his responsibility. After he did that, he'd take off in search of his heart.

He contacted Grayson and Chris.

I want you two to be sure those three make it off our land without any detours or little side trips. I also

*want this warehouse searched. I don't trust JT. Abso-
lutely none of what just happened makes any sense to
me. Maybe those two idiots were just a distraction. I
want security to search everything to find out where
JT was, and I mean everything. Both security tapes and
every inch of the entire warehouse. Not just in the area
we saw him appear from. My guess is he probably did
something elsewhere. I also want to know how they got
in, so get security—*

Gray interrupted, *They're already on it. Looks like
a newer employee made the mistake of letting the two
brothers pass through. JT wasn't seen, at least not by
the employee. Security is already reviewing footage
and we'll be looking for blind spots. We hadn't needed
to in the past. We do now.*

Everyone was entitled to a mistake here and there.
This was a biggie, but not enough for a new employee
to lose their job over. Or maybe it was. *Kelli, make sure
the employee understands all the policies. Also, let's
keep a watch for a little while, just to make sure we're
not dealing with an inside job here. I want it reiterated
to all employees that this is exactly why we require that
all visitors go through the front desk. Cassie can keep
out the majority of the riff-raff.*

Chris said, *Paranoid much?*

*You didn't feel Kate's fear when she had to face JT
again, Chris. It's not paranoia if they really are out to
get you.*

Gray said, *We'll take care of this. You take care of
Kate.*

Callan was already on his way to do that. He just
hoped he wasn't too late.

I plan on meeting you both back at the house for sup-

per. We can talk more then and you can catch me up.
I'm going to go spend some time with my mate.

It'd been weird, after all these weeks, having that constant stream of emotions, thoughts, information and conversations just shut down with no warning. Weird, and a little scary. Something had still been there between her and Callan, probably the mate bond, which seemed to exist outside of everything else, but all of their back-and-forth had been slammed shut.

If Kate had more experience in this world, more knowledge of what the hell she was doing, she might've been able to breech the silence via the mate bond. She might've been there for Callan, still.

But she didn't know what she was doing.

Not in this world where people became monsters and monsters lived and breathed as if they could roam the earth freely.

She watched them go from human beings—the one she recognized as Bobby, the unkempt guy from the river—to monsters with fangs and teeth and saliva and fur. So there were monsters in human skin and there were monsters in wolf fur. And sometimes there were monsters who could be in both human skin and wolf fur.

Those were the scariest.

No. Wait.

The scariest was the one who could shut down psychic pathways she'd always thought were a myth anyway. The one who could control other monsters with his mind. Just his mind.

The scariest one was the one who could know what someone else was thinking and already disarm the perp of his lighter. Had he been able to read her mind, beyond what she'd allowed him to know?

Allow. Such a funny word now.

Those wolves hadn't allowed Callan to take control of them, yet he'd done it anyway.

The scariest one was the one she loved. Yep, she loved him. And loving someone meant giving them her trust.

So what did that mean for her? Would he try to control her? Of course not. At least that's how he'd answer, because only an insane person would try answering any other way.

But could Kate trust him enough to believe that answer?

Or maybe he'd believe that answer, but wouldn't have a choice but to control her at some point.

That was the one thing she'd fought against for so long—helplessness. Or at least that feeling. She hated feeling helpless. She hated being helpless. But in this world, she very much felt helpless. She couldn't turn into a monster to fight other monsters. She couldn't control someone else with her mind. She couldn't even bare her teeth and growl in a way that would scare someone off.

She could feel Callan coming. That's how close they'd become. Everything in her was tuned into him now. Now that he'd brought everything back online.

Kate shook. She'd been strong because she'd had to be. Again. But that didn't mean she wanted to be.

Despair washed over her at what she knew she had to do. She pulled her bags from the closet and plopped them on the bed.

The bedroom door opened. "Katie, love."

She loved this monster. Which couldn't possibly be right, because monsters were frightening and horrible creatures who injured her friends and made Kate afraid for life.

Callan came to her and pulled her into his arms, squeezing her tight to him. His heart beat beneath her cheek, a bit faster than usual.

This monster loved her. She knew that deep down. But she couldn't live with a monster. She couldn't be where people could be human one second and a monster the next.

It just wasn't possible. It wasn't possible for her brain to wrap around that possibility, so that meant it couldn't happen.

"Say something, love. Anything. Let me know you're here with me." His white-blond hair, usually combed out of his face, fell over his forehead and into his eyes. The brown, a surprise so unique to him.

"I'm here." She wouldn't lie to him and tell him she was with him.

He jerked back just enough to look at her face. He took in her eyes and her mouth, over and over. His pale hazel brown eyes much more like the gold of his wolf now. His mouth, showing signs of strain at the edges of his tender lips.

Kate was going to break his heart. Her own heart wanted to break, was already breaking, but there was no way she would allow those emotions to show in front of him or anywhere near his pack.

Oh, God, the pack.

Grayson and Chris. She'd miss them. Chris, the prankster. He always had a goofy smile for her. Even the previous time she'd seen him in his monstrous wolf form, he'd hung his tongue out on the side of his mouth before loping away. But he'd been a monster today and far too close.

Yet not close enough to protect her from the waves of malevolence that had poured off JT like light rays.

"I can't stay here. I can't live in an area overrun with monsters. I just can't. It's not healthy for me and I'm not going to do it."

Callan staggered back as if she'd slapped him. "Monsters."

Chapter Nine

.

Callan's heart sank.

Kate closed her eyes and dipped her head. "I can't change who I am."

"And I can't change who I am. Part of that is taking care of my pack. The rest is me loving you."

She lifted her head and looked straight at him. "I know that."

"Then can't you see how much I want to spend my life with you?" Couldn't she see how he wanted to spend every waking moment with her? How he wanted to be beside her when they were asleep? Callan wanted to feel her working beside him, or at least in the same room with him, so that when he looked up and caught her eye, it was that much easier to deal with whatever it was that he needed to get through. He didn't want to go through his days without her strength, her bravery and, most of all, her love.

Tears filled her eyes.

He knew the punch of overwhelming loss was aiming straight for him.

"I can't be here, with you, as long as I view you and your pack as monsters."

Frustration had him opening and closing his hands. "But I thought you'd been getting better about that."

"I tried. I honestly tried." Tears streamed down her face.

Callan stepped forward to wipe them away.

Kate held her hand up and the force of her emotion stopped him.

"I've gotten to the point where I can separate the people from their w-wolves, so I can treat everyone with respect—"

"Katie, love, we aren't separate but equal. The wolf and me, we're the same person, just with a different set of instincts guiding us." At that, Callan knew it was well and truly over. Even more so when Kate looked at him in horror.

"I thought..." She shook her head.

"Thank you for trying, my love. I won't ask you to live in the land of your nightmares any longer." He picked up the bag she'd been packing. "Need anything else?"

Kate shook her head, her long ponytail swishing against the sides of her face and sticking in the tracks of her tears.

Callan would give almost anything to take away her pain and fear, but wishing he could be someone he wasn't had never gotten him anywhere, and it wasn't going to get him anywhere now. Once he said his good-byes, he'd let his wolf take over and run until he was exhausted. "Let's get you on the road and down the mountain before sunset and you can't see where you're going."

"'Kay," she sniffled.

He hoisted her duffel bag on one shoulder and laid

his hand along her lower back. She didn't flinch away, which gave him the tiniest sliver of hope. When they got to her car, he put her bags in the backseat, then turned her toward him. "Katie, love, I'll always be here, and you will always be welcome. You're pack now, whether you want to be or not. Like it or hate it. And everyone here is your family."

"But why?"

"Because I belong to you. I wish you belonged to me." He tried to smile at her, but knew he'd failed. "I'm not quite sure if I'm strong enough to fight my instincts when they say that yes, you do actually belong to me and I'm not letting you go. But even if you don't believe me, I love you and I do belong to you. You own my heart. You own my soul. And if you ever want to bring them back, I'll be waiting."

Kate reached up with both arms and dragged Callan's face down to hers. Their lips touched and their hearts took over. Their mouths locked on to one another while their tongues dueled for dominance, implanting this one last taste in the brain. Callan lifted her in a hug that had their hands tugging at each other's backs, her breasts rubbing against his chest.

He registered hands pushing against his shoulders and he lifted his head.

"Put me down," Kate whispered.

Callan set her down and stepped away. He would not apologize for loving her. He wouldn't. "Take care of yourself. Don't let anything happen to you."

"I won't. I know better." She gave him a small, watery smile and got in her car.

With that, his mate was gone. She'd walked away

from him. This wasn't supposed to happen. Callan had never heard stories of this happening.

He let all his frustration and anger and love transform him into his wolf mid-run down the mountain. He didn't care about the torn clothes he was leaving behind. He didn't care about anything except the love of his life, his mate, his very soul, driving down the mountain away from him.

Callan poured everything he was feeling into a howl that echoed through the trees and across the mountain.

Except it wasn't an echo. It was his pack, his family, answering him back, not leaving him to face his future alone.

The doorbell rang and Kate ignored it, just like she had all the texts, the phone calls, the voice mails and the many missed FaceTime requests. Cindy's car sat in the parking lot of the townhouse Kate was renting, but she didn't want to see her. Not yet. Kate still had too many things to work through.

Then the pounding on the door started.

Well that would get annoying. And Kate's neighbors probably wouldn't appreciate it much, either.

"Go away!"

"You can't just keep ignoring me, K."

"Yes, as a matter of fact, I can. I'm doing just fine so far."

"Open this door or I'll three-name you at the top of my lungs."

"You wouldn't dare."

"Kathryn. Mari—"

"Fine!" Kate opened the door and emotions flooded her. Relief. Happiness. Anger. Betrayal. Sadness. Love.

Cindy wrapped her in a hug that threatened to over-whelm Kate if it didn't suffocate her first. She abruptly turned loose and held Kate at arm's length. "I don't care how angry you are at me. How furious. We hash things out. That's what best friends do. Don't you dare try to hide from me ever again. I've missed you. I've needed you. And you deserted me. I get that you're angry—"

"Slight understatement."

"—but we're gonna face our problems, not hide from them, got it?"

Kate couldn't hold back her tears any longer. Tears she'd refused to allow to fall for the past few weeks had now broken through and she couldn't stop them. Cindy pulled her in for a hug and held on while Kate ugly-cried on her friend for what seemed like hours.

"Why didn't you tell me there were monsters in the world?"

"You already knew there were monsters in the world."

"No I didn't!"

Cindy shook her head. "Think carefully about what you just said to me, and think about the job you quit, and then tell me about the monsters you didn't know existed."

Kate fell back against her couch and sat with a plop. She felt dazed.

Of course she'd known there were monsters. She'd drawn them every single day in her job. Men and women described those monsters to her, and she'd ab-sorbed those victims' feelings every time she'd listened and turned their words into pictures that others could use to catch those monsters.

She'd even given herself a pep talk about having already faced some of the worst of society when she first met JT, and she hadn't even known then what kind of monster he could truly be. She was basing his monstrousness only on his behavior.

Monsters weren't what people looked like on the outside. Monsters came from within. And sometimes those monsters stayed in human form all the time. Or, as she now knew, sometimes those monsters turned into other forms, too. She'd now witnessed both.

However, she'd also met men and women who fought true monsters. Men and women who remained in human form at all times and fought human monsters, and men and women who took on wolf form and fought monsters who took on wolf form, too.

She knew all this.

Kate sniffed loudly and grabbed the tissues from her end table. In the time it took to blow her nose a gazillion times, she processed her thoughts. So if she knew all that, what was really going on? What was the real mental fight she was dealing with?

"Ah. I see you've figured some things out. What's the deal now?"

"Jeez. Are you reading my mind? I was just asking myself that same question."

"And what have you decided?"

Kate blew her nose one last time and dried the last of the tears that had streaked her face. "I think it boils down to control. The lack of it on my part and the fear I felt as a child. I couldn't stop the wolves that mauled my friend. I watched every second of it and there was nothing I could do. Nothing. I felt the fear and the terror and was completely frozen and helpless. Lots of people have dogs as pets. But in my mind, since Ellie called them 'big doggies,' dogs are then animals that will always have the chance to go feral and can attack or destroy something of mine. When the wolves change, that's what they look like—feral, out of control, dangerous, like they can attack and destroy not only something of mine but destroy me as well. And that scares me. Frightens me. Terrifies me. I don't want to live every single day in fear."

Cindy took a deep breath. "I can't help you get over your fear. You have to do that on your own. You have to get control of your own mind. No one else can. I believe you're strong enough to do that, but I can't help you with that. What I can do is remind you that they're not just feral wolves. They're people, too. And the people don't lose control."

"I know that on some level, just not on the most powerful levels of my mind."

"You'll figure it out. For now, let's call in a pizza and watch either a movie or binge watch a TV show."

"Sounds like a plan."

Two medium pizzas and three hours of twenty-one-minute sitcom episodes later, Cindy stretched and got to her feet. "I've got to get home so I can hopefully make it to work somewhat close to on time tomorrow morning."

"I'm sorry I kept you here so late."

"Shut up. I'm happy to be here and I'm happy you're talking to me again."

"I'm sorry about that, too."

"Shut up. One last thought I want to leave you with and then you're on your own with processing everything. Can you think of some times when the personality of the human was easy to see in the wolf? Whether it was protectiveness or humor or kindness or even playfulness, can you pinpoint some incidents where the personality of the person as a whole—human and wolf—easily showed through both forms?" Cindy gave Kate one last hug. "That's all I've got for tonight. Love ya. Send me a text tomorrow to let me know how you're doing."

"'Kay. I will. Thanks for everything. G'night." Kate shut the door, leaned her back against it and slid all the way to the floor on her butt.

Yeah, she could think of a few times when she'd seen Callan's family shine through their wolf forms. Okay, several times.

She needed her sketchbook and pencils.

Chapter Ten

Callan sat with his head on his desk. He changed positions every time the spot warmed up, which was often. It was better than working.

A pounding on his office door. "Hey," Chris called out. "There's a large box that needs your signature for delivery up at the front office."

"Why can't someone else sign for it?" Callan was annoyed with the interruption. He was annoyed with everything these days. There was nothing that didn't rub his skin or fur the wrong way, and people making him leave the comfort of his office was just one more annoyance he didn't want to deal with. Heck, he didn't want to deal with people at all. He kept hoping they'd get the hint. If he growled at everyone long enough about everything, maybe everyone would leave him alone. But no, these idiots were still showing up bothering him.

Maybe he needed to go for another long run by himself.

Chris barged in. "Your signature is the one required. Not anyone else's. Yours. It specifically says that you must sign for it. The delivery dude is waiting and you're holding him up from the rest of his route."

So much for locked doors and best friends.

"Yeah, well I'm being held up from getting work done."

"Dude, you've not gotten work done in weeks now. Everyone else is getting work done and we're just letting you think you're doing it all."

A growl rumbled in Callan's chest. No stopping it.

Chris came closer and even sat on the edge of Callan's desk. "Just calm down. We all get it. Now come up to the front office and sign for the package so we can see what the heck is making all of the noise in it. Griffin thinks it's a really huge set of overgrown Legos."

The maturity level in his pack seemed to be reducing by the day. That was probably a good reason for Callan to come out of hiding. Possibly.

He stood fast enough that his chair fell backward. "Fine. I'm coming." He punctuated the statement by throwing his pen down.

Maybe immaturity was contagious these days.

He followed Chris to the main building, cursing himself the whole time for being an idiot. "I need to get her back. I just can't live without her. I've tried, but this isn't living. Y'all are paying for my meager existence. I can't do it any longer."

Chris threw his hands up. "Well, hallelujah. It's about damn time. You're an idiot as well as a fool."

"Hey!"

"Well you are."

"I have a pack to run. A job to do. A cousin and his crap to deal with. I couldn't just run off and leave all of my responsibilities."

"No, much better to stick around and pretend like you're doing the work while instead you waste away inside. Yep. Much better plan."

Callan ran the rest of the way to the main building. He didn't need Chris or anyone else telling him what he already knew. He'd find Kate and go after her first thing in the morning. All he needed was a plan. And maybe a decent night's sleep. But he'd find her and he'd win her back. And if he had to make other changes in his life, well, then he'd cross those bridges as he came to them, because he couldn't go on barely existing like he was. This wasn't living. This was barely surviving, at least emotionally, because without Kate it didn't matter how much his pack, his family cared for him and loved him.

Their regular delivery guy was waiting for him on the front porch of the main building as Callan ran up. "Finally. I need you to sign for this package so I can get the proof of signature entered into the system by 2 p.m."

What the hell? They never had anything delivered to the resort, or even the distillery, that required only his signature. He always made sure Ginger or Kelli or someone else could sign in his absence. He'd barely finished his last name and the guy was off and running to his truck.

Callan turned to head back to his lodge so he could start doing a search for his Kate. He'd kept his word, he hadn't followed her, hadn't tried to keep up with her. But he needed to know where she was now and he needed to know right away. He wasn't going to waste another day.

"Aren't you going to open the box?" Several of his pack gathered on the front porch, looking at the big box.

"Huh? No. Y'all can take care of that."

"But the return address has KMB as the initials."

Everything in Callan froze. If she'd taken some of his things with her, then he would expect that maybe it was a box of the stuff she was returning. But from what he could tell, the only thing his Kate had swiped from him was the shirt of his that had been too long on her and she'd turned into a sleep shirt for the brief time she was in his bed. Then Chris's mention of Griffin's guess that it was a box of overgrown Legos jogged Callan's memory that the box itself must make noise when it was moved. Or shaken.

Callan had the top of the box shredded in less than a second, if anybody had been timing him.

Confusion greeted him in the form of what looked like blueprint tubes. Charcoal gray tubes stacked together in neat rows and columns were in the box. "Did someone order decor for the lodges or something?"

"Not that I know of," Chris answered, which was weird since Callan had thought he'd only asked himself the question and hadn't spoken it out loud.

"Open one already," someone else said.

He was too far deep in his own thoughts.

A thick folded piece of paper lay on top of all the tubes and Callan pulled that out first. He recognized Katie's handwriting immediately. At the bottom of the letter was a small hand-drawn picture of him and his pack in front of the building they were currently gathered at. She'd signed the picture with her very tiny scrawl she used on personal pictures.

"What's it say?" someone asked.

"Dearest Callan, I owe you and *our* pack an apology, and the only way I know how to show you it comes from my heart is by giving you all pieces of my heart. Enclosed you'll find portraits of each of you, of how I really see you, of how my heart sees you and not how my mouth claimed at one point to see you all. Please accept my apology and forgive me for being so stupid for so long. Remember, I'm only human… Ha! My love to you and ours, Katie."

Callan swallowed the huge lump in his throat that threatened to choke him in front of everyone before pulling out a tube labeled *Kelli*. He twisted the top off and drew out a thick sheet of paper, neatly rolled to fit inside. As he unrolled it, his audience gave a collective gasp. Callan had no breath whatsoever. His Katie had captured not only Kelli's human nature, with all her humor and bossiness rolled into one, but had managed to capture that same essence in Kelli's wolf form, and drawn the duality of her nature in the one picture.

Chris stood next to Callan while he studied Kate's talented handiwork, and Callan now carefully passed along the tube and the drawing for Chris to do something with it. He reached for the next tube, which was labeled *Anne Catherine*. He twisted the top off and once again carefully pulled out the drawing inside. Anne Catherine's caring nature, everything that made her a nurse in human form and such an excellent protector in wolf form was once again captured by Kate's talented fingers and the pencils she wielded.

The next tube he pulled out was labeled *Callan*. He wasn't sure he wanted to open this tube in front of an audience so he set it down and reached for another.

"I don't think so. Either you open it now or I will," Chris said.

"You wouldn't dare." Callan glared at him, but pulled back before he unleashed his alpha on his best friend.

"Wouldn't I? Do you really think it's going to be something horrible? She loves you, man, and she obviously loves your pack or else she wouldn't have gone to all this trouble. From what I can tell, she can capture a person's true nature. Their true essence."

"She saw me as a monster and walked away. I don't want to see that in person."

"She saw us all as monsters and walked away. But she's apologized and no longer sees Kelli and Anne Catherine as monsters. I don't think there's anything monstrous about those two drawings at all. Give your mate a chance. Better yet, give your heart a chance."

Callan shoved Chris. "Since when did you become the expert on love around here?"

"Since I've been keeping everyone away from you while you became a bear instead of a wolf."

"Funny."

"Not really. Open it."

Kate held her breath while Callan hemmed and hawed about the tube labeled with his name. She was downwind and had walked up from the parking lot, stopping at the edge of the tree line.

She could easily hear the voices as they were carried to her on the wind, and at the same time, she knew Callan hadn't picked up her scent yet. She also knew that so far, she'd been doing a good job of hiding her feelings as well as her *self* from him ever since she'd arrived in the vicinity.

That she'd hurt Callan so deeply and made him so jaded sucked royally. He didn't want to open the drawing she'd done of him. But as Chris said—and that might've only been because Chris could see her from his position on the porch—Callan needed to give her this one more chance to trust her. As she stood there, holding her breath, she hoped and prayed she hadn't ruined things so badly between them that he wouldn't give her this chance.

She wanted him to see with his own eyes that she no longer saw him as a monster.

That he was just... Callan.

Kate slowly let the air out of her lungs as he twisted open the top. She watched as he gradually slid the drawing she'd done of him out of its protective covering. He unrolled it and the love she felt from him through their bond flooded her. Overwhelmed her.

She gasped in air as her lungs burned for oxygen, reminding her she'd forgotten to breathe again. At the same time, not only did her gasp make a loud noise in the silence, his love for her tore down every teeny bit of shielding she'd thrown up to protect herself from his possible rejection. Instead, she returned every ounce of love he was giving her with the same love thrown back at him.

Callan handed the drawing to Chris and ran across the gravel parking lot straight toward Kate. She knew he could run like the wind and would catch up to her quickly, but she took off running toward him anyway. She wanted his arms around her just that much sooner, and she wanted her lips on his as soon as possible.

Lucky for her, he had the same ideas. Callan lifted her into his arms and slid her high enough for her to wrap her legs around his waist. Kate ran her fingers through his hair and held his face to hers as they took each other's lips in a kiss. Their tongues met and dueled for control, neither one backing off. His taste was like a homecoming to her, the taste of darkest chocolate, edgy and delicious.

They broke for air and then passion had them back

together, long kisses with tongues sliding against each other, soaking in each other's taste.

For a while, pack members called out to them, thanking Kate or welcoming her back or calling out their goodbyes, before disappearing into the woods and along the paths to go back to work or head back to their homes.

Kate turned to acknowledge them, but Callan stopped her.

"They're trying to interrupt us just to be annoying. Ignore them," he whispered, and kissed his way from her ear back to her lips.

"Hey, you know you two could get a room," Chris eventually called out. "We have plenty of them."

Callan grunted in response and returned to the kissing.

"Fine," Chris said, "I'll just take this box and deliver the rest of these drawings to their intended owners."

Kate and Callan ignored him.

Their *hello* could've been fifteen minutes or an hour. She had no idea just how much time had passed. However, the sun had made significant progress in traveling across the sky during their greeting.

"Hi," she said, shyly, although she had no idea why since she'd just attacked him with her lips and tongue.

"Welcome back." His deep voice rumbled through his chest and vibrated through her body.

"Can it be 'welcome home'?"

Callan's eyes widened, but the smile breaking out across his face was one of pure joy. "Is that what it should be?"

"Yeah, I think so." Kate dipped her head and kissed his nose.

"Then let me rephrase." He pretended to clear his throat. "Welcome home."

She couldn't stop the huge smile on her face. "Thanks."

"Not to ruin this homecoming, but I really want to understand why. Tell me about the drawings."

Kate tried pushing against his shoulders to get him to lower her to the ground.

He didn't budge. "Katie, I don't care what you have to say to me. I'm not putting you down. I may not put you down for a very long time. I need to feel you in my arms and know that you're here, with me. Whatever you have to tell me, you can tell me while I hold you."

"Fine, ya stubborn man."

She sighed. "I had a long talk with Cindy."

Callan's eyes widened and he raised his eyebrows. "Did you two make up?"

"Yeah, we did."

"I'm glad. I hated the thought of you losing your best friend because of all this."

He kissed her on the nose and the feeling of rightness, of belonging settled into place.

"I did, too, and she helped me see some things more clearly. Like the fact that I can see who Anne Catherine is as a human, a nurse, mirrored in her caring, protective nature in wolf form. She's still Anne Catherine. It doesn't matter whether she's in human form or wolf form."

Kate felt his hurt come across their bond, no matter how hard Callan tried to hide it. She knew exactly why and tried to explain. "You're the pack alpha. You're a scary person in human form to a whole lot of people. Not to me, maybe, but a whole lot of people."

He gave her a mock growl but nodded.

"That's who pack alphas are. They're scary people. And they're scary wolves. I couldn't see you, human you, in your wolf form because wolves are already scary to me. I couldn't see beyond that. I'm sorry. I'm sorry I hurt your feelings. I'm sorry I hurt you. And I'm sorry I hurt your pack—our pack—and your family in the process. I hope you can eventually forgive me, and I'm really hoping everyone else will be able to forgive me as well."

"I've already forgiven you, Katie, mine."

"But I still hurt you, and I'm very sorry for that." She kissed his forehead, his nose, and his lips. She tried to make the kiss on the lips a quick one so she didn't get distracted from her explanation, but Callan had a different idea. When they came up for air again, she continued.

"Where was I before you interrupted me? Oh, right, Anne Catherine. I had to start with someone who by nature doesn't have a scary personality no matter what form she takes. And then I moved on from there. I thought about some of the guys who have ridiculous senses of humor in human form, and how that plays out in wolf form as well. By the time I got to you, my love, I could easily see what my fear had been hiding. What I'd been missing all along, all the parts of your personality that are easily seen in both human and wolf forms. And then I knew."

"What did you know?"

"I knew this is where I belong. Here. With you. If you'll have me."

She held her breath, waiting to see what he'd say. All of nature surrounding them seemed to hold its breath too, waiting with her. She didn't hear birds singing or the typical forest sounds such as squirrels chattering and playing chase. Yes, he'd said he wasn't turning her loose any time soon, but she'd hurt him deeply. Could he really forgive her and accept her back?

His golden eyes were like flames. "Do you really think I'll ever let you go again? Of course I'll have you. From this day forward, as long as we both shall live." Callan punctuated his declaration with another kiss.

"Shew. I've missed your kisses."

"I've missed you." The truth of that statement blazed through their bond so that Kate had no question as to how much he meant it.

"I also knew something else," she said.

"What was that?"

"I knew I needed to actually package up and send all of the drawings I'd done as a huge apology to everyone. But y'all needed to see them before I got here so no one bit my head off when I arrived."

Callan chuckled and the sound rang like sweet music to her ears. "Ah. Hence the timing of the signature for the package."

"Yep. But I also realized one last thing."

"And that was?"

"Your cousin is a horrible person no matter what form he takes."

"Couldn't agree with you more."

"That was the other thing Cindy helped me see. That in my job as a sketch artist for the police department, I drew human monsters every day. That was my job. I worked with men and women whose job it was to find and capture those monsters. Your cousin just happens to be one of them who can also change into a wolf and

make that form even scarier than it already is to me.
I'll always be scared of him."

"As you should be. Because speaking of my cousin,
security ended up finding a couple bags of drugs planted
between the crossbeams of two different pallets in the
warehouse. They were found in different areas, one was
about a half pound of marijuana, and the other, a gallon
bag of crystal meth."

"Holy shit. JT planted drugs in the warehouse?"

"Yeah, looks like it."

"I'm so sorry."

Callan's shoulders sagged. "I am, too. I'd always
tried to be understanding toward him, what with his
mom being killed by revenuers when he was a boy,
but he's now gone beyond my uncle's 'sticking it to the
man' philosophy."

Kate wished she could take away the pain JT was
causing Callan. "I don't even know what to do with
that."

"You just need to know that he's as dangerous as you
always figured him to be. Keep clear of him, know that
he's out to destroy the pack by bringing down the warehouse and always let us know if you see him."

Kate ran her fingers through Callan's hair and looked
directly in his eyes to make him this promise. "I can
do that."

"We have some folks we've let know about the situation. You don't happen to have your own contacts
through the APD, do you?"

For once, the tables were turned. She sent as much
reassurance as she could through their bond. "I have
a few friends I can reach out to. I'll do that first thing
tomorrow."

"I'm glad you came back."

"I'm glad you're glad."

"And now I'm going to take you back to my—I mean our—lodge and welcome you back properly." He swung her legs up and over one arm, the other cradling her back, reminiscent of their very first walk through the woods.

"You haven't welcomed me back properly already? I'm certain that I feel welcomed back properly."

"Speaking of stubborn. Fine, Katie, love, I'm whisking you back to our lodge so we can celebrate you being home for good."

"Sounds like an excellent plan to me."

* * * * *

Acknowledgments

I never could've written this book without the help of so many different people. My best friends, Bozhena, Jenny, Kirsten (K-Oz) and Megan supported me every step of the way. Bozhena served as a sounding board and created opportunities for me to write throughout the summer, Jenny and Kirsten went from fans to beta readers in the span of a heartbeat and Megan took on extra work for the communications committee at school. I'm forever thankful to them for their help, their story thoughts and their extra effort.

The SFs and Smacs are always there for me with an encouraging word. Their support and love are as necessary to me as breathing.

My editor, Penny Barber, is amazing. She understood exactly what I thought I wanted to do with the story, and then gently guided me in the direction I needed to go to make the story stronger. Her edits gave me life and I've loved working with her.

Angela James, Stephanie Doig and the entire Carina Press team are wonderful to work with. I'm so thankful for this opportunity to write with them again.

And last, but certainly not least, my son, who finally went back to school at the end of August and stopped yapping at me so I could get this story written. I love him dearly.

About the Author

After a career in the tech industry, the birth of Shari Mikels's son led her to become a stay-at-home mom, spending her time reading to him and teaching him to read. While modern children's books are quite engaging, they do tend to be geared toward the…shall we say "younger" crowd. This helped her recall a lifetime love of reading that had been pushed to the background for too long.

The writers' strike in Hollywood during this time had her picking up books to get her fix of happily-ever-afters and vampires. Her voracious appetite for books came back full force, and she found not just paranormals, but romantic suspenses and contemporaries. She began proofreading for some of her favorite authors when her brain wouldn't let her skip over the typos. What they didn't know was that they were teaching Shari how to write the stories that lived in her head. Her second submission became her first industry-published book, Christmas Curveball, at the end of 2013. In the intervening years, Shari was busy publishing another genre under a different pen name. The chance to write the paranormal story she's had in mind since 2012 gave Shari the opportunity to come back to Carina Press.

Shari lives in North Carolina with her husband and son. She spends her days volunteering at her son's school and dreaming up scenes for the many characters who live in all the varied worlds residing in her brain.

Visit her on her website and blog, www.sharimikels. com, and sign up for her newsletter: eepurl.com/JqCTj.